WHAT DO WOMEN WANT?

To the age-old question, *Penthouse* has the answer: Great sex—lots of it—in every variation! Here, in these pages, you'll meet women of all ages and from all walks of life, with one thing in common. They're all open to erotic exploration with its infinite possibilities, whether it's having sex on the job, flaunting their charms in public, delighting in dreams and fantasy, yielding to the allure of the fetish, or finding passion with another female. It's girl talk at its most revealing, fabulously uninhibited and totally uncensored!

OTHER BOOKS IN THE SERIES:

Erotica from Penthouse
More Erotica from Penthouse
Erotica from Penthouse III
Letters to Penthouse I
Letters to Penthouse II
Letters to Penthouse III
Letters to Penthouse IV
Letters to Penthouse V
Letters to Penthouse VI
Letters to Penthouse VII
Letters to Penthouse VIII
Letters to Penthouse IX
Letters to Penthouse X
Letters to Penthouse XI
Letters to Penthouse XII
Letters to Penthouse XIII
Letters to Penthouse XIV
Letters to Penthouse XV
Letters to Penthouse XVI
Letters to Penthouse XVII
Letters to Penthouse XVIII
Letters to Penthouse XIX
Letters to Penthouse XX
Letters to Penthouse XXI
Letters to Penthouse XXII
Letters to Penthouse XXIII
Letters to Penthouse XXIV
Letters to Penthouse XXV
Letters to Penthouse XXVI
Letters to Penthouse XXVII
Letters to Penthouse XXVIII
Letters to Penthouse XXIX
Penthouse Uncensored I
Penthouse Uncensored II
Penthouse Uncensored III
Penthouse Uncensored IV
Penthouse Uncensored V
Penthouse Variations
26 Nights: A Sexual Adventure
Penthouse: Naughty by Nature
Penthouse: Between the Sheets
Penthouse Erotic Video Guide

PENTHOUSE: NAUGHTY BY NATURE

Female Readers' Sexy Letters to *Penthouse*

The Editors of

Penthouse

Magazine

GRAND CENTRAL PUBLISHING

NEW YORK BOSTON

Cover design by Claire Brown
Lips photo by Thomas Schmidt/Stone
Hips photo by J.P. Fruchet/FPG

Grand Central Publishing
Hachette Book Group USA
237 Park Avenue
New York, NY 10017
Visit our Web site at www.HachetteBookGroupUSA.com

Printed in the United States of America

First Printing: February 2002

15 14 13 12 11 10 9 8 7 6

Contents

Introduction

By Rachel Stokoe
Senior Editor, *Penthouse* on-line

"So, are they real?"

It is the question I am asked most consistently as senior editor of *Penthouse* on-line.

What is it about the Forum Letters that have such a pull on our collective imagination? They were an instant phenomenon after first appearing on the pages of *Penthouse* over thirty years ago. It was the first time a well-respected, mainstream publication gave readers the opportunity to write freely and candidly about their sex lives.

Now, these letters are part of our public lexicon. Indeed, their popularity shows no sign of abating. Every month *Penthouse* magazine and its web site are flooded with letters, all brimming with exciting encounters. No other magazine has had so many people willing to share their most intimate moments with an international audience.

For me, the most rewarding aspect of reading through the letters we receive is seeing how many come from other women. More so than men, women feel the weight of societal taboos surrounding sexuality, and are often too shy to share our private moments with even the closest of friends. Each letter teaches me something about the woman who wrote it, and about myself. They are unfettered explorations of passion, free and honest discussions that are so sorely missing in our everyday interactions.

The letters here represent the wide range of women who write. These women are from all walks of life and are all ages. Each account is colored by the writer's individuality: Each captivates us with a face, and an identity. The one thing they all have in common is an erotic openness.

Their recounts run the gamut, and reveal just what women get up to behind closed doors (or even out in public!). From one's first time to one's sexual reawakening years later, from threesomes to lesbian encounters, from illicit meetings to wedding nights, these confessions reveal just how all-encompassing female sexuality is. Each describes a life-transforming moment, when passion and reality collide, when a sexual tingle becomes earth-shattering.

Freud famously posed the question: "What does a woman want?" The stories collected here are clearly marked by the feminine voice, and offer readers a window into the female psyche, completely uncensored by external pressures. The women, in the security of the anonymity, lay bare more about their lusts and appetites than they would to a therapist. And, if their rendezvous are any indication, a woman's wants are not so dissimilar to a man's.

Penthouse Forum is truly a celebration of sexuality. The letters it contains represent that magical moment when fantasy becomes reality. These letters focus on the feminine perspective. For women, they provide a context within which to place their own experiences. For men, they give a rare glimpse of women's most private moments. For both, they offer the thrill and delight that is *Penthouse* Forum.

GIRL MEETS BOY

Love Thy Neighbor

This year being my first away from home, I never imagined moving into an apartment building near someone like Donald. As soon as I saw him, I could feel my animal-like desire pushing toward the surface. Several days later, I saw him again, and I knew I couldn't hold back. I wanted to uncover the bulge that I had been dreaming about.

I felt my pussy tingling with excitement and wanted to have his cock pounding deep inside me. My imagination was driving me wild. I was getting wetter and wetter, thinking about his throbbing unit fucking me like an animal. We went out that night, but it ended with only a little childish foreplay. I needed more than that. I needed to be fucked—fucked like a beast.

About a month into our relationship, we began talking about anal sex, which I found repulsive and inhuman. But if he wanted to try it, I would do it for his pleasure. I wanted him in me, but needed to be teased. My nipples were rock-hard, and he wasn't gonna let that stop. He licked, nibbled, and sucked until my cunt was begging him to touch it. He roughly threw me on my back and put his hard cock directly on my slit, driving me almost to an orgasm. Rotating his hips and stimulating my clit, he caused me to quiver with excitement. I needed him in me. Finally, he drove the head, then the shaft, deeper and deeper inside me. I could feel his balls slapping against my ass, which was wanting some attention, also. Almost instantly, I had an orgasm, thrusting and rotating.

I stopped and threw him on his back. Now I was in control. I placed the head of his rock-hard dick into my dripping cunt, teasing him until I could no longer stand it. I pounded away until I felt the intense quiver of an orgasm coming on. My pussy cried out for more, but I still craved the dual teasing that kept us both enthralled. I stopped and began rotating my hips until I felt his dick on my G-spot. I needed to feed my hungry pussy with his cock, but I didn't want to be selfish. My mind wandered to our earlier conversation on anal sex.

I needed to make him happy, drive him crazy. I removed his hot throbbing rod and gently placed it next to my ass. Teasing him, I spread my cheeks apart and put the tip of his dick in. Getting excited, I slowly eased down, yelping with pleasure and excitement.

Donald didn't know what to think. Feeling him throbbing inside my ass made my pussy drip. I wanted him in both holes at once. Thankfully, he began fingering my clit, which caused an almost spontaneous orgasm. I bounced wildly on his dick, carefully watching every expression on his face. Closing his eyes, he moaned louder and louder, causing me to come again. This time was more intense than any other.

We showered and cleaned up. I still needed him in my pussy, and I knew that he wanted it there. I placed his luscious prick in my hot, wet cunt. He came almost immediately, as did I. Our bodies cried for each other. Since that night, we haven't tried it again, but my mind is constantly next door, in his room, wondering if we ever will. God, I hope so.

—J. I., Illinois

Movin' In

I am a college student, and last year a few friends and I decided to rent a house together. I arrived at the house a few weeks before school began, expecting to be the first there, so that I could move in more easily. To my surprise, I found one of my roommates, Peter, already there. After he helped me carry my boxes into the house, he gave me the grand tour. We noticed that parts of the house needed some new paint, so we decided not to waste any time.

On the way to the hardware store, he couldn't stop staring at my 38D breasts, and I couldn't help but notice the large bulge growing in his cutoffs. Just watching him change the gears was making me wetter by the second. By the time we got back to the house, I was so horny I was about to burst. But I didn't think I should start off my relationship with my new roommate with sex.

I went to my bedroom and changed into a baggy white T-shirt and cutoffs. When I got back to the living room, Peter had already covered the floor with newspapers and begun to paint. I admired his beautiful, muscular back, but I knew I had to control myself so I picked up a paint brush and began on the opposite wall.

After a few minutes, I felt his strong hands from behind me, sliding around my hips and up my shirt. By the time he found my breasts, my nipples were already rock-hard, so he let his hands roam down into my shorts where he found my dripping-wet pussy. He slid his finger into my warm slit, and the instant he touched my clitoris I exploded in orgasm and drenched his hand.

He turned me around and pressed me up against the wall (into wet paint), where he gave me the hardest kiss I had ever had. Then he pulled off my shirt and sucked my nipples until my pussy began to ache for his hard cock. He slowly moved down, dropped my shorts to the floor, and began flicking his masterful tongue in and out of my pulsating cunt until I came again.

Then he stood up and dropped his shorts to reveal his beautifully engorged member. He pressed my hands against the wall, and I wrapped my legs around him so that he could slide his dick into my waiting pussy. His hard, deep thrusts were almost more than I could handle, but kept me wanting more. We fell to the floor and fucked on the newspapers, in more positions than I ever knew existed. Each position we tried seemed to allow his rod to go farther and farther inside me until it felt like one continuous, euphoric orgasm. When he finally reached his plateau of ecstasy and exploded inside me, we were both so exhausted we just lay in the pool of spilled paint, sweat, and mingling love juices.

Later we took a long, relaxing bath together and fell asleep in each other's arms. All I could dream about was painting the bedrooms the next day.

—A. P., Alabama

Feels Like the First Time

The first time I made love was about two years ago, when I was twenty-two. One of the guys who took the same bus to college as I did was looking at me. One day I smiled back, and his face went all red. He was sitting to the rear of me; but when the bus reached our stop, I just sat there and let him walk past me. He was holding his books in his lap, and I could see that he was trying to hide a real bulge in his pants. My physical reaction was odd. My forehead got warm and my pubic region got quite wet. It gave me quite a bit to think about. As soon as I got into the building, I went to the ladies' room and had to wipe the moisture. The guy's name was Darryl. Later, one of my girlfriends told me he was asking about me.

I play tennis. I really love the game. The next day he showed up at the courts and asked me to play with him. After the game he had to go home. This was a Friday night. Early Saturday, he phoned me and asked me if I'd come to his house for a swim. It turns out his parents are loaded, and they had left for the weekend. Of course, he didn't tell me that.

At about two in the afternoon I arrived at his house. When he opened the door, he was wearing racing-type swimming trunks. You know, the skintight type. Well, you could see *everything*. And when he turned around, he had the cutest butt I had ever seen. Well, I went wet again and had to go to the bathroom. While I was in there, I changed into my bathing suit. When I came out, he had opened a bottle of champagne. I tasted it; it was good. About halfway through the bottle, we went to the pool and sat on the steps in the shallow end. He kissed me on the lips, then tried to put his tongue in my mouth. After three tries, I let him. I looked down at his swimsuit, and saw that he had a very big hard-on. My body temperature must have jumped twenty degrees. I was shocked at myself, because I wanted desperately to put my hands down in his trunks. But I resisted.

He began to lick my ears and blow in them. I thought I was going to die. He was hugging and kissing me, and, as he squeezed me to him, I could feel that huge organ of his pulsating against me. He tried to put his finger inside my suit, but I kept moving away. He would always come back, and I felt that giant tool of his pulsating against me.

Finally, I got out of the pool and sat on the edge. He was still in the water. He came over and began massaging my feet. Then he worked his way up to my knees and began kissing my upper legs and thighs. My pussy got so wet, and I got so hot, that I thought I was going to explode. He began to work his tongue under my swimming trunks, but I slipped back into the water. I don't think I could have stood that.

He had slipped his trunks off. He was so cute I again thought I was going to die. He squeezed me, and I put my hands around his neck, then slid them down until I had my hands on the cheeks of his gorgeous butt.

The suit I had on was one of those two-piece things, and he had the bottoms off before I knew it was happening. He began nudging his dick between my legs. The contrast between the cool water and his hot throbbing dick made his equipment feel even more exciting. Frankly, I knew I wanted that thing inside me. We moved up to a pad on the pool deck and he began licking my pussy. He was in a sixty-nine position, so I had a good look at his throbbing, red, shiny dick. I blew hot air on the end of it, and a strange-looking fluid appeared on the very end. I touched it, and it was slick. I ran my fingers around the head, using that fluid as a lubricant. My God, it got even bigger.

He pulled the top of my suit off so my bazooms were pointing straight up. He moved his equipment between them, holding them together, slipping his penis back and forth. Then he slid farther down and began trying to enter me. I was very small, and I guess he was really average in size, but it seemed like it was the size of the space shuttle. It was really tight, but there was something compelling about it. I really wanted that big thing inside me. I put my legs around him, tightened my teeth, and pulled him all the way in. It felt like my insides had caught fire. I let out a groan that the neighbors could've heard. Within a few minutes, the difficulty had gone away, and we began that dance of love. It felt s-o-o-o good. We must have been screwing for about a half hour when all of a sudden he tensed up, pulled out of my vagina, and came all over my stomach.

We went swimming, and then into his bedroom for at least another hour of lovemaking before I had to go home

—*S. S., Online*

Morning Jog

I like hot, steamy, sweaty sex. I also like relaxing, quiet sex after some long, sexy foreplay. I like surprising quickies. I like . . . you name it.

When it comes to the steamy-and-sweaty type of sex, I've found the perfect partner. Twice a week I do some gardening in our front yard. Some months ago, a jogger started to pass by, huffing and puffing and groaning a painful hello. He wore a T-shirt and skintight bicycle shorts. The second time he passed by, I noticed a tremendous bulge up front, and I began to wonder. His efforts made him sweat profusely. His shirt clung to his muscular chest, and his shorts showed wet spots in the crotch. He looked outright sexy and appetizing.

I smiled, and he stopped. While we exchanged pleasantries, I could not keep my eyes off his crotch. He noticed, because he started to survey my body. I felt he was undressing me. I asked him in for some fruit juice, and as soon as I closed the door, I fell into his arms.

I kissed his sweaty face and smelled the primeval scent of the male. All my senses reacted at once. I felt weak at the knees, my skin yearned to be touched, and my pussy started to moisten. My desire made me almost delirious as I sank to the floor and stripped off his shorts on my way down. My heart almost stopped when I saw his tool. It was huge! I've had an eight-and-a-half-incher, and my husband is a respectable seven and three-quarters, but this one was nine and three-quarters, as I later measured. And it was thick, very thick and roughly veined. I almost swooned, and I rapturously held it in both hands. Clear precome lubricant oozed out copiously. I touched it to my face, and then I couldn't wait.

"Let me have it. Fill me up with this wonderful cock," I moaned, spreading my legs wide.

Then I felt the great monster split me apart. The pleasurable sensation was so intense, I started to orgasm immediately, and it lasted and lasted—longer than I had ever experienced before. "Do it hard," I whimpered, and he started to work in and out—slowly at first, then increasing the speed until he finally banged so hard, I almost lost consciousness. Only the joy and the pleasure kept me aware. I reached the highest level of pleasure and just stayed there. My lover's sweat dripped on me, our bodies smoothly gliding against each other as the wetness served as the lubricant. Then he fiercely fucked me, until he shouted, "My God, I'm bursting!" I felt him melt inside me, and the swishing and slurping sounds became more intense as much of his come had filled me and squished out. What a sweet mess it all was. The smell of raw sex filled the room.

I held on to him, and he stayed inside me and did not wither. I slid my hands down to his buttocks and into the crack of his ass. He responded and resumed fucking. I met his thrusts, and we worked ourselves into another frenzy. Since our bodies were covered with sweat and my mouth was dry, I licked the salty moisture from his face, neck, chest, and arms.

He went wild, and it took a deliciously long time until he collapsed on top of me, spilling his second load into me. I was in an unbelievable state of arousal, and finally simmered down to sweet reality.

He rolled off me, then he looked at me and said,

"Oh boy, if my wife knew." I told him that my husband and I have been happily married for more than twenty years, due to the fact that we have had an open marriage for several of those years. The more juicy stories I told him, the more interested he became, until, finally, he rose to the occasion again. Rock-hard, he entered my wet, swollen pussy and did some more powerful fucking. We both reached that beautiful plateau of pleasurable release again.

Two weeks and four more visits later, he asked me to meet his wife and talk to her about our lifestyle. Well, I did, and we have become good friends and bedroom partners.

—*T. W., California*

Personal I.D.

We sat in the restaurant and talked for well over an hour. I felt an incredible attraction to this man. I wanted to touch him, to kiss him, to have him kiss me—I wanted him! After he excused himself and left, I noticed he'd left his wallet behind with his driver's license in it. I smiled . . . this would be the perfect excuse for a reason to see him again.

The next evening I did just that. I explained to him that I had gotten his address from his license and I was in the area and decided to return it quickly, in case he was in need of it. He invited me in for a drink. The next thing I knew, he was standing only inches away, with one hand behind my head and the other on my breast. He bent his head and kissed me gently, trailing smaller kisses across my cheek, then whispered softly, "I left my wallet in hopes that you would return it personally."

That was all it took to make me melt in his arms. His kisses were long and deep, his hand was gently caressing my breast, kneading its tip, while the other skillfully unbuttoned my dress, letting it fall to the floor. Soon after, my bra and panties followed. He stopped for a moment, looking into my eyes as if to ask if he should continue. I reached for the buttons of his shirt and was stopped short when he scooped me into his arms and carried me to his bedroom.

A brief flash of guilt crossed my mind, but it was soon forgotten when the kisses commenced once again. His lips were warm on my skin, and when they reached my breasts, I shivered. A slight moan escaped me. The kisses he bestowed on my body sent my senses reeling. They traveled to the junction between my legs. My first instinct was to stop him. I reached down, only to have him grab my wrists and hold them firmly at my side.

When at first his hot tongue touched my most private spot, I thought I would lose my mind. All sanity was removed. The only thing that mattered was the gentle assault this man was making on me with his tongue. My breathing became erratic. I could feel the perspiration forming on my brow. The ache between my legs became overwhelming. I wanted to explode! Never had I thought I would have such overpowering sensations.

Just then, he left me. A sigh of protest escaped my lips. He stood at the edge of the bed, smiling down at me, and removed his clothes. Soon he was naked before me. His body was exquisite and well-defined. His penis was extremely large compared to my husband's, and for a moment I thought it might be difficult to get this man inside me.

The look of worry must have crossed my face, for a second later he was lying next to me, whispering words of comfort in my ear, followed by more soft kisses.

His fingers worked their magic on my mound, massaging little circles on my clit, then diving deep inside me. Soon the twinges came. I closed my eyes, wanting only to revel in the ecstasy. He stopped, and when I opened my eyes, he was poised above me. In that instant, he entered me. It only took my body a moment to adjust to his size as he moved slowly inside me. His penis filled me completely. I could feel its tip reach deep inside me with each stroke, as an intense urge for fulfillment came over me. My hips swayed, matching each plunge. I held his buttocks, pulling him deeper. When his fingers reached between us and found my clit, the explosion began, a shudder coursed through my body, and spasms gripped his penis like pulses. I held him fast as my back arched and my body convulsed beneath him. I soared through clouds, then fell back to earth. He moved more rapidly now, his muscles tense, and with one last thrust, he collapsed on top of me.

"You're a wildcat," he said, looking into my eyes. I hadn't realized that I'd left marks down his back until he got dressed. I said I was sorry. He bent and kissed me. "It was worth it."

—V. B., Utah

Little Drummer Boy

After reading *Penthouse* recently, I knew I had to share my story from a few months ago—my encounter with a very talented musician.

After a long day of business seminars, I sat in the lounge of the hotel where I was staying. As I sipped my margarita, I noticed the drummer of the band that was playing—I was looking at him, looking at me. By the time the last set was finished, I knew what he wanted.

His kisses were so passionate, I was instantly wet and ready for him. He licked and kissed me all over, then softly whispered, "You taste so good." We began to undress, and I saw his manhood in all its glory. As I sucked his cock, he moaned with pleasure. When he asked me if I wanted to be eaten, I quickly said yes and sat on his face. He put his tongue in my aching pussy, licking and sucking furiously until I almost came, then he entered me. I could feel him ramming his rod into my cunt. It was sheer ecstasy! For hours we experimented with several different positions until we both collapsed from exhaustion. This "little drummer boy" had given me the most enjoyable evening of my life.

—M. H., Louisiana

Marital Bliss

The sky was dark, the water in the hot tub boiling and steamy. The mist swirled in the air around us. My naked breasts rubbed against his chest. His hand touched my sensitive clit. He rubbed it between his fingers, causing me to moan softly. My hips rose to meet his probing rhythm. My pussy became wet with desire, and his huge cock sprang to life. I straddled his lap and slowly lowered my slippery pussy onto his pole, my breasts bouncing in the cold air and making my nipples hard. I moved faster as I felt my pussy pulsating around his cock, and began to feel an orgasm coming on. My pussy tightly grasped his cock as my body shuddered with a shattering orgasm.

We decided to move to the bedroom and resume our activities. Once there he lay back on the bed. I knelt between his legs, gently took his balls in my mouth, and sucked and licked until he moaned with pleasure. My tongue moved up to the head of his slippery cock while my fingers tickled and stroked his balls. I kept sucking until he was almost ready to explode—tempting as it was to have him shoot on my face so I could taste his hot come, he grabbed me, pulled me on top of him, and rammed his cock deep into my wet hole.

He shoved his cock in so deep I thought I would split—he felt even longer and harder than usual. He rolled me over to the edge of the bed and pulled my legs over his head. While he pumped me with his massive cock, he rubbed my clit with his finger until we both exploded in a massive orgasm. Another awesome night with my sweet, loving, and incredibly *sexy* husband.

—J. K., Ohio

What a Muscle!

I proceeded to remove Alex's tank top, khaki shorts, and briefs. I was pleased to discover the largest penis I'd seen in my four years of exploring. It was about nine inches long and thicker than my ankle, and I wondered if he'd be able to fit it all inside me. When I giggled, Alex asked me what was funny. I told him I'd been hoping he was well hung. I quickly took off my shorts and blouse, and let him do the honors with my bra and panties. After getting me naked, he gently went down on me, running his fingers and tongue through my soft blonde hairs until he found my clit. I needed no foreplay, but Alex worked me into a frenzy anyway. My wetness was spilling onto his face and hands.

I rolled over onto my stomach, and Alex began rubbing his dick along my slit to pick up some lubrication for the task ahead. He pulled me up onto my hands and knees and prepared to enter me from behind. His large cockhead nestled inside my lips, and I relaxed my vaginal muscles. I opened them as much as I could as Alex began his entry. I can't describe how wonderful it felt to have his huge, warm organ sliding into me for the first time, although it hurt a little. It felt as if someone was pouring a hot mold inside me, as his cock was filling every available space in my cunt. His rod finally reached the back of my pussy after about a minute of positioning. I looked underneath me and saw his balls resting up against my now sopping mound. Knowing that I could fully accommodate his large member, I asked Alex to fuck me hard with his beautiful prick. He began to thrust, and after three or four minutes of furious fucking, he shot a healthy load of come deep inside me. I needed no further servicing—my crotch was completely drenched, and my body was tickling all over. We lay there for about ten minutes—I just wanted to enjoy the feeling of being so filled up. When Alex finally withdrew, my insides had to completely reposition themselves.

He cleaned up and left me to myself—my energy and arousal completely spent.

—*C. S., Texas*

Seduction

My roommate's boyfriend came over, so my date Jerry and I went into my bedroom to listen to some music. We sat on my bed—drinking beer, talking, and listening to some powerfully sexy music that I had selected especially for the occasion. Eventually, we began to kiss, and things started to get very hot. All of a sudden, he stopped and said he didn't feel right having sex with me on our first date. I had no intention of letting him get away after he had gotten me so horny, so I apologized and excused myself to get another beer.

I went to my roommate and asked if I could borrow something sexy to wear. She gave me a short blue-silk nightshirt that buttoned up the front. I quickly went to the guest bathroom and changed into the nightshirt, making sure I left enough buttons undone so Jerry would be able to see my breasts when I bent over to hand him his beer. I got the beer and went back into my room. The look on his face when I bent over was one of sheer longing. He took a sip of his beer, and I kissed him again. A moment later he mumbled something about my not playing fair and kissed me passionately, pressing his hard cock against my stomach as he did so. When I felt his cock, I knew it would only be a matter of time before I had it inside my hot pussy.

He unbuttoned my shirt and began kissing his way down my body, beginning at my neck, which drives me crazy. I stopped him when he got to my breasts and helped him out of his clothes. When I saw his beautiful, rock-hard dick I was delirious. Then he resumed kissing and sucking my body, beginning at my hard nipples and slowly working his way down to my hot pussy. When his warm, wet tongue reached my clit, I began to writhe on the bed. He was moaning as well, and I could tell that his cock was aching to be caressed. I told him to turn around so I could suck that nice organ, which he gratefully did.

I began to gently lick the slit of his cock to the rhythm of his licking of my pussy, knowing that I couldn't hold out for very long. I began to suck his tool in earnest, gently circling the head with my tongue as I did so. I came explosively as he moaned his own approaching orgasm. When he came he bucked so hard that I had a hard time keeping him in my mouth. His come dribbled down my chin, and when he pulled himself from my mouth, I licked my lips to make sure I got all of his tasty sperm.

We lay there for a while, exhausted and elated. We fell asleep in each other's arms and awoke a short time later. He kissed me gently, and I could feel him hardening again. I stroked him while he fingered my clit. Then he turned me over, put a pillow under me, and entered me from behind. It felt so good; and I started gently squeezing and tugging at his balls while telling him to fuck me harder. I came quickly, but he held back. He started fucking me faster, and once again the feeling of his cock and balls sent me into the best orgasm I ever had. My moans must have pushed him over, too, because I could feel his cock swell. The warm jet of his come followed. It was the most incredible sexual experience I ever had, and I hoped it would lead to many more similar encounters.

Since that night we have tried almost every position known to man, and I can honestly say that I have the most perfect lover in the land.

—J. L., Oregon

Mare in Heat

I'm a freshman at a small Southeastern college. It hasn't been easy meeting men, but one guy, Jay, paid a lot of attention to me, and we went out a couple of times. Somehow our conversations always turned to sex—I guess it was because of mutual attraction and lust. At times the size of the bulge in his pants made me soak my panties. I knew I would soon have him between my legs.

He asked me to a Halloween party, and I said that I would love to dress up for him. I borrowed a very short black skirt, got some fishnet stockings, a black bustier, my five-inch red heels, and a little apron. My roommate said I was the sleaziest-looking French maid she'd ever seen!

At the party, my pussy tingled as we drank, danced, and partied. Soon he was stroking my cunt, and I insisted we leave for his place right away.

We were hardly in the door when I pulled his pirate tights down, unleashing what I later measured to be a ten-inch sword! I gasped as it sprang up and hit my chin. I took the bulbous head down my throat and pumped him with my hand. He held my head and fucked my mouth with long strokes. I held his balls and pumped thick rivers of jizz all over my heaving tits.

At that point he carried me to the bedroom and put me in one of those swing things. As he diddled my dripping cunt, I melted into passion and ended up begging him to fuck me good. He held my ass, my legs spread wide around him, and pushed that huge cock up my open pussy all the way to the base. I shrieked as a violent orgasm ripped through me. He held me tight and proceeded to fuck me unmercifully through a wonderful sea of screaming, thrashing climaxes—my slick snatch impaled like never before. He fucked me like this until I passed out from exhaustion. When I came to, we showered together, and then he took me home.

Now I'm in total lust with that huge cock of his, and we've been fucking steadily ever since that night. I, for one, believe what they say about size—my pussy may be stretched out, but if this is what it's like to be a horse-cock lover, I'm a mare in heat!!

—C. B., South Carolina

Slippery and Wet

I heard him in the shower, and after hours of thinking about his rock-hard, satisfying cock, I knew this was my moment. I quietly opened the door and entered, stripping off my clothes. I climbed in, surprising him when I grabbed the soap and started washing off his dong. I slowly stroked, switching from soap to hand stroking, and finally some sucking action. I ran my tongue up and down his increasingly hard shaft as I gently rubbed and squeezed his balls. Then I started to suck and nibble on the very end of his cock, hardening my grip on his tightening balls. When he moaned I took his entire shaft down my throat, increasing the tempo, water running down my back. I could feel my own clit getting wet and throbbing with anticipation.

Just as I could feel him starting to come, I gently started over, licking up and down his shaft, occasionally nibbling his balls. That teased his cock enormously. Since I had started fingering my clit, my own excitement mounted. When he couldn't take any more, he ordered me to bend over. I gladly obliged, loving the feeling of his superhard cock when he first drives it into my soaking pussy. He started driving his cock into my throbbing pussy, water spraying down on us as we both moaned in ecstacy. As he drove his shaft deeper and harder into my pulsating vagina, I couldn't take it any longer. The feeling was too intense. I came in waves, letting out a scream of passion, cresting and breaking the waves of desire. As he felt my pussy tighten and listened to my screams of delight, he could take no more. I felt his own pulsating organ explode as he drove it as deep inside me as he could, moaning in pleasure, pumping his cock in and out of me until we both collapsed, weak-kneed and happy. I turned around and put my mouth to his cock again, starting from the base and working my way up. When I reached the head, I ever so lightly rolled my tongue around in circles, slowly and gently, licking and licking until I felt myself begin to get aroused once more. Judging from the size and hardness of his cock, so was he.

He grabbed me, carried me out of the bathroom, and threw me onto the bed. Passion burned in his eyes as he commanded me, in a husky voice, to lie on my back. I gladly obliged, and once more he drove his cock deep into my wet, silky depths. I moved my hips to match his, watching his body gleam with sweat, knowing that this man was mine. As I felt myself getting ready to explode again, I drove my hips into his, once again groaning with pleasure at watching his cock entering me, driving in and out, my wetness covering his shaft. And I exploded with multiple orgasms that came in ripples, like waves crashing onto the shore. Feeling those multiple vibes was too much for him, and he drove that beautiful shaft deep into my cunt, which only extended my pleasure, making me drive my hips into his with such a fury, I thought at least one of us would have bruises. As we came down from our passion-filled glory, he collapsed on top of me, kissing me deeply, driving his tongue down my throat. I never feel happier or more satisfied than I do after making it with my lover. If only I could get him to experiment with the kinkier side of sex, though I can't imagine it getting any better than it is now.

—R. P., Vermont

Letter to a Friend

I am writing this with the hope that a very special person will see it and know how much I need him in my life. The day I decided to become my friend's lover was one of the best days of my life. My husband had always said I was frigid because I couldn't come with him—but my friend showed me that wasn't true.

We decided on a hotel for the first night we would be together. He arrived first and arranged for everything we would need. When I got there, the first thing he did was compliment me on how I looked. Then he kissed me and made me feel very special. He didn't rush me at all. First he kissed my lips, then my neck. He worshiped my large breasts and nipples, then he sat me on the bed and proceeded to eat my pussy for hours. He never once pushed me into having sex with him. He was content just to caress me and eat my pussy all night long. I fell asleep at some point during the night. When I woke up, we made love slowly. I came twelve times that night—pretty good for a frigid woman. Thank you, my friend. You will always be very special to me.

—R. E., Colorado

Country Copulation

My boyfriend and I have been involved for about one year now. We are each married to someone else, so our sexual encounters take place only about once every two months or so. When we are together, we like to take our time to really make love.

About two weeks ago, we met one Friday morning. We each brought along a few items. One bottle of Evian, one blanket, the most recent issues of *Penthouse* and *Penthouse Letters,* and some ideas! We headed north to a small, remote resort I had visited once before. Along with regular rooms, they have cabins which they rent for weekends. As we were checking out the cabins, Anthony tried his room keys in the lock. With a little patience, he was able to open the doorl What a neat surprise. The furthest thing from my mind was making love to him in a romantic log cabin during the day.

We quickly locked the door behind us. The excitement of possibly being discovered added to my extreme horniness. Anthony has a fine body, with the best-looking ass I have ever seen. He had on skintight Levi's. As we slowly began to kiss and caress each other, I could already feel my pulsating clit start to make my cunt moist. I could feel his rock-hard member straining to be released from his jeans. When our tongues met, I just melted all over. As we removed all of our clothes, I ran my hands all over his gorgeous body. His cock stood tall and proud, begging me to wrap my moist lips around the tip to slowly suck him off. I slowly licked his neck, then nibbled and sucked my way down his chest and all around his thighs. I enjoy giving head so much that I almost came before he even touched me. As my lips engulfed his long hard cock and my pussy lips massaged his leg, I could feel the tension building inside me. I licked him as if he were a cherry Popsicle, caressing his tight balls with my tongue and lightly twirling them in my mouth.

Anthony always does an incredible job of lasting for hours. We decided to make full use of the brass bed that we had found. He pushed me back, and I could hardly wait for him to thrust the head of his cock inside me. He entered me nice and slow, massaging all around my pussy lips with his thumbs. The anticipation and the sensation of feeling his dick all the way inside me was so incredible, I came about four times, with the most intense orgasms I have ever experienced.

My juices were flowing. Anthony loves to tease me with slow strokes in and out until I beg him to fuck me harder. We enjoyed trying all different positions. Once he lifted my back off the bed and slowly moved his cock in and out until I exploded again. I could not believe it when he took my hand, lightly rubbed it across my lower stomach, and said, "Feel me inside you." I could feel the head of his dick as he pushed all the way into me. I couldn't wait any longer. I wanted to taste my juices all over his cock.

I pushed him back on the bed and sucked him dry, never missing a drop of his hot, sweet come as he shot it deep down my throat. It was the most memorable experience I've shared with Anthony so far, and I hope he can read this in *Penthouse* and realize that this is my way of saying thank you.

—*M. H., Texas*

Sunday Night Sex Session

The weekend was coming to an end—it was Sunday evening. We were lying on the sofa watching television. The movie was quite boring to me, so I began running my hands all over my boyfriend's chest, gently caressing him. He appeared to be enjoying my touch, so I slowly moved my hand down to rub his leg, then back up to his chest. Slowly I inched my hand along his inner thighs until I was rubbing his cock. I felt it grow hard under my caresses. Then I removed his shirt, pants, and underwear and began kissing him and rubbing him all over. But I wouldn't suck his dick—I just licked his balls and inner thighs. After several tantalizing minutes of this, I slowly began licking his hot, throbbing tool, running my tongue up and down the shaft, paying special attention to the head. By the time

I inserted his dick into my mouth, he was squirming with desire and begging for me to go down on him. He was preejaculating like a gusher. I licked all his juicy love potion and continued to suck and lick his hot, swollen member for several more minutes. Then we retired to the bedroom for my turn.

I threw myself down on the bed, and my boyfriend ordered me to take off my clothes. I hastily removed my panties and the T-shirt that I was wearing. Then he attacked me, rubbing my breasts and sucking my nipples until they were hard and red. He then kissed my stomach and caressed me with his strong, knowing hands.

Next he started kissing, sucking, and biting my inner thighs while his hand massaged my cunt. As he continued to rub my breasts, he put his tongue inside me—making me scream with pleasure. I started rubbing my clit. I was so excited that I came within minutes. Then he instructed me to raise myself up with my feet and arch my back, supporting myself with my hands so I was in a position similar to a back bend. He continued eating me.

I was grinding myself against his face, trapping him between my thighs, begging him to stop, but praying that he wouldn't. My juices were spilling out onto the bed and onto his face, running down his chin. I'm not sure how many orgasms I had, because I lost count after three. Then I threw him off me, swearing that I couldn't stand it anymore.

I grabbed his cock, inserting it into my mouth, and

slowly began licking and sucking. Then I made him lie down on the bed so my mouth and tongue could pay full homage to his body. After he was totally out of control, I mounted him and stuck his penis into my hot, wet pussy. I exploded instantly. My boyfriend, however, is a very experienced lover, so he turned me over onto my back, and we started moving together. He was thrusting his tool deep inside me. We were moving as one, simultaneously, and I was screaming with delight while he moaned with ecstasy. Then I turned over so he could enter me from behind—his favorite position. He entered me quickly and began thrusting deeply. I moved my hands between my legs, caressing his cock as he thrust it inside me. That's when he lost all control and came inside me. We both stayed still for a few moments, enjoying the aftermath. We were both so weak, our knees were shaking. That Sunday night sex session was something I'll never forget.

—S. P., Tennessee

Making the Grade

I have always wanted to fulfill a sexual fantasy of mine in a remote mountain cabin during a gentle snowfall, next to a warm fire. After six months of learning enjoyable lovemaking from my teacher and special friend, Jack, it was time for my final exam.

Upon arriving at our mountain retreat, we

unpacked and settled in for a cozy weekend of love. I sensuously stripped down to my lacy underwear, then I took the shirt off Jack's back. He stepped outside to gather a load of firewood while I slipped his shirt on. Underneath the flannel, my nipples hardened through my clingy lingerie as my excitement grew. I anxiously waited for Jack to return.

After Jack started the fire, I snuggled up to his handsome body to begin my final lesson on a warm bearskin rug. I started to massage his muscular back and chest, then I moved my hands down to feel the firmness of his thighs and tight butt while gently kissing his neck and ears. Noticing the swell of his cock, I began playfully to lick his nipples. Next I unzipped his jeans and moved closer to rest his large cock against my cheek. Feeling the warm glow from his cockhead, I began to gently lick and nibble the sensitive underside of his dick. I started slowly sucking his cock until I felt a hot jet of thick, sweet come splash the back of my throat.

When I had licked up the last of the come from his still hard cock, Jack slowly removed my shirt. His hands reached around my back to unclasp my bra, our tongues darting in and out of each other's mouths. When my breasts were freed from their lacy confines, Jack massaged them with one hand. With his other hand, he started to insistently tug my panties off. Once I was completely naked, Jack's hands moved slowly toward my wet, hot box. His stimulation of my clit made me want to feel the warmth of his body on mine.

I wanted him to fuck me, to place his dick in my pussy. As he glided his hot rod firmly in and out of me, I begged him to pump faster. Waves of orgasm overcame me from his deep, penetrating thrusts. Looking into his hazel eyes, a twinkle told me that my final grade was an *A*.

—*E. B., Washington*

Camping, Yes!

It was late, probably around 1 A.M., and I was alone with my love in the lush mountains on our first camping trip. The fire outside beautifully illuminated the inside of our tent. I was awfully horny, but apparently he wasn't, since he was already trying to go to sleep. Well, he wasn't going to get off that easy. Ever so gently I leaned over him; my naked breasts hung down, lightly touching his arm. I slowly kissed him, first on his cheek, then his lips. He turned over and looked up at me. I smiled and began kissing him all the way down his chest, onto his belly, then only his inner thigh. I sucked hard on his thigh, watching his excited cock grow. It bobbed as if asking me to take it in my mouth.

I slowly ran my tongue up and down the length of his hardening cock, softly, then with more passion. I took it between my lips and let it ease into the warm wetness of my mouth, his moan urging me on. I increased the pressure of my lips, creating a tighter vacuum, and slowly fucked him. Gently, I slid his cock out of my mouth and covered his balls with my lips. I watched as he threw his head back in ecstasy, wanting me to swallow his cock again, but I had other things in mind.

Pulling him onto me, I started licking his neck and ears. He put the head of his rock-hard cock at the entrance of my tunnel and began teasing me by slipping just a little of it in and then pulling it out. He then started to rub it around my clit while I shivered from the sensation. I started to get hot flashes, the excitement was so incredibly overwhelming.

He slowly eased his cock inside me, as deep as I could take it. In his frenzied, passionate state he began thrusting harder and deeper into me. He threw my legs up behind my head and pounded even harder. Tugging at my breasts, he slowed his pace, then with one last incredible thrust, he had us both coming.

Our energy drained, and I opened the tent flap for some cool air. It felt good against our sweaty flesh. The fire had died down, and we rolled over in our sleeping bag into each other's arms. I hope all our camping trips are this good.

—0. F., California

Fantasies Do *Come True*

Four years of erotic fantasies finally erupted into one hot, passionate night for both of us. I've been trying to think of a way to thank him for giving me the most incredible sexual experience I ever had—and putting this letter in your magazine is the perfect gift for a perfect lover.

The fantasies started more than four years ago, when we began working together. I used to dream of seducing him every time we met, but my fear of rejection always won out. Then he moved farther away—leaving the telephone as our only form of communication. As luck would have it, we were both traveling to the same city for a convention. I arranged for my company to book me into the same hotel as him, even though I had no idea if I was ever the object of any of his desires.

I was just about ready to give up on seeing him—cursing myself for expecting anything to happen—when, finally, late in the night, there was a knock at my door. It didn't take us long to realize that our attraction was definitely mutual! He leaned over, and our lips finally found each other. It was a slow, sexual kiss at first, then it turned into a passionate, sultry kiss that I prayed would last forever. My body felt like it was on fire, pressing against his. I unbuttoned his shirt and undid his pants, running my tongue down his sexy, smooth chest to reach my final destination—the swelling in his pants. As he undressed me, I kissed every inch of his body that I could reach. He lay me down on the bed, kissing my neck and shoulders, stopping to suck on my breasts, working his way down to the ache between my legs. I've never had a tongue do to me what his did—exploring every crevice of my soaking-wet cunt. I had to beg him to stop so I could feel him inside completely. As he entered the territory, he pleaded with me not to move—he didn't want to come yet. That's all I needed to hear, and I started bucking fiercely against him until he exploded.

Now I knew this definitely was not going to be the end of our adventure. We had a lot of lost time to make up for. After a few minutes, it was time to let my tongue do the work. I teased him by ever so lightly licking his cock. He responded immediately, as I very slowly took him in my mouth—feeling him grow hard against my tongue made me wet and willing to do anything to satisfy him. I wrapped my lips tightly around his dick, sucking every inch while torturing him with my tongue. He grabbed my legs and had me straddle his face in a sixty-nine. I could feel my juices flowing down my legs as I ground my pussy against his face while he fucked my mouth. Then he told me to sit on his cock. I turned around to face this gorgeous man. Kissing him, I could taste my own juices as I guided him into my own cunt. I arched my back and slowly glided up and down his rod as I reached behind to fondle his balls. Both of our hands caressed my tits, making my nipples painfully erect. He placed his hands on my hips and pounded me harder against him. We came together in another harmonious climax.

Little did I know there was more to come. As he was saying how worn-out he was, he kissed me long and hard. Before I knew it, he was on top of me and his cock—as hard as could be—was finding its way home between my legs again. I told him I wanted him to fuck me from behind, so I could feel him deep inside me. Getting me on my hands and knees, he squeezed my ass tight with his hands and slipped his erection into my wetness. When he told me to touch myself, I didn't hesitate for a second. I rubbed my clit while feeling his hard, wet cock thrust in and out of me. He was tracing his tongue lightly up and down my back and neck, causing a sensation I'd never felt before. His hand joined mine, as he brought me to the most glorious orgasm I've ever experienced. He came inside me with as much strength as the first two times.

We collapsed in each other's arms, agreeing it was definitely worth the wait.

—K. F., Pennsylvania

ON THE JOB

It Works!

After reading Xaviera Hollander's October 1991 column containing the letter from N. L. in California, I was wild with desire. My pussy lips were already slickening in anticipation of the orgasm I would have in the "frog" position, and I couldn't wait to try it out. I was just hoping I could find a man to oblige. As luck would have it, our office Christmas party was the next day, and I'd had my eye on a certain coworker named James ever since he started working there. I made my way over to him for some small talk and the conversation quickly turned sexual. I intentionally brought up the *Penthouse* article about the frog position, and to my surprise, James said jokingly, "Hey, what are we waiting for . . . let's try it." "Right here?" I giggled.

The party was far from over, and most of our coworkers were milling around, including our boss.

We set our drinks down and James led me by the hand to his office. He kissed me hungrily as his hands grabbed my ass. I could feel his manhood pressing against my thigh and could tell I was in for quite a time. We moved some papers off of his desk and he lay down on his back as I described the position to him step by step. I was so hot by this time, I almost said the hell with the position. I wanted his cock inside me right then and there.

I knelt down while James moved his legs out from under me and I slid his cock deep inside me. His cock felt so good, and I began to rock back and forth so it would press on my clit. The combination of my sexual attraction for James, our friends and coworkers down the hall, and this froggy style made my body begin to shake almost instantly with a massive orgasm. I could have sworn the desk actually moved.

Just then there was a knock at the door, and before we could make ourselves decent, the door opened. Our boss had wondered why James was still working and not at the party. We thought we were both immediately fired, but instead, our boss set his drink down, unzipped his fly, and placed his cock in front of my waiting mouth. I took him inside while I continued to rock away with James's ever-growing prick inside my soaked pussy.

I sucked my boss's cock as James pumped his load deep inside me. I was approaching another orgasm and began to grind down on James. I reached up and gently squeezed my boss's balls and took him even deeper into my mouth. I knew he couldn't last much longer, either, and just then I felt his cock begin to pulsate. He shot his thick jism into my mouth and I eagerly swallowed every drop as my own body shuddered with a second orgasm.

We cleaned ourselves up and went back to the party. Thank you, *Penthouse* and Xaviera, for informing us of the frog position. I definitely found not one, but two Prince Charmings that evening.

—*M. N., Virginia*

Steel Mill Stud

I am one of the very few women who work at a steel mill. Sometimes I find it hard to work around mature, good-looking, well-built men without having sexual fantasies. One of my handsome coworkers, Brian, always came across as very shy, but I fantasized that underneath that coy boy there was a passionate beast. One day my dream came to life.

We were assigned to go on the overhead crane and dust the cabinets. It was a hot August day, and the temperature was beginning to make me hot in more ways than one. Seeing the sweat roll down Brian's masculine chest and smelling his seductive cologne, I was getting hot and wet.

I think he sensed my thoughts, but it was obvious from the way I was undressing him with my eyes. He started to loosen his shirt, and I couldn't control myself any longer—I had to have him right there. I grabbed him by the shirt and thrust my body against his. His warm, moist lips teased me as our tongues raced back and forth. My hands slid down to his perfect ass and squeezed his hips next to mine, inviting him to take me. I could feel his pulsating cock through his jeans, and it was driving me wild.

I started to unbutton his jeans. Meanwhile, he was massaging my sensitive neck with his tongue, licking back and forth. I released his cock from confinement and gently massaged his throbbing manhood. By this time I was dripping wet and overcome with ecstasy—my wildest fantasy was coming true. I took a second to stare into his alluring hazel eyes and run my fingers through his auburn hair, then down his massive chest.

He began to unbutton my shirt and playfully nibble at my neck and shoulders. He slipped off my jeans, and we dropped down to the platform. He worked his tongue up and down my body, focusing on every sensitive spot until he reached my clit. Massaging my pearl with his tongue, he gently fucked me with his forefinger. After what seemed like an eternity of erotic movement, I reached the most incredible climax I'd ever dreamed possible.

Next he worked his way back up to my lips and kissed me hard as he penetrated me with his massive cock. The humidity was almost unbearable yet stimulating. Our bodies clung together with every thrust, and I grabbed his ass and drove him deeper. Our moaning grew louder. As I begged him for release, it seemed to make him want me more, and his thrusts became harder.

Just when I thought it couldn't get any better, the crane clicked on and started moving down the mill. Apparently, the operator didn't know we were up there. Every little bump the crane hit drove me wild. After we both climaxed, we collapsed into each other's arms. He gently kissed me. We were drained from the heat that we had created. Remembering that we were at work, we quickly got dressed and returned to our jobs. Later we met in the parking lot for more of each other, but I'll save that story for another time.

—P. E., Pennsylvania

Lust for Lunch

Recently, my boyfriend and I had an interesting and very enjoyable lunch hour. He is one of the sexiest men I have ever known and is very creative, which means our sex life is far from dull.

On this particular day, he called me at my office and said he would meet me at my house in an hour. As soon as he arrived at my house and bolted the door behind us, an animal magnetism drew the two of us together. Our tongues explored each other's mouths, barely letting us breathe. We made our way to the bedroom with our clothes falling in heaps along the way.

I bent down and locked my mouth around his raging hard-on. I sucked his hard cock into my mouth and tongued my way down the length. As my tongue swirled back and forth across the tender spot just below the head of his penis, my hands pumped his thick shaft. He lifted my head off his hard tool, lay down on his back, then pulled me on top of him. I put his cock into my very wet and waiting cunt. I slowly rode him up and down, then bounced wildly on his cock while he rubbed and squeezed my tits.

Then he rolled me over onto my back without his hard erection ever leaving my hot, dripping box. I wrapped my legs around his waist and thrust up to meet his every stroke. He lifted my legs even higher as he pumped in and out.

After he positioned my legs on his shoulders, his prick sank in to the hilt. We fucked fast and furious until I started to come, my body convulsing against his. Suddenly he shoved his thick prick deep inside my wet, throbbing cunt, and I had another mighty orgasm.

Then he lowered my legs, and once again I wrapped them around his waist. Ever so slowly he pushed the head of his cock into my pussy, then he stopped. Without warning, he plunged his cock into my tight slit. I moaned loudly and raised my hips to take all of him. I was approaching climax again. I lifted my head to kiss him, and he opened his mouth wide. His tongue swirled with mine until I shuddered and writhed ecstatically. He rammed his cock into me time and time again.

Just when he was about to come, he removed his prick from my pussy and proceeded to spurt hot, thick jets of come all over my chest and in my mouth, some splashing on my neck and tits. We collapsed, exhausted, in each other's arms. That was by far the best lunch hour I'd ever had, and I can hardly wait until my lover's next creative moment!

—S. W., Michigan (Aug. '93)

Counting with Cynthia

I am presently employed as a grocery-store cashier, and one recent Sunday we had to do inventory on all of the stock. I was assigned to work with Cynthia, my fellow checkout girl. We were in the manager's office counting all of the tobacco products. I couldn't help noticing Cynthia's very sexy legs, which were revealed by her short pink skirt. She was braless, and her pert nipples stuck out through her blouse—she was quite a sight.

I had climbed up on a stepladder and was counting cigarettes when I asked Cynthia to hand me my inventory sheet. She climbed the ladder and stood behind me, nonchalantly placing her hands on my shoulders to give me a gentle massage. "Oooh, that feels good," I said.

"Does it?" she asked. "If we put our heads together, we can make each other feel *really* good." Then she grabbed my hand and seductively ran her tongue over my fingers. I couldn't believe how good it felt. I was really getting turned on by my sexy coworker. Her hands ran up my shirt and over my breasts. I put my hands over hers, and we both caressed my boobs while she began to nuzzle my neck. We couldn't stand it any longer and got off the ladder and headed to the compressor room, knowing that it would be the only place for lusty, uninhibited sex.

We met in the middle of the room and each clutched our arms around the other. Our mouths met, our tongues exploring. I ran my hands under her blouse and felt, fondled, and squeezed her firm breasts. Cynthia unzipped my trousers and pulled them down—along with my now soaked panties.

Next she unbuttoned my shirt while her other hand diddled with my wet pussy. She unzipped her skirt and took off her blouse. We French-kissed and fell to the floor, not caring how dirty it was. As I lay on my back, Cynthia ran her tongue up my leg, slowly working her way to my cunt. "I want to taste you," she purred as she opened my legs wide and buried her face in my twat.

Her tongue worked magic on my wet clit as she licked in a circular motion, making me squirm. She licked faster and faster, then slid her tongue into my hole, exploring every crevice. I couldn't believe how horny I was. She continued to please me for another fifteen minutes, and then climbed on top of me so we could kiss some more.

She rose up above me and brought her pussy down so I could taste it. She went up and down, moaning as

I fiercely sucked her pussy for another quarter of an hour. Then she ran her tongue over my breasts, sucking them ever so gently, making my nipples stand out, rock-hard. I caressed her ass as she made love to my breasts, and we continued our lust for the next hour. Needless to say, it was a very profitable inventory.

—*R. Y., Nebraska*

Business Meeting

I love to tease, so if Jenna wanted to fuck around on her girlfriend, I decided to let her have a little fun. Whenever I came to her office, she would give me gifts like flowers, candy, or sexy panties she would imagine me wearing. She would even hold all calls and lock her door when I was there. This girl sure had the hots!

She wasn't about to get my pussy right away. She spent several of our "meetings" kissing me and trying to either take off or pull up my skirt while I warded her off. She was very aggressive and quite adept at wooing, nibbling, and kissing. But I taught her who the boss was, and only let her get so far each time. I was driving her crazy, but told her that she could just go back to Mary and forget our little get-togethers if she really wanted to. But she wanted me, so she had to go at my speed. I was in control.

It was erotic being in her office, having this very intelligent young woman going bonkers over me. I felt very masterful, realizing what the powers of the flesh held over her. She'd always wind up on her knees with me sitting on the edge of her desk or in her leather swivel chair, my skirt hiked up while she massaged my legs and kissed my inner thighs or my tummy. She had already nicknamed me "The Bod," and she loved to explore every inch of it. I had let her loosen my top a few times and go wild on my breasts, which she couldn't seem to get enough of. That felt pretty nice. I liked watching her looking at me as she licked and sucked my tits. She adored them, and they had her panting.

Finally, one day—wearing a see-through mesh top under a light blazer, with no bra, a short red skirt, garterless black mesh stockings, and a pair of black thong panties—I sat on the edge of Jenna's desk, and as she fell to her knees, she begged me to let her lick me. She had wanted it long enough, and I relented. Soon her tongue slipped right into my pussy. Her tongue licked my honeypot as if there was no tomorrow, and as her face buried in my muff, she looked up at me as if she was in heaven.

I teased her, asking, "Who tastes better, me or Mary?" I could see her smile as her head went up and down and side to side, tasting my muff for all she was worth—I could tell it was no contest. Boy, could she give some head! Her cheeks were literally slapping against my inner thighs as her tongue circled over and around my clit. Making her wait had heightened her excitement more than I could have imagined.

I liked seeing her head down there and seeing her

nose pressed up against my pussy hair. While she was busy eating me, her hands roamed all over, either pushing my knees apart or wrapping around my outer thighs or firmly holding my ass while her tongue did its trick.

I liked getting licked by Jenna, and sat back and let her do all the work. She never asked me for anything in return. I felt sorry for her when the phone would ring or if she would have to meet with someone and let them in. One time she took a call, talking to the person in between licks of my pussy. She was very annoyed that she couldn't just hang up the phone.

Jenna introduced me to a very exciting experience, and needless to say, I enjoyed it very much.

—L. J., New Jersey

Home Improvement

After thirty years of marriage, my husband died suddenly, and I found myself, at fifty, sleeping alone, very well off, and set upon by every gold-digging lounge lizard in California and points east. After a year of this, I decided to sell the house and move, but I needed to fix it up, so I started taking bids. I must have seemed like the perfect target. I look forty—full breasts, wide hips, long legs, sensuous mouth, dark eyes, black hair, olive skin—and have a great deal of money. Prices from the contractors were outrageous, and all of them thought I would jump into bed with them. Finally, a chance meeting with an old girlfriend provided me with the number of Marty. I called him, and he came over.

He was a handsome man in his forties, black hair going gray, big brown eyes, warm, humorous, and very honest. He said we should start with something small and see how it went, so he gave me an estimate on the guest bedroom, and he started the next day.

I had errands to run, and when I came back, he was stripping wallpaper. To my surprise he was wearing cutoffs, no shirt, and sandals. I couldn't help but check him out—it had been *so* long.

He had a great body—strong legs, a firm, round ass, flat stomach, strong arms and chest (salt-and-pepper hair on his chest and stomach, glistening with sweat). His sweet, musky scent caught my nose, and I could feel my nipples harden, my heart start to thump, and my mouth water. I hadn't planned on this. My mind went blank.

He gave me a big smile, and said, "Ah, the woman of the house." My heart just melted, and I wanted him right then and there. He was standing on a ladder, facing out, his waist about level with my head, and I could see his cock pressing against his Levi's. He saw where I was looking, and his cock lengthened and thickened down his leg. God, how I wanted it.

Without saying a word, he unsnapped and unzipped his cutoffs. I stepped forward, pulled them down, and his cock sprang out and up in my face. The shaft was blue-veined, the swollen glans was deep red, almost purple, and I proceeded to swallow it whole! A delicious cock—a good seven inches and full balls.

I was nipping the head, stroking the shaft, and driving him crazy. He moaned deep and full like an animal, one hand buried in my hair, the other steadying the ladder against the wall. I continued deep-throating him and squeezing his hard buns until I thought he was going to come, but he displayed great control. I was glad, because I wanted his load in other places besides my mouth.

I stepped back and unzipped my blouse, freeing my swollen breasts, my inch-long nipples jutting out at him. I stepped closer and wrapped them around his hard cock, giving him a breast fuck while I licked his belly and squeezed his great ass until he moaned again—a real man, completely masculine and natural. I was in heaven. I brought him to the edge again and stepped back; offering him my breasts in my hands. I undid my skirt and let it drop, pulling the thong aside to reveal my wet, hot, purple-lipped cunt to him, spreading the folds, fingering cunt honey onto my hand, and putting my fingers in his mouth. He licked them clean while I sucked his cock, rubbing another handful of cunt honey on his cock, covering his balls with it. He went wild.

He pushed me back onto the bed and stepped down between my legs. I was spread wide for him, everything in a haze, blood pounding in my brain, every inch of my being on fire! He took his full, hard, swollen erection in his hand and ran the head up and down my wet, hot slit, the opening at the head of his cock kissing my fully stimulated clitoris. Up and down, again and again. He was working me so good, making me want it so bad. It was never even close to anything I had done with my husband, and I always thought we'd had a good sex life. Was I wrong!

I couldn't stand it anymore. I reached down and spread my cunt to him, imploring him to fuck me. He looked deep into my eyes and slowly put the head in—I was in bliss. I wanted it hard, but he had other plans, only giving me an inch at a time. With his hands moving up and down my body, massaging and squeezing my swollen breasts and nipples, thumbing my clitoris as he sank his hard shaft completely inside me, I came!

Then he started to really fuck—long strokes, short strokes, combinations, fucking my brains out, fucking me into ecstasy. I had a multiple orgasm, coming three or four times in a row, and he was just incredible. I had never come so hard and fast and often at one time. It was like I was in another world, out of my senses, just aware of his being and his cock and his hands taking me to new heights, an orgasmic wave carrying me along. Wanting it from behind, I turned over, head down, my bottom up in the air. He gave it to me, fucking me like a dog—I was a bitch in heat. The tempo picked up and I was gone, finished, history. I came twice more and picked up his rhythm, working my ass against him, bringing him closer and closer. Then, with a deep roar, he started coming.

Quick as a whip, I pulled away, turned, grabbed his erection, and took his full load into my open mouth, catching his hot, sweet come on my tongue, letting his sap run down my throat until he collapsed between my legs, his tongue going inside my cunt, lapping up my love honey, eating my throbbing pussy until I came again.

Then we both passed out. We woke up laughing, his laughter matching mine until our mouths met in a long, wet, come-mixed kiss. Then we got into the shower and fucked standing up. Afterward, he carried me to the bed, and we slept until dark.

I woke up in the early evening, his erection against my rump. I eased it in while he slept, fucking him with my cunt muscles, and he came in his sleep, even though his eyes opened and looked into mine as he did, his orgasm matching my own—heaven!

He spent the night, and the next, and after three days, we were together. Needless to say, the work on the house is progressing slowly, but I am his apprentice. He is teaching me about renovation and about all the positions and techniques of advanced fucking. I am teaching him a few of my own talents. He is the kind of man every woman dreams of—a stud, a stallion, a lover, a friend, intelligent, fearless, a great sense of humor, and heaven to sleep with.

—M. G., California

Hired Help

I am not an avid reader of your magazine, but I have read a letter or two from your "Forum" section. The letters always seemed a bit far-fetched to me, and I believed that they were only the imagination of a lonely soul. But after this event, I am a firm believer, and would like to share it with your readers.

I am recently married, and am now living up north. I am from a small Southern town, and I left all my friends to move to Pennsylvania. My husband is away a lot—his job takes him out of state for days at a time.

On this particular weekend, my husband was out of town, and I was getting our town house painted by Tai and Ray. I was very bored, so I decided to go through my summer clothes. I found one of my favorite outfits that I thought I had lost. Wondering if it still fit, I decided to try it on. As I started to undress, I felt as if I was being watched. On the closet door in my bedroom I have a full-length mirror, and in the mirror I saw the reflection of the two painters standing on the scaffolding outside my bedroom window.

Knowing they were watching my every move, I decided to give them a show. Wearing only my French-cut panties, I grabbed the feather duster from my closet. Propping one leg up on a shelf, I ran the duster up the back of my leg, starting at my ankle, then over my calf and across my long, silky thigh. I started to work the duster back and forth across the crotch of my panties. I soon forgot who I was doing this for, as I was very much into the pleasure I was giving myself. As I ran the duster over my belly and to the undersides of my breasts, the tingling sensation from the feathers sent a wave of chills across my body, which made the nipples of my large tits stick out. Then all of a sudden, I heard a loud thud, and that made me remember my Peeping Toms.

Throwing a robe on, I headed to the window. I asked them if they were okay. Tai had twisted his ankle. I told them to come in and that I'd be back with some ice. When I returned I told Tai to take off his boot so I could check it out. He was reluctant, saying that he thought it would be all right. Finally, he did, though. As I removed his sock, I told him that it didn't look like there was anything wrong, but that I'd better check some more to make sure nothing was swollen. My hands made their way up his pants to his crotch, and I said, "Well now, this seems to be very swollen. . . . And I know just how to fix it." The two men gave each other high fives and were out of their clothes in a heartbeat. I took off my robe and panties and got down on my knees in front of Tai. His cock was brick-hard and pointed straight up, with a slight curve to it. His cock was on the small side, so I was able to take all of it in my mouth.

As I sucked Tai's cock, I felt Ray slide between my thighs and lower me onto his face. His tongue worked masterfully on my dripping pussy. After a few minutes of this, they wanted to switch positions. Tai lay on his back and I straddled his head, rubbing my juices on his face. Ray stood in front of me. When he pulled his shorts down, one of the biggest cocks I'd ever seen leaped out at me. It was at least eight inches of thick, dark meat. Being a woman who loves big cocks, I eagerly took his pole into my mouth. I have been told that I am an expert cocksucker, but I was only able to get about half of it in. I sucked his cock hard, and Tai licked my pussy for about twenty minutes. Needing something hard inside me, I turned around, and Ray slid his huge black cock into my pussy. My cunt felt as if it would split end to end as his dick filled every inch of it. I felt something rise inside me. My whole body was an active volcano, and I erupted into an incredible orgasm. I think I had four fabulous orgasms that day. As I started to get hot and wet again, I told them to get up and jack off. My juices started to flow as I watched them stroke their cocks. Tai was moaning like crazy as come flew from the head of his cock and landed all over my tits. As he massaged his come into my tits with his cock, Ray put his hand on my face and turned me toward him. His cock was only inches from my lips as he pumped it furiously. Being what you could call a junkie, I wanted every drop of his come. He jammed his dick into my mouth, and I felt the hot come splashing in my mouth. Not wanting to waste a drop, I sucked every bit of his cock. There was so much come, it seeped out of the corners of my mouth. Ray used his finger to scrape up what was on my chin, and I licked it off his finger. After lying on each other for a few moments, they put their clothes back on and headed out the window to finish their work. I just stayed there for a while, savoring the taste in my mouth and the smell of sex in the air. I hope everyone enjoys reading this as much as I enjoyed living it.

—L. D., Pennsylvania

Turnabout

For the past four years, I've earned extra money as a phone-sex operator. Most of the callers want me to do all the talking, but last week a very special man named Jack called, and here's how it went. . . .

Me: Hi, Jack. My name's Roxanne, and I'm twenty-two years old. I'm five-foot-two, with red hair, long legs, a small, round ass, and big tits. I'm a C cup, and my measurements are—

Jack: Do you like to have your pussy licked?

Me: Yes. I—

Jack: I bet you do. I'd love to bury my face in your little red cunt. I'd suck your lips into my mouth and run my tongue up and down your slit, stopping only to tickle your little pink clit. Would you like that, Roxanne? [At that point I noticed myself beginning to squirm in my seat. My silk shorts were getting moist. Most callers are passive and let me talk, but Jack barely let me finish a sentence. The role reversal was very exciting.]

Me: Do you like to have your cock sucked, Jack?

Jack: I'd love to run the tip of my seven-and-a-half-inch cock all over your face. You'd be on your knees, naked. I'd sit on the edge of the bed. You would lick the shaft until you got to the tip. Then you'd stand up and sit on my dick. I'd fuck you hard and fast. [By then I had my hand in my shorts, fingering my very wet slit.]

Me: Oh, yes.

Jack: Touch yourself, Roxanne. Fuck your own cunt.

Me: I am.

Jack: Stick two fingers in.

Me: Okay.

Jack: Now bring them up to your mouth and lick them. They taste good, don't they? Now with your other hand, I want you to pinch your nipple and rub your tit.

Me: Oh God, yes, yes.

Jack: Now keep rubbing your nipple and fucking your cunt. I'm going to come. I'm going to spray it all over your face.

Me: In my mouth, baby. Come in my mouth! [I heard Jack coming for a second, but my own orgasm was too loud for me to hear much more.]

We thanked each other and said good-bye. Jack has yet to call me back, but I'll bet he's making some other phone-sex operators as happy and satisfied as he made me.

—R. M., Maryland

Muscle Madness

I work in a men's clothing store. Having a good Midwestern work ethic, I check every order before sending it to the factory, even those taken by other managers. It was while doing this that I noticed what seemed to be a big mistake.

I found an order for a man who was, apparently, fairly heavy for his height—215 pounds at five-eleven. His neck was over eighteen inches, his chest was fifty-one inches, and his waist was thirty-two inches. Either some of these measurements were wrong, or this guy had one hell of a physique. On the off chance that this was the right information, I knew I wanted to meet this Goliath.

You see, ever since I can remember, I have hid a real weakness for guys with big muscles. I loved to watch all those old *Hercules* movies and pretend that I was the young slave girl who would be rescued by the strength and power of the huge muscle man. More recently, I've become a big fan of *American Gladiators*. The sight of those big guys just gets my pussy juices flowing!

I decided to call this guy, Marty, to come back in for a refitting, claiming I wanted to make sure we had all the right information. I said I was the new manager and wanted to take personal responsibility for every aspect of my job. I suggested he stop in sometime near closing. To my delight, he said he appreciated the extra effort and would be happy to stop by the next night after his workout.

Upon hearing him say "workout," I became overwhelmed with excitement! This was not a potbellied guy—this was, in fact, a real muscle man!

I carefully decided what to wear for my first encounter with a *real* bodybuilder, wanting to show off my very firm, five-foot-five, 115-pound, 37C-23-35 body. I decided on a simple white-silk top that clung to my firm breasts and a short black-leather miniskirt that showed off my great legs. Of course, I wore no bra and my skimpiest panties.

Just around closing the next night, I looked up and saw him. He looked even bigger than I thought he would. He was wearing a Gold's Gym sweatshirt and baggy muscle pants. His enormous shoulders tapered to the tightest ass you can imagine. He was in his late twenties, about my age, very well groomed, with dark brown hair and deep blue eyes. His rugged good looks fit the rest of him perfectly.

I thanked him for stopping in and suggested we step into the fitting room to take his measurements. I had to stretch my arms to get the tape measure around his enormous chest. While doing this, I could feel how rock-hard he was. His pecs felt like slabs of granite, his back muscles rippled right through the thick sweatshirt. Wanting to see more of his body, I thought quickly and pointed out that we could get the best results if he would slip out of his shirt. He was more than willing to accommodate. I think he was catching on to my little game, as he noticed my nipples harden.

It was staggering! I was standing in front of my

very own Hercules—deep tan, bulging muscles, and the smoothest skin. This guy was awesome! I continued my job once again, measuring his chest and his tight little waist. I said I wanted to make sure the suit we ordered would have enough room to accommodate his big arms, so I asked him to flex to get the right measurement. As he flexed, I held my breath as the tape stretched to over twenty-one inches.

I couldn't help myself. I asked him to flex his entire body for me. He was certainly on to me now. It was all I had to say. Without breaking eye contact, he slipped off his muscle pants, revealing the teeniest bright blue bikini briefs. His thighs looked like they were carved out of tree trunks. As he went from one pose to another, I became hotter and hotter. Almost instinctively, without really thinking, I slipped off my top, revealing my big, firm tits. I cupped them gently in my hands, playing with my hard nipples. He smiled as he saw me getting pleasure out of worshiping his huge body. He looked down at my miniskirt. Without saying a word, I knew what he wanted to see. I writhed out of it, stretched my hands above my head, and displayed my body for him. His cock showed me that he liked what he saw.

I moved closer to this mountain of muscle. I got down on my knees and slowly removed the last bit of clothing between my mouth and his cock. His shaft was as well developed as the rest of him. When I took him into my mouth, he groaned with pleasure. As I worked on his muscle shaft, he continued to pump and flex. His body was now covered with a thin film of sweat; it made him even more beautiful. As he flexed and I sucked, we were surrounded by images of ourselves from all angles in the fitting-room mirrors. This added to our excitement, as we got off on our perfect bodies.

I looked up at him and whispered, "I want you to be my Hercules." He smiled and said that nothing would please him more. He spotted the big chains that we use to secure the security bars on the loading dock. He asked me to wrap them around his enormous chest. I knew exactly what he was doing—he was going to act out one of my favorite scenes from the movies.

As he towered above me, his cock deep in my mouth, I saw him place his hands on his waist and breathe deeply—his chest expanded, his pecs bulged, his lats flared out, and the chains fell from around my Hercules. As he broke free, he came in my mouth. His load was thick and hot, just like his body.

It was incredible. Since that time we have played out many other fantasy scenes. The sex is really great when two gorgeous bodies merge in muscle-crazed passion!

—D. M., Illinois

Cleaning Up

We can finally afford a housecleaning service. That gives me time for myself and some pet projects. But I soon learned another major advantage of having a crew clean my house. In our case, the work is done weekly by two young guys from the Philippines. From day one, I not only admired their easygoing efficiency, but also their exotic faces and muscular bodies. From day two, I not only lusted after them, but also devised a strategy to seduce them.

Cleaning day number three saw me parading around the house with mini cutoffs that exposed part of my cheeks and a flimsy T-shirt that brought out the best of my shapely breasts. The result was almost immediate. One fellow dropped his cleaning bottle and the other bumped into the furniture with the vacuum cleaner. I teasingly scolded them and threatened the appropriate punishment. Their smiles nearly melted the lower part of my body, and I wanted to fuck them right then and there. But I savored a slow approach. I derive much pleasure from the tease and anticipation, as well as from a prolonged, built-up sexual tension.

In the fourth week, I acted like I had just gotten out of bed. My hair was down, and I wore a sheer baby-doll nightie. Their eyes were popping as they ogled me. As I moved around, the silky fabric stuck to my skin, showing my erect nipples. I bent down to show them the dark crack of my ass. I sat down on the couch to read the paper, spread my legs to let them see up my thighs. From the cool air, I could feel that they were able to see the furry part between my legs.

But now I was moist and wantonly hot. With a low voice, I asked them whether they perform *other* services. They asked, "What do you have in mind, lady?" I leaned back, moved the fabric of my panties aside, slowly spread my cunt lips, and proceeded to insert one finger inside of me.

The two men dropped their cleaning equipment, sank to their knees in front of me, and started to caress my body. Their hands were all over me, softly stroking my thighs, kneading my tits. As soon as I removed my hand from my pussy an eager tongue lapped broadly from the bottom up to my clit. Every time he touched my knob, I felt closer to coming. One thick finger slid between my swollen pussy lips, and I almost dissolved in a shattering orgasm.

They had undressed and showed their other equipment. Their dark, smooth bodies were almost hairless. Their cocks stood straight up near their bellies. I leaned forward and licked one of these beautiful tools while holding the other in my hands. I opened my mouth, took it all in, and started a slow pump, which turned into a fast pump until an enormous eruption shot down my throat. I took a deep breath and continued the same treatment on the other cock. All this had taken but a few minutes, and I wasn't through yet, by a long shot. In fact, I burned with desire. I led the two men into the bedroom and sucked them alternately to a renewed state of action. I took the deep pounding on my back with my legs over their shoulders. I was in sex heaven.

Two men in bed is my favorite, surpassed only by more men in bed, including my husband. Like always,

I told my husband what I'd been up to, and he joined us a couple of weeks later.

—T. W., California

Behind the Scenes

Imagine a beautiful neighborhood in Oregon with trees, white picket fences, and annual barbecues. This is the type of neighborhood that Larry and Debbie live in. They are the model neighbors in everyone's eyes, but behind the bedroom door there is a different side of them.

Their bedroom is a *Penthouse* wonderland. The bed has a beautiful oak canopy with mirrors on the top and sides. At the foot of the bed (which vibrates), there is a stationary video camera for recording all the fun and adventure.

You see, I'm their housekeeper. One day while cleaning their bedroom I found one of the tapes they had made together. I put it in the VCR that was in the bedroom and began to watch it. I couldn't believe my eyes. The ever-so-perfect couple was doing things I have only dreamt of. Debbie came into the room in a little string bikini and lace cover. Larry was sitting on the bed with a bulging hard-on. Debbie went to him and stripped each piece of clothing off. Once she was at his feet, she began to suck his now even larger toy.

As I was watching this I began to get wet. I wasn't

sure what was turning me on more—his huge penis or her beautifully shaped breasts. I began to finger myself while watching more of the tape. Debbie stopped sucking and Larry lay back on the bed. Then she sat on his face and he began to eat her out. I couldn't stand it—I began to masturbate. Just as I was close to coming, Debbie and Larry came into the room. I was so embarrassed . . . I wasn't sure what to say or do. As I started to get up, Debbie came to me and began rubbing my breasts. She asked if I wanted her to eat me out, and I told her that I wasn't sure. She just smiled and guided me down onto the bed. I could tell that Larry was getting quite turned on by the way his penis was growing in the fastest way. He began to rub himself.

Debbie was sucking my tits and rubbing my clit and my breathing was so wild I couldn't control myself. Larry came over, sat on the bed, and turned on the mattress. The more it vibrated, the wetter I became. Debbie started to lick my cunt, and Larry suggested that I close my eyes so I wouldn't be able to see what was happening. I could only feel that there were two people on me. One of them was sucking my tits and the other was eating me out. The feelings were so much more intense because I couldn't anticipate what was going to happen next. Larry stuck his long, hard cock into my mouth and his precome tasted so good. He then put his penis into my wet cunt and began to bang me. He started slowly, then worked his way up to a fast, pulsating hump. I screamed as I climaxed.

When they were done, I opened my eyes. They were both sweaty, and when Debbie asked how I'd liked it, I just smiled. Larry invited me over to enjoy their company anytime. Now I can't wait to work for them again next Tuesday.

—H. H., Oregon

Working the Worker

My fantasy begins like this: There are men working in our house. I find one in particular very attractive. My husband is also home. I am going about my business in the kitchen, working at the counter and sink, preparing our dinner. I am wearing a half shirt with no bra and a denim miniskirt with nothing underneath. From behind me I hear someone working. A few minutes later, my husband is standing behind me, sliding his hands up my ribs underneath my shirt to gently grab my breasts. His fingers feel their way to my already hardening nipples. He lightly pinches them, and they harden all the more. While he plays with my tits, I let out an approving moan to let him know in yet another way that what he is doing is just right.

My nipples are like stones between his fingers, and now I can feel my cunt throbbing because of what he is doing to me. I am getting wet and slippery between my legs. The anticipation of waiting for him to discover my wanting cunt with a finger is killing me. He is so excited—I can tell by his breathing. I reach behind me and feel his excitement through his jeans. Finally, ever so gently, his fingers find my hot cunt. He is so surprised when I spread my feet a little farther apart. His finger finds my moist entrance and teases me. I want his finger to enter me, but he continues his game. While he is playing with my entrance, I quickly bend my knees so his finger is forced to slip inside. Again I give a most approving moan. He slides his finger in and out of me.

I need to take him to my room, so without even turning around, I take his hand and lead him up the stairs. One of the other workers spots us and gives us a thumbs-up. When we enter the bedroom, I turn to close the door. To my surprise, the man is not my husband but the worker I was admiring earlier! I can't stop now. Even if I wanted to, he is already sliding his hands around me to find my ass, hiking my skirt up to feel my cunt from behind. Then he kisses me, softly at first. I open my mouth to his, and our tongues meet and explore each other. Wow, does he taste sweet! Now my curiosity gets to me, and I need to see the bulge beneath his pants. I slide my hands slowly from his shoulders to his not-too-hairy chest. It's hot, and I can feel his heart racing beneath my hands. I slide my hands down to his navel and use one finger to trace the hair from his belly to the thing I've been wanting since he first touched me. I unbutton his pants and ask him to remove them. He is wearing normal white briefs, but they are so sexy on this man. He is breaking through the elastic waist. I stroke him through his underwear, then I pull them down to reveal a soft yet very hard cock. He sits on the edge of the bed. I love the taste of man, so I can't resist him. I lick his cock to get it wet all over, then grab the tip of it with my lips and slide them down the length of his bulging cock—tugging, sucking, and playing with it with my tongue.

Now it is his turn to let out a moan. Sucking and licking and kissing, I love the feel of him in my mouth. I can feel that he is ready to explode, but I am not finished yet, so I slow down and gently kiss his cockhead. He lies across the bed—I lean over him and let him play with my hanging tits, the nipples still showing my arousal. I swing my leg around so my cunt is above his face. I let him look and, finally, explore with his fingers. I can't see his face, but I can feel his pulse accelerating to an incredible speed. I know he must love watching his fingers disappear and reappear from the depths of me. I reach around my own ass, and with my fingers I spread my cunt open even farther for him. That I would let him look at me in this way excites him so much, and it excites me to know that I am able to do this to a man. I lower myself to him so he can reach me with his mouth, and I feel his hot, wet tongue lick the area around my cunt, finally tasting all of me as he slides it in and out. I shudder as I feel my juices rush into my loins. I moan, wanting his tongue to be farther inside me, wetter, hotter—my heart is beating so hard and fast, I'm sure it will somehow escape from my chest—exploring, licking, thrusting until my entire body trembles in an incredible climax.

He licks me softly now, tasting me again, knowing it was he who drove me to such wild passion. I move my body down to touch his cock with my still wet cunt. I rub it, covering him with my juices. To his surprise, I slip his cock right into my opening, but only the tip at first. I love to tease! As I am coming down so slowly onto him, he jerks his body up, and the length of him is buried inside me. My cunt seems to tug on his cock, as if I want to feel him deeper. We thrust our bodies together and, since I am on top, I make sure my cunt swallows his entire cock—in and out, up and down. Once again his hands find my flopping tits—pinching my nipples in such a way that it feels as if I am being fucked in two places! My cunt is just throbbing, this is incredible! We roll over to the missionary position, and I grab my legs to give more thrusting power. I feel his hands on my ass as our bodies are turned into one. Again I feel my body shuddering below—his is doing the same. Thrusting deeper into me, it seems as if he is going to put his whole body inside me. I *want* his whole body inside me. I feel his body tremble, and I know that his climax is about to happen, just as my second one is. Together, deep, hot, wet, I realize I have been screaming softly. I feel his cock throb and pulse as he shoots his magnificent seed into my barren body. With no worries, I reach the point of ecstasy with him. We kiss, then smile at each other. I tell him there is a lot more work to do and that we will be needing him until further notice. *I* will be needing him.

My husband knows of this fantasy and is turned on by knowing that I actually imagine this when we have sex.

—L. M., Wisconsin

Love Is Blind

Here is a story that I would like to share, even though in so doing I have to make a few embarrassing admissions.

First let me say that I am thirty-seven, unmarried (sigh), and work as a secretary for the most wonderful and gorgeous man in the world. Although I have a nice bust line and shapely legs and fanny, I am not what you would describe as beautiful, with the result that my social life—and yes, my sex life—is nil.

Anyway, I have this mad crush on my boss, and I have had it since I started to work for him, five years ago. But do you think he notices me? Not in the least. Oh, I've tried, let me tell you, but nothing seemed to work.

Then one noon a couple of months ago, I had a quick lunch in the cafeteria, then returned to the office for a package I was going to mail at the post office. His office door was closed, and thinking I'd ask him if I could get anything for him while I was out, I opened the door . . . and what a sight I saw.

There they were on the floor, my boss and Martha, the receptionist, going at it like crazy:

I was utterly shocked and, at the same time, hypnotized by what I was watching. He was stretched out on his back, completely nude, with Martha, also nude, astride his midsection, pumping away, her little breasts bouncing and flying about with every mad thrust. She was riding him for all she was worth, and the very thought of it drove me insane with jealousy. They were positioned so that she was facing me, but she didn't see me, as her eyes were closed. Then, suddenly, something must have registered, for her eyes blinked open in recognition. After the first grimace of shock, her face melted into a broad smile, and she winked! The sight of the two of them so unnerved me that I was trying to back out of the doorway when Martha made a motion for me to stop and, pausing not the least in her rhythm, she pointed to his head and made hand motions for me to come in and undress.

I looked down at him, and for the first time I noticed that his eyes were tightly closed. Despite her urging to the contrary, I was going to back out and leave them alone when the thought struck me: *Why not? An opportunity like this doesn't come often in my life.* So, my decision made, I slipped into the room, closing the door softly behind me, and quickly stripped nude.

Martha motioned me over and, as she did so, she leaned over close to his ear, telling him quietly that she wanted to do it to him orally and he should keep his eyes closed. With that, she eased herself off his pelvis, revealing the most gigantic male organ I had ever seen, even in the magazines. Inexperienced as I am in such matters, I couldn't even begin to estimate the dimensions—it was simply *huge*.

Glistening moistly, it stood there, erect and waiting for further attention. Bending over, Martha grabbed the back of my head and pushed my face right down on the top of its gleaming wetness. Under her expert, albeit silent, tutelage I began to fellate him, licking at the stiff organ for all I was worth. After two minutes of this my crotch was dripping, I was so randy. I'm sure Martha must have sensed my hunger, for, aided by her deft hands, I squatted over his erection. Apparently, gently easing down was not the way to do it. Martha grabbed me around the hips and shoved me down. With that, his entire length pierced into my unyielding flesh, dilating me like I had never been before. I felt so full!

What happened afterward was one wild race to orgasm. My breasts, flopping about with unaccustomed lack of restraint, seemed to be a force all their own. I hit peak after sensational peak, and I was just about to add another to the score when he stiffened, arched his back, and came in a whoosh, spasm after spasm. He was just barely gurgling to a stop when Martha motioned me off. Panic-stricken by what I had been doing, I managed to get my blouse and skirt on, and then, slipping into my shoes barefoot, grabbed the rest of my things and dashed for the ladies' room, thankfully unseen. Once there, I stood in the stall for a long time, savoring the throb of my stretched muscles and his moisture running down my inner thighs.

Nothing was ever said about the episode, even by Martha. I truly long for an encore, but even more, I wonder over and over if he ever knew.

—Name and address withheld

OVEREXPOSED

Our First Nude Beach

My roommate Connie and I had never been to such a place before. I was very surprised when she suggested it. But there we were at the gate to a small nude beach in California. We could see the naked bodies on the beach beyond the sand dunes.

"Let's go, Jennifer," my friend said as she strode onto the warm sand. We walked toward the ocean. There were lots of people on the beach, more than I expected. When we found a spot, Connie spread out our blanket and lay down. "I can't do this, Connie," I said. "Sure you can," Connie said as she removed her T-shirt, exposing her breasts. "You have a wonderful body and nothing to be embarrassed about," she added, removing her shorts. I looked at my naked friend and thought, if she can do it, I can, too. I stood up and stripped. It felt like everyone on the beach was watching me, although I'm sure they weren't.

Connie asked if I wanted some lotion. I agreed and she began to coat my body with it. Her hands felt wonderful as they slid across my hot flesh. She spread the sun cream on my shoulders and breasts, on my stomach and legs, even in my pubic hair. "Do me," she then said. I poured the lotion into my hands and smeared it onto her back and ass. I always felt that Connie had a wonderful body, better than mine. I found myself enjoying the feel of her rounded bottom and smooth inner thighs.

We lay on the beach for a while, watching the men and women, and then decided to go for a swim. "Hi there," said a fellow swimmer. "Hello there," I responded. He introduced himself as Ron, and the three of us swam together for a while. He followed us back to our blanket, and although I tried not to notice, I couldn't help seeing that his body and penis were quite large. I noticed that Connie was watching him, too.

After the three of us had talked for a while, Ron suggested we all walk down the beach. He said the nude area was about two miles long, but most everybody stayed at this place. We picked up some bath towels and headed down the coastline. Soon we were completely alone. Ron wanted to swim again; we declined and watched him walk toward the water. The moment he was out of earshot, Connie said, "Did you see the cock on him? I'd love to get a ride on it!" I found myself laughing and nodding.

Ron jogged back to us, his penis bobbing from side to side. When he got to us, his cock was at eye level, only feet from our faces. "Listen, Ron," Connie said seductively, "Jen and I were wondering if you'd like to fuck the two of us." I looked at Connie, surprised at her boldness. Ron looked rather surprised, too, but before he could answer, his penis said yes. It started to grow, and it continued to grow until it was at least twelve inches long.

"I don't know about you, Jen, but I'm not impressed," Connie said with mock seriousness as she took his cockhead and several more inches into her mouth. She wrapped both hands around the rest of him and began to pump. Ron moaned in ecstasy. Connie was sucking him as if she hadn't had a drink for weeks!

My pussy was getting wet, and I began to rub myself. "Looks as if Jen wants to be fucked, Ron," Connie said, and she was right. I was horny as a cat. I lay on my back, spread my legs, and Ron eased his cock into my inviting pussy. I never had anything that big inside me. Inch by inch he slid it in, until his entire length was filling my cunt. He fucked me for several minutes, and I had the first of many shattering orgasms. After about my fourth, Connie yelled, "My turn." She got on her hands and knees, and Ron slid into her from behind. I watched, fascinated, as he fucked her good. By the time he finished, Connie was screaming with joy.

Our well-built friend stood up, his still-hard cock bobbing in the air. On my knees, I started to suck his enormous log. I sucked the end, and Connie licked the base and his balls. Within seconds he was shooting cream all over my face, chin, and tits. I just smiled as I felt the warm liquid run down the front of me. Connie crawled over to me and began licking the come off my face. Her tongue swirled over my cheeks and into my mouth. I had never kissed another woman before, and boy did I love it!

Ron sat down and watched us lick each other's face. We soon moved our mouths to each other's pussies. We sucked and finger-fucked each other long and hard, barely hearing Ron say he had to go. He left us locked in each other's legs. Since then we haven't enjoyed another penis as much as Ron's, but we're enjoying each other a lot more!

—J. A., Pennsylvania

Playing Doctor

It was late Sunday afternoon and the hospital was quiet. Just forty-eight hours before, my lover had had surgery on his foot. Now we were sitting on a bench outside the hospital, his hand was inside my jeans playing with my dripping-wet pussy, and mine was inside his shorts giving his forever-hard dick a hand job. No matter the situation, we are two people who can't get enough of each other.

As the wetness between my legs was beginning to

make its mark on my jeans, and our playing with each other was getting far too hot for the bench, we decided to try out the deserted cardiology ward. Because of his crutches, his movement was limited, and I was able to have my way with him. As he braced himself with a handrail, I knelt in front of him, unbuttoned his shorts, and released his huge throbbing dick. Taking him into my mouth, I nibbled, swirled my tongue, and thoroughly encompassed that gorgeous rod with my mouth. He says I give the best blowjobs, and I was determined to do justice to those words.

Soon we heard voices and decided to head out to the car in the parking lot for some privacy. As soon as we got into the car, I couldn't stand it anymore. I quickly shed my pants and climbed on top of him, pushing his shorts to the floor. I was dripping wet, and he was as hard as a rock—that cock was just waiting for my pussy to bring it home. Sliding my wet lips back and forth over his dick and then stopping to rub my clit over the tip of that glorious head, I slowly lowered myself on his dick, taking every bit of him deep inside of me.

His mouth worked mine feverishly, and then he pulled off my shirt. He took each breast in his mouth, gently biting the nipples and sucking hard, the way I like it. All this time I was riding him like there was no tomorrow. Somehow he managed to get on top of me, and he was suddenly ramming me from above. I held on to him, digging my fingernails into his back, causing him to groan and sigh.

By this time all of the windows were fogged up, so we opened the door to cool off. The cold evening air felt so incredible on our hot, glistening bodies, so we climbed out—both of us naked—and continued to work each other over on the grass. He finger-fucked me until I grabbed his dick and placed it against my clit—an indication that I wanted to be fucked, immediately! With my juices dripping down my ass, our bodies melted together, his fantastic dick riding high in my love canal—we were one with the night. In fact, we were so into each other that we hadn't even noticed that another car had parked next to us while we were there.

—F. I., Massachusetts

The Art of Fencing

We were standing in front of a chain-link fence that surrounded a school yard. Suddenly he turned to me and started kissing me passionately. I responded by putting my arm around his neck to hold him closer. I could feel his hands starting to move across my hardened nipples. I couldn't help but let out a short, soft moan. I just wanted him to take me. He was so sure of every move, almost as if it were a plan of attack. He lifted my blouse, exposing my soft white breasts. Softly touching me, fondling my nipples, kissing my breasts, and caressing my ass, he kissed his way down my body and finally reached my hungry, waiting snatch. With every part of me turning to Jell-O, he continued to kiss my clitoris until I had to beg him to stop.

At last I had a chance to begin making him feel as good as I could. We began kissing as I undressed him, unzipping his pants and putting my hand around his hard, warm cock. I couldn't believe how perfect he was, such a round, plump head and a long, thick shaft—just right for sucking.

I slowly started to move up and down his shaft, burying my nose in his pubic hair. I could taste the drops of sweet precome as I went back up. He seemed anxious to get started as he pulled me to my feet.

To add a little spice to the situation, I climbed up onto the fence. He immediately followed, coming up behind me, kissing my shoulders, and trying to find a good hole to bury his hard cock in. I took his tool in my hand and directed it into my soft, wet pussy. His rolling motions got me so hot, I began to offer myself to him by bucking my hips and pressing myself against him. I could feel him growing harder, so I slowed the pace. Then, with a sudden burst of energy, he exploded deep inside me.

Suddenly, he went calm and released his grip from the fence. Waiting for me to join him on the ground, he helped me down. We hugged and kissed, then he whispered how much he'd like to try this playground again.

—*J. H., Virginia*

Stealing the Show

I knew it would be a memorable evening—a romantic French dinner, live music, and a night of intense lovemaking. What occurred during the evening could not have been anticipated in my wildest fantasies.

My boyfriend and I began the evening with a delicious meal over candlelight. We sat at a private table tucked away in the back of the restaurant. With the exception of occasional waiter visits, it felt as if we were the only people around. As the meal progressed, my desire for Sam grew more intense. His flirtatious gestures, sexy brown eyes, and captivating smile, coupled with intriguing conversation, left my mind wandering in a wonderfully naughty direction! How I would have loved to sneak under the table, wrap my lips around his dick, and cleanse my palate with his sweet, hot semen! How was I going to last through the performance without satisfying my craving?

We continued to tantalize and tease each other throughout the meal, to the point that we were late for the show. There was no doubt that we wanted to skip the performance and devour each other at home, but we chose not to waste the tickets. We settled into our seats, awaiting what promised to be a great production. What we didn't realize was that *we'd* be the best entertainment.

The lights dimmed, and the music began playing. I tried hard to concentrate on the singing, but my thoughts kept returning to seducing Sam. My hands began gliding over his firm thighs. Knowing that those muscular legs powered the thrusts of his hard cock into me—something I wanted very badly right then—made my pussy swell with desire. Feeling his large bulge was too much. There had to be a way to have him!

During intermission I slipped into the ladies' room and slipped off my panties and stockings. With only a miniskirt on, Sam could have easy access to my starving box. Almost instantly he noticed my bare legs. He gave me a mischievous smile and whisked me to the balcony. Within minutes we were settled in a secluded section that must have been reserved for us. Sam spread my legs and revealed a sopping pussy. I covered my fingers with creamy juices and slipped them into his warm, soft mouth. His skillful tongue and succulent lips savored every drop.

Wasting no time, he buried his fingers in my swollen cunt, teasingly finger-fucking me to near orgasm. Occasionally, others would glance over, but the tempo was picking up, and I just couldn't be stopped. I felt Sam's shaft—it was very firm and very ready to be swallowed up by my quivering pussy. Pulling my miniskirt to my waist, I straddled him and was enraptured by the feeling of his rock-hard cock plunging into me. I gripped his thighs and held on as he thrust in slow, deep pulses. Sam continued rhythmically gliding in and out, bringing me closer to climax with each stroke. I could barely keep from screaming with pleasure, but I had to. Others' stares forced us to slow our pace, though we never stopped. Sam stroked my clit and caressed my erect nipples. When there were no eyes on us, he pulled my skirt higher and resumed fucking me. As all of my sensations peaked, I moaned in ecstasy as I came, pouring juices down Sam's balls. I sank back, cushioned by his muscular body, and relished the tingling feeling throughout my body.

The last moan of delight must have been pretty recognizable. In no time, someone turned around and caught us in the act! Slipping down to my own seat, I couldn't help but think that we had the best entertainment . . . and who knows how many others in the audience thought the same!

—M. E., California

Love in the Lav

My boyfriend Tom and I always have wonderful vacations. Not only do we travel to some great destinations, but we have many erotic adventures along the way. On our last trip to the Caribbean, our adventures started on the plane ride to San Juan.

On the plane I was wearing a short skirt and T-shirt with no bra. The anticipation of our vacation was making me especially horny, and I wanted Tom to be as excited as I was. While he was reading I placed a blanket over my lap and removed my panties. I slid them over my feet and showed them to Tom. He closed the book and smiled.

He reached under the blanket and moved his fingers lightly up and down the inside of my thighs. I leaned back in my seat and spread my legs wider. I looked across the aisle to make sure that the attention of the other passengers was still on the movie, and then began to rub my nipples through the fabric of my shirt.

I let out a small gasp as Tom's fingers brushed my swollen clit. He expertly rubbed my twat and slid his fingers in and out of my hot, wet box. After ten minutes of this I was on the verge of orgasm, but I wanted to come with his huge cock inside of me.

I grabbed Tom's hands and led him down the aisle to the lavatory. I was so hot that I didn't care who saw us go in together. We locked the door and exchanged a long, passionate kiss, while I unbuckled his belt and unzipped his pants.

Tom's cock was bulging from the top of his briefs. I released his stiff, nine-inch rod by sliding his briefs to the floor. I knelt down in front of him and opened my lips to accept the swollen, purple head of his cock.

His cock slid in and out of my mouth until I started to taste his precome. I normally like the taste of Tom's come as it shoots down my throat, but today I wanted him to shoot his load inside my cunt. I was ready to feel his stiff, large dick inside my hot box. I sat on the edge of the counter adjacent to the sink and spread my legs in invitation. I pleaded, "Fuck me, Tom. Fuck me now!"

With one quick thrust, he slid deep inside and began pumping with long, smooth strokes. I moaned softly, and he quickened his pace. I asked him to squeeze my nipples, and he squeezed each of them between his thumb and forefinger. He continued to slide in and out of my dripping pussy.

I could sense that he was getting closer to orgasm and I begged him to pinch my nipples harder. He began to moan as his thrusts became deeper and more powerful. His first shot of come spurting deep inside of me pushed me over the edge as wave after wave of ecstasy washed over my body. My contracting pussy muscles squeezed Tom's cock and milked him of every last drop of semen.

We caught our breath and cleaned ourselves up. As we left the lavatory to return to our seats, a flight attendant gave us a knowing nod and a smile of amusement and envy. This was the first of many adventures on our vacation, but I will write about the others in future letters.

—*L. L., Michigan*

The Ride of Our Lives

Our trip began early one morning as the sun rose in the Las Vegas sky. My husband and I were reluctantly coming to the end of a fantastic weekend. We rose very early to begin our drive to San Francisco. We put the convertible top down and headed west. I took a short nap and awoke incredibly horny from a hot dream. I glanced over at him and realized that I couldn't resist the temptation to "christen" our new convertible with this gorgeous man.

I undid my seat belt and reached over to kiss his neck. He smiled, thinking it was just my normal friendly kiss. I continued kissing his neck, moving closer to his ear. I love to lick his ear, because it always provokes a sexy moan. I moved around to his lips and French-kissed him hard. He looked a little surprised, but he definitely did not want me to stop. I began to rub his legs and continued kissing his neck and ears. I could see him growing hard, which made me even hotter. I undid his shorts and took out his cock. I rubbed it slowly and leaned over to get my mouth closer. I love to rub my face all around him—he smells so manly. I tongued his balls, making him groan. I'm big into noisemaking, and hearing him so horny turns me on even more.

I started to suck him softly, moving my tongue all around. As he grew bigger, I sucked harder. Just when I knew he was getting close, he stopped me. He pulled me up and kissed me, whispering, "I want to see you come." I smiled and leaned back in my seat—he loves to watch me bring myself off. I was already close, so I knew it wouldn't take long. I slid off my shorts and panties and spread my legs on the dashboard, giving him a good view of my pussy. I started teasing myself with my finger, then I plunged my finger deep inside me. I withdrew it slowly and licked my fingers, savoring the taste of my own juices.

My husband was having a difficult time dividing his attention between what was going on outside the car and what was going on inside the car. I leaned over and let him suck my fingers. I imagined his tongue licking deep inside me, tasting what I had tasted. I spread my lips wide, fully exposing my clit. I began to rub myself, and within minutes I was close to what I knew was going to be an awesome climax. I tilted my head back and closed my eyes, moaning as I came and shuddering in the total openness of the convertible.

I slowly opened my eyes and looked at my husband. His glazed look and the bulge in his shorts told me he had enjoyed my performance. I reached over and slowly stroked his cock while licking his ear. "I'm on the cliff," he said hoarsely, which is our code for being close to orgasm. I suggested we pull over, so at the next exit, we quickly found a gas station.

I checked the ladies' room and signaled for him to follow me. I could barely contain myself—I wanted to taste his come. I pulled him into one of the stalls while ripping down his shorts. He sat on the back of the toilet, and I began to suck him hard. I could tell he was close by the size of his dick and the sound of his moans. Just as he seemed ready to explode, a woman entered the rest room. I slowed down my sucking so I could fully enjoy his orgasm. The woman took forever and no doubt wondered why a pair of feet were facing backward in the stall. When she finally left, I wrapped my fingers around his cock, cradled his balls in my other hand, and sucked for all I was worth. He came almost instantly, spurting what seemed like an endless stream of come into my mouth and on my face. I swallowed as much as I could while he groaned wildly. Then I kissed him so he could experience the sweetness of his come. We exited the bathroom just in time to meet the bewildered stare of an older couple in their car. We were on the road again before they figured out what happened. Thoughts of that experience left a permanent smile on our faces.

—J. S., California

Thick Dick

I'm a married woman who reads your letters with my husband on a regular basis. While our sex life is good, I have developed a craving for thick cocks. My husband's is, let's say, average. He is sympathetic to my cravings, and he even bought me an eight-inch dildo that is more than two inches thick. It helps, but it's not like the real thing.

Well, a couple of weeks ago, the annual rodeo was in town, and my cravings were finally satisfied. It all started when my company had its annual rodeo party after work. In the past I'd done a little dressing up for the event, but this year I decided to go all out. I bought a denim skirt that was split up the front and held shut by two snaps, a denim shirt with snaps, and some new boots.

The day of the party was a hot one, so I left my bra at home. The party turned out to be a great big bore, and I left at around seven. As I walked by another party, somebody whistled at me. Always willing to acknowledge a compliment, I turned around and saw a man I do business with from another company. Bobby was at his company party, and he was apparently having a great time, as I would have expected, since he's a real looker. At well over six feet tall, he has a fantastic body, well muscled and proportioned, topped off by a great personality. His wife is equally splendid as well, unfortunately. Bobby brought me into his party, and soon we had taken over the dance floor. Eventually, a slow song came on, and Bobby reached out, wrapped his powerful arms around me, and pulled me toward him. This caught me a little off guard. Actually, what caught me off guard was the lump in his pants.

Because of our height difference, his cock was rubbing my belly just below my breasts. It was massive. Soon I found myself rubbing his cock with my tummy as we made our way around the floor. As I felt it grow in his jeans, he moaned softly, then he leaned down and whispered in my ear that I was going to get in trouble. I responded by lowering myself a little bit so my breasts were against his groin. He took my hint and pulled me closer. After the dance, we sat down at a table. Reaching over, Bobby took my hand and placed it on his groin, which now housed a truly impressive erection. When I squeezed it through his jeans, he responded by slipping his hand up my split skirt. After gently massaging my lips through my soaking-wet panties, he pulled his hand out and slipped a wet finger into my mouth. I have always enjoyed the taste of my pussy, and tasting my juices on a relative stranger's fingers made my cunt throb.

We hurriedly left the party and headed to the river's edge, where we could see other couples in various stages of intercourse. It seemed like many people had the same idea! In the seclusion of the trees, Bobby and I kissed passionately, our tongues entwined as he lifted me off the ground. I wrapped my legs around his waist, his cool silver belt buckle pushing against my soaked panties. Holding me up with one hand, he pulled my skirt from me and let it fall to the ground, then he reached up and pulled my blouse open, exposing my breasts to the cool evening air. I had never felt such wanton lust for any man.

Dropping to the ground, Bobby pushed me back onto my skirt, and as I raised myself to my elbows, he pulled my panties aside and ran his tongue up the length of my pussy. I gasped and fell back, thrusting my pussy up to him. He slid two fingers into me as his tongue went to work on my clit. Lying there in erotic bliss, I could hear the music from the party intermingled with the sounds of other secret lovers along the river. Soon I had my legs wrapped around his shoulders as I erupted in orgasm. As my shudders subsided, I looked down to see Bobby on his knees between my legs. Sitting up, we kissed, the taste of my pussy covering his face. He massaged my breasts as I tugged at his belt, then at the buttons of his jeans.

He was wearing boxer shorts, and as I pulled his manhood through the opening, he slipped his fingers into my open and eager cunt. His cock sprung up at my face, its purple head easily the size of a plum. The shaft was as long as the dildo my husband bought me, but it was much thicker. As Bobby worked his fingers in and out of my soaking pussy, I wrapped my hands around his enormous shaft. Bobby reached behind my head and pulled me forward. I needed no further encouragement—my lips parted, and his manhood penetrated my mouth. For anyone watching us, it must have been a very erotic sight, this petite woman sitting naked on the ground in front of this man, eagerly accepting his flesh in her mouth as he worked his hand over her cunt and breasts.

With the cold night air blowing over my body, I shuddered in orgasm again as his fingers explored the reaches of my vagina. Pulling his cock from my mouth, Bobby gently pushed me back and positioned himself over my eager frame. Looking down between my legs, I saw drops of precome seeping from his cock. In the moonlight they glistened as they formed a small pool on my womanhood. I instinctively wrapped my legs around his waist and pulled my soaked panties aside. I was so horny, I was ready to beg for it.

My flesh opened for this monster, and I screamed out in desire as his shaft sank into my pussy, stretching my flesh to previously unknown limits. As his groin pressed against my clit, I erupted again. I continued to come as he pulled back, then sank back into me. Leaning forward, we kissed passionately, my breasts mashing up against his muscled chest. Bobby had magnificent control, and he continued to fuck me for what seemed like hours before rolling us over.

Pulling me up, he sat me on his dick. In the distance I could see the party as I fucked him to my final orgasm. I collapsed on his chest, too exhausted to move, his cock still throbbing in my vagina. After a moment's rest, Bobby pulled me off and positioned himself behind me. Once I was on my hands and knees, Bobby pulled down my panties and entered me once more, his organ filling my void. With each thrust, my body was pushed forward. Hanging my head down, I could see the glistening shaft protruding from his boxers, and with each stroke, it sank deeper into my eager flesh. With one last powerful thrust, he held himself in deep as he spilled his seed into my loins, grasping my breasts for balance.

—G. M., Alberta

School's Out

Throughout the summer semester, we'd flirted heavily and innocently touched, but everything came to a climax on the last day of class. He left immediately after taking the exam, and I thought I would never see him again. What a surprise when I saw him standing next to my car! Without a word he took my purse and books and placed them on the ground next to us. He gently pinned me against the car and stroked my huge breasts though the thin T-shirt I was wearing. The whole time he was staring deeply into my eyes, letting me know without words how much he wanted me. His mouth overpowered mine and our tongues met. He put his hands between my legs, and I saw his surprise when he realized I was wearing nothing under my tight miniskirt. We both groaned as he thrust his fingers up my cunt, then made me lick my own juices from them. Even though we were in a fairly dark part of the parking lot, we still didn't want to be seen. I fumbled with the keys, and we both jumped into the passenger seat, unable to wait a moment longer. I pulled off my shirt and straddled his lap. He lifted my miniskirt, and while he sucked and teasingly nibbled on my hard nipples, his hands were working their magic on my hot, sticky cunt. I groaned as he bit my nipples and thrust his fingers up my hot hole. He watched me spasm in the greatest orgasm I'd ever had. Then it was his turn.

His tight jeans, wet with my juices, came off. I pulled his underwear off with my teeth and smiled when I saw the biggest rod I have ever seen. His cock was hard as a rock and ready to explode!

My mouth savored the huge treat, and I licked and sucked his shaft as he fondled my ass. I straddled him again, and when he lay back in the car seat, I pumped and ground against him until we both came. Sweating, with our juices all over each other, I was in heaven. He continued to play with my breasts, sucking and nibbling them for quite a while. There was no end to the ecstasy as he pushed me into the backseat and opened my legs. He licked and sucked my clit, thrusting his tongue up my hole. My pussy was dripping wet. Then he French-kissed me, allowing me to taste my own sex again. He flipped me over so I was on all fours and squeezed my hard nipples, making me cry out in a mixture of pleasant pain and ecstasy. I begged him to fuck me again. He entered me from behind and rammed me until we both came again.

—E. P., Connecticut

Dancing Fever

Recently, my boyfriend and I went to a dance club. We usually hang out at sports bars, but we really wanted to try something different. After being at the club for a while, my boyfriend was getting tired of dancing, but I wanted to continue. He sat at a nearby table, and I danced where he could watch. The dance floor was very crowded, and as I danced, another girl kept nudging up against me. Soon we were moving close to each other, and ultimately, together. Since I was alone and could have used the company, I didn't mind her dancing with me. She was very attractive and mysterious-looking, with a real sex appeal. She looked sultry in the tight black-cotton shorts that didn't even cover her ass and a white shirt that revealed her flat stomach and shapely breasts. Her nipples were so hard they were almost poking through the clingy top.

We continued to dance, and when the music picked up, she moved closer to me, putting her hands on the back of my waist right above my ass. She ground her body into mine and slowly slithered up and down to the pulsating rhythm, staring me in the eyes the entire time. So many thoughts were racing through my head. I'd never been with another woman, but this one seemed so attractive and seductive—I really wanted her. I looked over at my boyfriend, and he just smiled deviously. I guess the situation was exciting to him. Instinctively, I grabbed her and pulled her hard body close. I gazed into her eyes and we French-kissed passionately. Our tongues played and our bodies rubbed together. Then she hiked up the hem of my dress until it was around my back so she could place her cool hands on my uncovered ass cheeks. Her hands felt sensual as she explored my body with them. As we moved to the beat, she pulled down my panties and let them fall to the floor, completely exposing my entire lower body to everyone on the dance floor.

You can't understand how turned on I was by all this. For the first time, I was experiencing another woman, in the middle of a club, in front of my boyfriend and who knows how many others. It was completely exhilarating.

The stunning beauty then brushed the back of my

moist pussy with one hand and lightly rubbed the front of my mound with the other. Then she spread my ass cheeks and crotch with one hand and inserted her fingers into my hole from the back. Her penetrating fingers felt so good inside me. I instantly came, and as I did, she grabbed my ass so hard I felt her nails digging into my skin. I whimpered as my juices poured out of me and down my inner thighs. She continued to kiss me and slid the straps of my dress off my shoulders, revealing my tits. This unknown goddess sucked my hard nipples and licked my breasts. My dress, which was wrapped around my stomach, soon slid to the floor as she relished my entire body. I was totally naked, and held her body close to mine so I was not completely visible to the now staring crowd. Her forceful tongue darted in and out of my mouth, and I kissed and licked her neck, longing to taste more of her. As we danced I was dizzy with passion and lust. It got the best of me and made me come again right there, completely forgetting where I was.

Just as I came, I noticed some of the bouncers and security guards walking toward us. Suddenly, my boyfriend grabbed me and pulled me away from the mysterious woman, whom I never even said a word to. She smiled and winked good-bye while my boyfriend and I scurried through the crowd, the bouncers closing in on us. I didn't even have enough time to pick up my clothes. My boyfriend threw his blazer over me, and we fled the club.

During the ride home, I wore nothing but the blazer.

We were so hot that we had to pull over twice and fuck before getting home. I haven't had sex with another woman since then, but I can't wait for it to happen again. My sex life is much better now that I am bisexual.

—*J. L., Illinois*

Viva Las Vegas

This year my husband, Gerard, and I decided to take a trip with our close friends Nadia and Albert. The excursion took us on an eventful trip to Las Vegas.

Flying in at night, we could feel the anticipation growing as the plane circled for the landing. The city lights had only been visible for about ten minutes, but we had already planned our itinerary for the next three days.

Albert and I decided to go sight-seeing while Gerard and Nadia gambled, so we drove out to the Hoover Dam and then picnicked at Red Rock Canyon. I had been attracted to him for as long as we had been friends, but the feeling was never as strong as it was that day when we were overlooking the water.

The passion began to surface that afternoon on the cliff of the painted sandstone. Albert could sense what I was feeling, so he walked over, put his muscular arms around me, and pulled me closer. Then he gently tilted my head up and began to kiss me. His tongue gently caressed my mouth as mine graciously welcomed his entry. Every fiber of my being felt the intense passion that had been bottled up inside us, awaiting the moment when our feelings could erupt. Our bodies were aching to join together, and it was a feeling that we could no longer control.

Albert began to unbutton my blouse and gently caress my body with his soft kisses. His tongue found its way to my breasts, and he began to suck my nipples as his hands carefully found their way to loosen my shorts. Then he laid me back on the rock—placing his shirt under my head—and began to let his tongue trace the curves of my body. "I'm going to love you all over," he told me. My mind holds the echo of his softly spoken words. My body quivered as he lovingly kissed his way down my stomach to the top of my pink lace panties. Stopping there, he rubbed his hands down my legs and removed my shoes.

Starting at my ankles, he licked and kissed his way to the inside of my thigh. He ran his tongue under the edge of my panties, the suspense driving me to the brink of climax when he stopped. "I've wanted to do this for a long time," he whispered, as he knelt between my legs and slowly and delicately began to lick my clit. The passion soon overwhelmed us as he started to make love to me with his tongue. Soon I felt his fingers exploring my wet pussy, which was so swollen with desire, I cried out in passion as he brought me to my first orgasm of the afternoon.

"My turn," I said as I sat up and knelt over Albert's toned body. "Let me spoil you," was all I said as my hands massaged the bulk of hard flesh trying to stay concealed in his hiking shorts. When I removed his raging hard cock from its confining prison, I was amazed at how beautiful it was—nine inches of muscle waiting to thrust itself into my mouth and down my throat. I'm a bit of a tease; so I took my tongue and licked around the head and then lightly down the shaft and back up. Then I placed only the head in my mouth, softly sucking and twirling my tongue around it. Then it was finally time for what both of us had been waiting for. I placed his hands on my head and let him thrust his nine inches into my mouth. His flavor was as sweet as honey and as addictive as drugs. We developed a rhythm that should have been documented. "Oh, Fran, I've got to have you now," was all he said as he removed his cock from the warmth of my mouth. He sat up, and I climbed onto his lap. I felt every inch of his cock as it drove into my swollen pussy. My legs were wrapped around his waist as he pounded me with his hot flesh, my body flinching with passion as he brought me to yet another orgasm. Quickly, he lay me on my back. Placing my feet on his shoulders, he drove his luscious cock into a climax that we both shared.

Almost exhausted from this three-hour love fest, I began to lick his cock. Our juices were mixed, and the flavor was intoxicating. Albert removed his hardening cock from my mouth and kissed me. He could taste the flavor of our love on my tongue. Then, without saying a word, he placed me in the doggie-style position and fucked me.

I can't remember how many times he brought me to orgasm that day, but every time I see an ad for Vegas, I get weak in the knees and wonder if we will ever again unleash our animalistic desires.

—*F. M., Texas*

The Friendly Skies

On a recent flight to Europe, my husband and I realized one of our fantasies. During the in-flight movie, I secretly removed my panties under the blanket and motioned for Paul to follow me. I led him to the back of the plane and into one of the bathrooms, and we quickly locked ourselves in. Without a word I bent down, lifted my skirt, and offered my dripping hole to him. He entered me from behind and we slowly fucked ourselves to a beautiful, satisfying orgasm.

Outside the rest room stood a man whose jaw dropped when he saw both of us coming out. While I went back to my seat, my husband stayed behind to stretch his legs a bit. Half an hour later, he returned, sat down, and said, "How would you like a repeat performance with that nice fellow back there?" I looked at Paul's roguish grin and nodded.

That's why I love him so much. He finds joy in my pleasure, and we have become tolerant of each other's feelings and wishes. We have an open marriage, and we always know about each other's bed partners.

Paul had started a conversation with the man, Donnie, and told him what we had done in the rest room. Eventually, he asked Donnie if he would like to do the same. Now Paul told me that Donnie was sitting a few rows behind us. I was to walk to the rear, and he would follow. I did, and we arrived together.

After we locked the door, he tenderly embraced me and kissed me. I stood with my back to the sink and held him and caressed his neck and back. Soon I felt his hard cock against my abdomen, and my juices began to flow. My arousal made me feel like jelly. I pushed him away, hoisted myself onto the sink, and raised my skirt. I felt the cool air on my puffed-up, wet pussy and smelled the just-fucked scent. My hands guided his head and adjusted the pressure on my cunt until I built up to that intense approach of an explosion-like release. I pushed his face to my sex with all my strength, then I moaned loudly as I slowly relaxed.

Then it was my turn to return the favor. We switched places, and I pulled down his trousers and shorts and relished his splendid equipment. His balls were heavy, and his cock stood up at an angle from his belly. I felt the delicate skin, the thick veins, and the smooth head with its broad rim. Thick lubricating fluid oozed out of the top. I formed an *O* with my index finger and thumb and lightly rubbed it over the head. My husband likes that very much, and it always makes him beg for mercy. Donnie mumbled, "Oh, that feels so good." Then I deep-throated him. The feel of his prick in my mouth, his balls in one hand, and my other hand between his ass cheeks made me very hot. While I was squatting, I squeezed my legs together to increase that delicious pressure on my pussy lips.

I finally stood up, turned around, and positioned myself as I had done about an hour before with my husband. Donnie impatiently rammed his tool into me and fucked me wildly. I met his powerful thrusts and heard him bang his back against the door with each stroke. He increased the pace, pulled me tightly against his groin, and we both reached the top of our orgasm.

We straightened up and opened the door. Outside was a line of wide-eyed people, some of whom smiled knowingly. Those smiles were nothing compared to the looks some of them gave us when they later discovered us sitting with different partners.

—T. W., California

On the Road Again

My husband and I own a trailer, and we frequently travel to various campsites for a weekend, or, if time permits, we will travel farther if we can camp for a week at a time. I really enjoy the camping part, but I've found the travel part to be very boring. On one of the trips we took, I decided to do something to break up the boredom. That particular morning, instead of my usual conservative pullover top with a bra underneath,

I only put on a sheer cotton top without a bra. I could tell that it had an instant effect on my husband, because he kept staring at my perfectly shaped 36C tits. He would, from time to time, reach over and gently brush the nipple of my left boob and cause it to stand out as firm as the large cock pressing against his shorts.

However, what he wasn't aware of is that before we left the campground that morning, I had inserted a set of ben-wa balls into my shaven pussy. I couldn't believe the sensations I was having. There I was, sitting in the cab of our truck, feeling all the road vibrations right in the center of my sex! Usually, I couldn't wait for us to get back onto a smooth road, but that day I wanted us to be driving down a washboard.

As we started down a rather bumpy section of highway, I leaned forward a little bit and pressed my hot pussy into the seat. I knew I was only moments away from a climax, but then the road smoothed out again. I could've screamed—I mean, I was so close to coming, I gave serious thought to pushing the leg of my loose shorts aside and fingering myself to the climax I needed. I didn't want my husband to know what I had done until I could handle his beautiful eight inches, so I decided to continue the tease trip that I had put myself on.

I said to my lover, "Have you ever wanted me to expose my tits to a truck driver as we pass?" He said that he thought it would be a big turn-on for him, and suggested that I unbutton my blouse and allow the world to see what great tits I have. As I unbuttoned my blouse, I could not believe how sexy I felt. I began to rub my titties and pull on my nipples, and soon they stood out like the erasers on a pencil.

As I continued stroking my very sensitive breasts, the road turned bumpy again. And as we passed a big truck, I could feel the climax begin to overtake me. The pleasure of mind-shattering orgasm spread from my gushing cunt and filled my whole being. I leaned back in the seat and continued massaging my breasts with my eyes closed, allowing a loud sigh to escape my lips.

My husband was having a difficult time keeping our truck and trailer in our lane as we passed the truck and he watched me come. He said, "God, you came, didn't you? I mean, playing with your tits as we passed that truck brought you off, didn't it?" I looked over at him with a flushed face, smiled, and told him that it did and that it was a great turn-on for me to do it. To this day, he does not know about the ben-wa balls stuffed inside me and the feeling that the rough road gave me.

—C. B., California

THREE, FOUR, AND MORESOMES

Three's Not a Crowd

My husband and I have been married for eighteen wonderful years. One thing that we share is great fantasies. We decided recently that it was time to live out one of our fantasies—for me to share an experience with another woman. I had always wanted to know what it would be like to touch another woman's body, and my husband was dying to watch.

Heather, a close friend of ours, came by our house to have a few drinks. Before we knew it, she and I were lying on the couch together, caressing each other's thighs, while my husband sat across from us watching.

Heather's breasts felt soft, yet so firm and sensuous. I slowly raised her blouse so I could play with her large nipples, and she put her hand under my skirt and began to spread my lips apart. As she fondled my cunt, I begged her to suck me while my husband watched. I began to drip hot juices, and I told Heather that I wanted to pussy-fuck her. As our two twats touched, I could not contain the excitement that went through my body.

We didn't want my husband to feel as if three is a crowd, so we invited him to join the fun. Heather and I licked his cock, taking turns sucking it while the other licked his ass. My husband could not believe how much I was enjoying myself. I felt that Heather should do the honors and drink his come while I proceeded to suck and lick her pussy until she came in my mouth. Our activities continued until the late evening, and now this takes place at least once a week.

—I. B., New Hampshire

Women's Studies

My name is Stephanie. I am a senior in college and am planning to attend graduate school. Good grades, therefore, are vital to my undergraduate education. This past quarter I was enrolled in a particularly difficult course and wasn't doing well. Toward the end of the quarter I decided to visit my instructor, Ms. Crowley, who is a very beautiful and intelligent woman. I wanted to see if there was any chance of improving my grade.

As I approached her office I noticed another student entering ahead of me. It was late in the afternoon, and the building was empty and quiet. The warm light from the office was inviting, and I was persuaded to enter the doorway, hoping for a quick, dual conference. As it turned out, I received much more than that.

Entering the room I encountered the most unexpected situation. There was Ms. Crowley, passionately French-kissing one of my gorgeous fellow coeds. I recognized the girl, a fiery redhead from her class named Ginger. They turned around simultaneously, their faces rosy with passion and embarrassment. I stammered a feeble apology and turned to go. "Please wait," I barely heard Ms. Crowley call. I had never seen two women together, and I'd never even entertained such an idea myself. My head was swimming with confusion, and I was dimly aware of a tingling sensation beneath my panties.

She took my hand and led me back into her office as I continued to apologize. She shut her door and asked me to sit down. I noticed Ginger sitting on the edge of Ms. Crowley's desk, blushing and looking at the floor. She began to cry, and I felt genuinely sorry for the embarrassment I had caused her. I went to her, put my arms around her, and began stroking her long red hair. It smelled fresh and clean. I'm not sure how things started, but the next thing I knew I was kissing her face and cheeks. I tasted her salty tears, and our lips met. My breasts are large and firm, and my nipples pushed through the fabric of my soft sweater. As we explored each other's mouths, I felt a pair of hands caress my ass. Hot breath descended upon my neck as Ms. Crowley drew herself close behind me.

Within minutes we were all stripped down to our bras and panties. My box was pulsating with wet anticipation. Ms. Crowley led me to her desk, cleared it off, and instructed me to lie down on it. I did as I was told, shaking violently. Ginger released my aching tits from my bra as Ms. Crowley slid my soaked undies down to my ankles. Ginger climbed onto the desk and straddled my face, at the same time pulling on my rock-hard titties. Meanwhile, Ms. Crowley was busily working two fingers in and out of my slippery love hole. My tongue lapped at Ginger's swollen clit as I breathed in her musky scent.

For the next half hour we sucked, licked, and stroked each other into a fucking frenzy. All at once Ms. Crowley instructed us to bend over the desk. We did as she asked, and she proceeded to reach down and diddle with our twats. Ginger and I bobbed and ground, the rhythm gaining momentum. I finally came in a quaking orgasm, and a moment later Ginger swiveled into multiple orgasms of her own. We collapsed, exhausted, onto the desk.

When we turned around after catching our breath, we were treated to the sight of Ms. Crowley reclining in a chair, fucking herself furiously with a ten-inch dildo! Her eyes were glazed with lust, and she came with a shaking cry. After slowly removing the love toy, she offered it to Ginger. Ginger deep-throated it, her soft lips tasting the teacher's hot come. I began lapping it as well, savoring the fragrant aroma of Ms. Crowley's snatch.

I forgot to explain why I had come to her office, but I received an *A* anyway. Moreover, Ginger and I have become roommates and frequently visit Ms. Crowley for dual conferences.

—E. W., Minnesota

Fantasy Fulfilled

My fantasy has always been to have two men at the same time. After I married it seemed impossible, but my husband and I have great sex, so I didn't mind putting my dream on the back burner.

While we were making love one evening, I ventured to tell Don my fantasy. To my surprise, he too had fantasized about sharing me with another man. The thought really turned him on, and gave us many enchanted evenings just talking about it.

Then, while watching movies at a friend's house one night, we had our chance. It was getting late and everyone had gone home, leaving Don and me to watch the end of a very steamy movie with Joe, a very attractive, longtime friend of ours. As the movie came to an end, we teased and joked about having an orgy like the one in the film. My eyes met Don's, and he raised an eyebrow.

I leaned over and kissed Joe deeply, right in front of my husband. He enthusiastically returned my kiss. I slowly kissed my way down his chest, working down to his jeans. As I removed them, I watched my husband—who had by then taken off his own jeans—pull on his lovestick. I took Joe's cock in my mouth and sucked to the same rhythm that Don was jacking off.

My husband couldn't stand it any longer. He moved behind me and lifted my skirt. As his cock entered my wet pussy, I exploded with the best orgasm of my life. It wasn't long before I felt both cocks inside me begin to swell. At the first taste of come in my mouth, I felt the warm streams running between my legs. And that was just the beginning of a wonderful night!

—V. R., Kansas

Two-Man Job

I knew when my best friend Tammy invited me go on a double date with her boyfriend and his roommate I was in for a wild time, but I had no idea how wild it would be.

Tammy's boyfriend Rick is a good-looking blond guy. From what Tammy had told me, I gathered that he was forever horny and pretty damn creative when it came to sex. I had never met his roommate, Bill, before our date. I was beginning to wonder if it was a good idea for me to go. When I met him, I was glad I did. He turned out to be an absolute hunk with dark hair, blue eyes, and a great body! As the evening progressed, I got the impression that he was pleased with me, too. We went out for dinner and a movie, then back to the boys' apartment to watch a little TV.

Bill and I sat on the couch while Rick and Tammy sat on the floor. Before long they had their tongues plunged deep inside each other's mouths. I leaned over and gave Bill a long, deep kiss. His tongue was inside my mouth, but I wanted more. Our friends had already taken most of their clothes off. Bill's cock was bulging in his jeans, so I pulled down the zipper in order to free him. His penis was of average length, but nice and thick. He gently removed my shirt and fondled my breasts. My nipples got very hard, so he started to lick and suck them.

By that time Rick and Tammy were furiously doing the horizontal tango on the floor. I needed to feel Bill inside me, so I pulled off his pants and lay down to let him ride me. He got on top and began fucking me with powerful strokes that made me quiver. I came several times before he shot his load deep inside me.

We didn't want to leave yet, but we didn't want to get dressed either. So Bill went to the fridge to get some food, and Rick got up to change the channel. If there's anything I like better than a good-looking guy walking around in the nude, it's two good-looking guys walking around in the nude. Bill brought out some gelatin squares, and we started eating them. It wasn't long before Rick started playfully rubbing the gelatin along the outside of Tammy's pussy. She made him lick it off, and that gave him a major hard-on. He was ready for another round, but that time he suggested we switch partners.

That was all right by me. Rick has an incredible physique and a beautiful thatch of amber-colored pubes above his dick. While Tammy and Bill got to know each other better; we went at it. I got on top and slid up and down on Rick's pole as he moaned in appreciation. I came first, but just as I was finishing, he started coming, and that got me going all over again. When our night of fun was over, we made arrangements to "double date" again a few days later.

—A. R., Illinois

Topless Treat

I have a story to tell. I recently experienced one of the best sexual encounters of my life.

It all started when Jessica, Rich, and I went to a topless-dancer club. I sat there between the two of them through six or seven dancers, and by the third one I was already aroused. I think we all were because I could feel the sexual tension building between the three of us. By the time the sixth dancer came on, I could take it no longer. I could feel my pussy throb and moisten with each thrust of the beautiful dancer's body. I looked over at Rich, and I knew that I wanted him, but I wanted Jessica as well.

That is when—to my surprise—Rich suggested that

we go back to his place for drinks. When we were walking out of the bar Jessica's beautiful breasts brushed against my shoulder, and I felt the electricity fly through my body. I knew what was in store for me, and I could feel my cunt get wetter and wetter by the minute.

As soon as we got to Rich's apartment, he grabbed me by the crotch and pulled me toward him—making me explode automatically. He unzipped my tight blue-jean shorts and slid his fingers into my throbbing, wet hole. I felt my shorts fall to the floor and looked down to see Jessica get on her knees and lick my shin. I could feel my sweet nectar drip down my sweaty legs. My love box was dying to be licked. We proceeded to the couch, where I lay down. Jessica licked my erect nipples as I thrust two fingers into her juicy cunt. Rich was now sucking my clit. As he slid his tongue in and out of my hole; Jessica moved so I could eat her perfect pussy. I could feel her clit swell between my tingling teeth.

Unable to take this any longer, I was ready to be fucked out of my mind. Rich stuck his joystick into my pussy, and I went crazy. We writhed in pleasure, and I looked over and saw Jessica fingering herself vigorously. I motioned for her to come over to the couch. As she approached, I got on top of Rich so that she could situate herself on his face. Finally, Rich showered my insides with his hot jism. He then moved on to Jessica. She rode him for nearly ten minutes as I watched her lively titties bounce freely. Afterward we lay spent on the floor.

That was the first threesome that I had ever participated in, but I can assure you that it won't be the last.

—*W. A., Mississippi*

Blind Date

Blind dates usually end in disaster, but this one was certainly an exception. My fiancé and I set up two of our friends to go out on a double date with us. Jake showed up first, and we sat around waiting for Linda. I was having really naughty thoughts with two incredible guys sitting in my living room, and I secretly hoped Linda wouldn't show. She finally got there, though, and we went for drinks.

The evening dragged on—the two of them had nothing in common. Linda said she wanted to go home at ten-thirty. We drove back to my place, and she left. It was still early, so we invited Jake in for a beer. Those naughty thoughts immediately popped back into my head, and I wasted no time acting on them.

I went inside and changed into nothing but a button-down shirt, deliberately leaving it *un*-buttoned. When I joined the guys, they were both reading *Penthouse*. I could see the bulges in their pants getting bigger as I sat down next to my fiancé. He noticed that my tits were in full view, and he couldn't keep his hands off me. He reached under my shirt and was soon sucking on my boobs. He slowly worked his way down to my clit, and then began fiercely sucking and licking my cunt.

When I remembered that Jake was sitting there watching us, I reached over and unzipped his pants. I pulled out his huge cock and sucked down to his balls. He was a little surprised but had no problem enjoying the action.

I begged my fiancé to fuck me from behind while I sucked off his friend. He slid his big, hard cock into my cunt and fucked me harder than ever before. Jake guided my head up and down his shaft, but stopped suddenly and said he wanted to taste me. I lay on the couch, and Jake put his tongue on my clit and sucked my cunt juices. My fiancé stroked his cock as he watched me being eaten out. He came over to me and began fucking my mouth with his cock. Jake licked my clit until I almost came, and then he took his cock and rammed it inside me. My fiancé shot his load in my mouth, which made me come all over Jake's cock. He came next, and as he did, he pulled out and shot his load all over my clit.

We all sat around afterward, wishing we hadn't even bothered with the blind date. But we agreed that things had worked out fine anyway.

—T. T., New York

The Perfect Getaway

This summer my best friend and I decided to go on vacation. We wanted to get away from home and all of our problems—including our boyfriends. We decided to go to Hawaii. After we arrived and got settled in, we frequented the beach. Katie and I each wore one-piece bathing suits that consisted of straps connected in the back by a G-string. The suits barely concealed our nipples, and our asses and hips were completely exposed. I have to say that Katie's tight little ass looked especially hot. I'd never noticed that she had such a sexy body.

After lying out one day, we decided to hit the hotel's poolside bar. I was in awe when I saw the bartender. He was very good-looking and muscular. Wanting to see more of this stud, Katie and I stayed at the bar all afternoon. After a while I confessed that I was thinking about being with him. She thought it was a good idea, so we invited this beefcake up to our room.

Katie and I went to shower up, and by the time we were done, there was a knock on the door. We both answered the door completely naked, which completely shocked our visitor, but he didn't hesitate to come in.

I didn't say a word to him, but just took off his shirt, pulled down his pants, and caught his hardening cock in my mouth. Katie came up behind our new man, sank to her knees, and began licking and kissing his back and ass cheeks. Then she spun around him, took his hard dick out of my mouth, and started sucking him, too. We were sharing his long, pulsating cock.

Then, to our surprise, our man stopped us. He sat in a chair and asked if we had boyfriends. We said yes, and he said that he wanted our boyfriends to know exactly what our vacation was like. He said I could start by setting up the video camera that we had brought. I did as I was told, and once everything was set up, he instructed Katie and I to sit on the floor in front of him. Then he began to masturbate and told us to stick out our tongues. We did so, and he jacked his come all over our mouths: I sucked as much of his cock as I could, and when I looked over at Katie, she had a single drop of come glistening on her cheek.

The stranger told me to lick it off of her. I obeyed and began licking Katie's cheek, but my tongue accidentally slipped into her mouth. I looked deep into Katie's eyes and, without hesitation, kissed her full on the lips. I had never really thought about her in this way before, but when she snaked her tongue into my mouth, I was incredibly turned on. We started sharing the taste of his come, and the thought of him watching while our video camera taped made me come.

Katie's sweet kisses made their way down my body until she found my aching pussy. She dived right into my moist box, licking and teasing my clit until I came all over her face. I needed to taste her, and so she straddled my face—I began eating her delicious cunt. Katie started bucking and moaning furiously as I grabbed her ass and pulled it toward my mouth. She started screaming loudly, rubbing her pussy up and down on my face until she exploded in ecstasy.

As we got up, we noticed that the bartender was gone but the camera was still taping. We were so elated by our new discovery that we didn't leave our room for the rest of the week. . . . Well, just a few times, for a fresh supply of videotape.

—*J. K., Illinois*

Graduating with Honors

My husband, Kurt, and I had a party to celebrate my graduation from college. Brenda, a good friend of mine, arrived at the restaurant with a cake and a bottle of champagne. Because we didn't get around to drinking the champagne during the party, Brenda suggested we go back to our house afterward and drink it. The three of us sat on our bed and talked for several hours.

The conversation turned to female actresses, and Kurt asked Brenda what she would do if she was alone with Kim Basinger. Brenda smiled and didn't say anything. Kurt encouraged her by asking, "Would you like it?" Brenda, still smiling, breathily answered, "Yes!" At that point I was shocked, because I had no idea that Brenda was attracted to women. While I had been getting to know her better over the preceding few months, I had become very attracted to her. I never thought we would actually get involved sexually, but here was my chance! Kurt continued to ask her more probing questions, and I started running my fingers through her silky blonde hair. I was so excited, I was having a hard time breathing!

Brenda turned and kissed me—tentatively at first, then quite passionately. Her tongue played with mine, and I was in heaven. I was trying to take it slow because I didn't want to scare her, but she grabbed my hand and put it on her breast. *Okay,* I thought, *this is really it!*

I pulled off her jacket and shirt, then her bra. *Mmmm,* she was tanned all over. I rubbed her small tits and sucked on each nipple until they were both hard. She took off my shirt and bra and fondled my 36C tits. I pushed her back on the bed and lay on top of her while I kissed my way down her body. When I got to her waist, I pulled off her shorts and her lacy panties. Her pussy hair was neatly trimmed, and I could see her wetness. I rubbed her juicy pussy, then I licked it. Brenda pinched her nipples, and cried out, "Oh, yes!" I continued licking and sucking that sweet pussy while I finger-fucked her. Brenda grabbed my head and pushed my face in deeper while yelling, "Tanya, Tanya!" over and over.

I was so into eating her pussy that I forgot about Kurt until I felt him pull my pants off from behind. I lifted my ass into the air, and Kurt stuck his rock-hard cock into my dripping love hole. He fucked me from behind while I ate Brenda's pussy. She bucked her hips, and loudly cried out, "Oh, Tanya, I'm coming!" I furiously licked her until she was through. Then I lay down next to her, and she touched my pussy. I kissed her so she could taste her pussy juice, and she sucked on my tongue. Kurt sat there looking kind of unsure, so I pulled him up to Brenda. I wanted to watch my handsome husband fuck this blonde beauty.

Kurt proceeded to kiss Brenda and suck her perky tits. She grabbed his ass and ground her pussy against his cock until he put it inside. I tried to move back on the bed a few inches to get a better view, but Brenda grabbed my arm and pulled me to her. She writhed and moaned, begging Kurt to fuck her harder. He, happy to oblige, rammed his cock in and out of her soaking pussy. Brenda cried out and came. What a screamer! Neither Kurt nor I had come during this interlude, but we had a great time with Brenda. She got dressed and kissed me good-bye. I promptly got back into bed and fucked Kurt until we came together. What a graduation present!

—T. C., Indiana

Blame It on Reno

A couple of months ago, my fiancé, Sam, and I took our first vacation together to Reno, Nevada. The first two evenings were really fun, but in no way could they compare to the final night. Sam was on an incredible roll at the blackjack table. By the time he quit, he was up $2,500. Upon celebrating his win, he looked at me, and said, "This money is going to fulfill your wildest fantasy." The first thought that came to my mind was that I'd always wanted to go to a brothel. Although I have never had any trouble getting men or women, the thought of picking through a large group of women, paying for one, and knowing she'd do anything I wanted was extremely exciting. It didn't take long to find out where the best whorehouse in the city was.

When we got there, it was better than I ever could have imagined. As we walked into the large lounge area, there were sexy and beautiful women everywhere. It was thrilling to have them staring at me, walking by me, and saying "Hello" while intentionally brushing against me. The eagerness on their faces showed how much they wanted to be with us. While Sam was dealing with the woman in charge, I made my rounds, looking at all our hot options. I was already so turned on with anticipation, I could feel my pussy getting moist. Then I looked back at the doorway, and there stood my fantasy. She was absolutely breathtaking. She was wearing a cherry red teddy with a black garter belt, matching nylons, and black spike heels. Her silky dark hair lightly covered her firm breasts, exposing just enough of them for me to know I had to see more. She wouldn't take her piercing blue eyes off me, looking at me as though she knew exactly what I needed. I approached her, and said, "You're the most exciting thing here. I guarantee, tonight will not seem like work." She replied, "I knew that the second I saw you walk in."

She introduced herself as Yolanda and invited Sam and me back to her room. By the way she carried herself and by the way other people were treating her at this house, it was clear that she had a certain prestige. When we got to her room, Sam and I sat on the bed and instructed her to do a striptease for us, which she gladly did. She slowly pulled her teddy down, exposing her mouth-watering tits. Then Yolanda dropped the teddy to her ankles. Seeing her closely shaved and hot pussy put me over the edge. Judging by the bulge in Sam's pants, he was loving it as much as I was. Yolanda approached me and started slowly undressing me, at the same time giving me gentle kisses all over my body. Feeling turned on, we pushed Sam onto the bed and stripped him naked. As his rock-hard dick stood at attention, Yolanda and I licked and sucked him together, our tongues occasionally meeting. That was driving me wild, and my pussy started aching for attention. Yolanda then led us into the Jacuzzi on the other side of the room.

She immediately started sucking my rock-hard nipples while her fingers found their way to my throbbing snatch. I lifted myself onto the edge of the tub, spreading my legs wide open. As soon as she put her lips on my pussy, I went crazy. It was the most erotic feeling I have ever experienced. I guess practice makes perfect. While Yolanda was eating me up, Sam went behind her and thrust his cock deep inside her meaty pussy. She was making the most satisfied and sexy moans. It was such a turn-on. After playing around in the Jacuzzi for a while, I grabbed their hands and led them back to the bed. I was dying to taste Yolanda's sweet juices. I had her lie on the edge of the bed while I probed every crevice of her cunt with my fingers and tongue. Sam rubbed and sucked her tits, then inserted his stiff shaft into her mouth. She went wild and started screeching and bucking against my hand. Within seconds my hand was drenched with her come, her face showing total ecstasy. She said, "Believe it or not, I haven't climaxed like that in years!"

Yolanda proceeded to pour warm oil over my body, then she and Sam rubbed their hands over every inch of me. The feeling of four hands rubbing my skin was incredible. Yolanda would rub her tits on mine, then rub them on Sam. Then she lowered her pussy onto my tits and slid up and down from my tits to my snatch. The mood was playful and fun, but so intense.

Yolanda pulled out a strap-on dildo and stuck it into my mouth. I love being fucked in my mouth and my cunt at the same time. She was fucking me like there was no tomorrow. I remember gasping for air at times. My pussy started quivering, and then I experienced the most exhilarating climax. Yolanda said my come literally shot right out of me, soaking her dildo and dripping down onto her own snatch. I quickly tried to pull myself together because it was Sam's turn to reach ecstasy. I eagerly went to work, sucking and stroking his dick while Yolanda licked his entire body and talked erotically in his ear. I bent over the edge of a table, and Sam thrust his dick into me from behind. Listening to his moans, I knew he was about to come, so I pulled him out and had him shoot his wad in my mouth.

We lay on the bed for a while, softly rubbing and kissing. We knew the time was running out. Afterward, Sam asked me if my fantasy was as good as I thought it would be. All I could say was that we are going to have the most exciting and erotic life together. One fantasy down, many more to go.

—*K. S., Minnesota*

Three's Company

Your magazine has been instrumental in solving a problem that my husband and I had for the last six years of our eight-year marriage. Your article on troilism and the "Forum" letter describing a sexual encounter with a woman hitchhiker combined to provide the solution. Perhaps it will be of interest to others.

I married my husband when I was quite young and a virgin. The marriage caused me to cut short my college career after barely beginning. Within two years I began to resent the marriage because it had happened too soon. It had denied me the sexual experimentation that I had always believed to be an intrinsic part of a college education. This resentment culminated in an arrangement to have a motel owner send me lovers during weekends that my husband was away. I sexually satisfied over a dozen men, but strong feelings of guilt prevented me from reaching an orgasm. Your troilism article caused me to realize that while I desired sex with other men, I could not gain any satisfaction without my husband's participation.

After disclosing the motel affairs to my sympathetic and intelligent husband, I have, for the past few months, enjoyed sexual threesomes with hitchhikers. Our method, though clumsy and self-conscious at first, is really quite simple and very exciting. We have an automobile that seats three in the front. A U.S. Marine training base some distance from our home provides an abundance of young, handsome, and clean hitchhikers. A touch on my husband's leg signals my approval of the hitchhiker and the start of our mutual seduction.

It is not difficult to get a young Marine involved in a chat about sex. We encourage this by telling him of our own experiences, and never fail to mention troilism. The conversation is deftly directed to my legs, and my husband raises my skirt to demonstrate his point. Then, illuminated either by daylight or a dashboard light, our young friend is treated to a view of sexy panties or the very smooth mound of a shaven pubis. The dialogue of sex increases, as do my passions.

Then my husband starts to masturbate me, in partial view of our new friend. This is not enough to encourage assistance from my right. It takes a whispered "Play with me, too," which almost always results in the man starting to fondle my breasts. There seems to be a universal aversion to one man touching another, even while both are being satisfied by the same woman.

When I sense that our hitchhiker is aroused, I will have intercourse with him in the backseat while my husband drives and listens. Several times I have found the man to be so exciting that we spend the evening in a motel, during which time the only limit is our joint imagination.

Our threesomes are lessening in frequency, from two or three an evening to about once a month. I feel that I have made up for lost time, and now it is just another sexual variation to us—important, but not our prime outlet.

—Name and address withheld

A Voyeur's Dream

I am an incorrigible exhibitionist. Within a reasonable margin of safety, I love to show off my body in some sexy fashion. It may be my bouncing tits in a partially unbuttoned blouse, or much of a leg. It is exciting to see men's surprise and wanton looks.

The other day, my fetish got the better of me with

thrillingly satisfying results. My husband, Paul, and I hosted a meeting of Little League baseball umpires in our house. There were about a dozen men and two women. As the talks proceeded, I offered some hors d'oeuvres and drinks and then joined the group. Charlie sat across from me. He is a single parent and has a wonderful relationship with his and all the other kids.

Soon I realized that his eyes frequently dropped to view my legs. I also saw he was the only one in a position to see more. With increasing heartbeat, I casually opened my legs a bit. He noticed. I changed my sitting position slightly and showed him more of my inner thigh. I wore a short skirt. Then I covered my lap with a bunch of papers while, with one hand under this cover, I teased my inner thigh and slowly moved up to my crotch, rubbing my pussy through my panties. I caught him looking intently and smiled at him. He blushed.

The meeting ended and more social conversations ensued. I managed to quickly tell my husband what I was up to. As Paul escorted people to the street, I asked Charlie to stay for a while. Paul finally led the last visitor to his car. By that time, I was very excited and hot, and bluntly asked Charlie if he liked what he saw. At the same time, I slowly pulled up my skirt until it was all ruffled up at my waist, exposing myself in my tiny panties, and asked Charlie to treat himself to the goodies. "Your husband!" he gasped.

"Don't worry. He knows," I answered.

He fell to his knees. I slid forward on the couch,

spread my legs far apart, and let him lick and suck me. I was rushing into ecstasy. I took his head in my hands and controlled the pressure on my pussy. I came quickly.

"Your turn," I whispered. He stripped, sat down, and I delivered an intense blowjob. I started to lick up and down his gorgeous meat. Paul had come back and, looking up, I saw Charlie's relieved smile when Paul asked, "Are you two enjoying each other?" Before long, he came up behind me and started playing with my wet cunt. Ah, I was in one of my favorite, heavenly positions—with two gorgeous men servicing me. As my tongue explored the hardness, the veins, the velvet ridge, and tasted the precome lubricant of Charlie's meat, I felt my husband's motions on my juicy pussy. He reached around and tickled my clit until I couldn't stand it any longer. I came and came as I felt the pressure of Paul's touch against my innermost parts. And then Charlie gave his best to load up my throat with his come. Boy, did he come. "Oh, it's been so long," he moaned.

We went to the bedroom. Charlie never went limp. I had him lie on his back and impaled myself on his superhard prick. I reached for some lubricant and liberally doused Paul's cock and balls. He likes to be masturbated. A new wave of pleasure surged through my body as I moved up and down. My tits bounced freely. Sucking and slurping noises emanated from my pussy and from ministrations on my husband's equipment, and mingled with the moaning and groaning of the three of us in the heat of passion. The intensity of our collective orgasms was borne out in our collective outcry. I again felt the stream of love juice fill my inside and squish out, and Paul's come shot high up, to fall on his stomach. I fell forward, embracing both men.

Paul took a shower. But I had not had enough. My hands still full of lotion and come, I gently handled Charlie's cock and balls, rubbing and squeezing until he stood at full attention again. On my back now, I raised my legs over his shoulders as he slid between my swollen pussy lips. I asked him to fuck me real hard. And he did, his balls slapping against my ass, his pelvic bone crushing against mine, sending waves of pleasure up my spine as my clit felt the impact of each push. Again, we rushed toward this sweetest of releases that culminates in the greatest pleasure of all.

We have been inviting Charlie for occasional threesomes. One time we invited Bonnie, a neighbor, to a foursome. Bonnie and her husband have been our friends and swing partners for the past few years. They are open-minded and know of each other's involvements. Eventually we will have both Bonnie and her husband join us with Charlie.

—T. W., California

All in a Day's Work

My husband, Howard, and I are middle-aged, small-business owners in a happy and, until recently, monogamous marriage. We deal with the public and various salesmen and deliverymen on a daily basis. My little adventure concerns one of these salesmen.

Even though I have three grown kids, I'm still slim with long, naturally red hair, green eyes, great legs, a nice ass, and smallish-but-perky tits. I love going out with Howard wearing a micromini, a skintight top, fishnet stockings, spike heels, and no undies. (Tramping, I call it.) I've been known to go out to dinner wearing a trench coat and heels and nothing else. This usually guarantees a good finger-fucking under the table at some point during our dinner. I get turned on by flashing truckers and teasing Howard's friends by "accidentally" flashing them or rubbing my tits against them.

My husband enjoys watching other men watch me, but recently I discovered that he wanted to watch them do more than watch me. This was due in part to some of the letters we've read and enjoyed in your fine magazine.

The other catalyst was when I told Howard about a dream I'd had about one of our salesmen, Greg. Before this dream, I really hadn't thought of Greg in a sexy way, but dreaming of him fucking me doggie style while I sucked my husband dry sure changed that!

Howard and I began talking about having a threesome with Greg. At first I thought my husband was either kidding or just talking out a fantasy, but the more we talked, the hotter the sex between us became, and soon all I could think about was being kissed, licked, sucked, and fucked by the two of them. It got so bad (or good) that I'd wake myself up in the middle of the night, caressing my tits and rubbing my swollen clit until I came several times and could go back to sleep.

With Howard's encouragement, I began my campaign. This was going to be a challenge, because we knew Greg was married, so I eased into it by wearing short skirts when I knew he was coming by our store and giving him a glimpse of my bare pussy now and then. I put on a temporary tattoo and innocently asked if he'd like to see it—it just happened to be on my breast. I really wanted him to do more than look, but he was being coy, so for a few weeks I had to be content with teasing and flashing. That was really no problem, since on the nights after Greg came in, I was so hot from flirting that Howard and I had some terrific sex.

One afternoon, when Greg was due to arrive, Howard and I decided it was time to escalate things. When Greg came in, I told him I had bought a new dress and that I wanted his opinion of it. He agreed to handle any customers that might come in, so I went to change.

The dress was black, very short—stopping just past my crotch—and clingy. I put on black thigh-high stockings, black heels, and a smile, then I strolled up to where Greg was sitting. He looked somewhat surprised, but appreciative, and he said I looked very nice. Not exactly the reaction I'd been hoping for, but he seemed a little unsure of the whole situation. To nudge him in the right direction, I turned around and leaned forward, exposing my round, lily-white ass. "Don't you think it's a little short?" I asked, with an invitation in my voice.

My husband was making complimentary and suggestive remarks during my little fashion show, but Greg still wasn't too sure of how to respond. To help him out, I sat down across from him and put one leg up on the table between us, giving him a close-up view of my steamy, wet, and ready pussy. He just sat there, so I took the bull by the horns so to speak, and told him he could do anything he might feel like doing.

In a heartbeat, he was on his knees, licking and sucking my juicy love hole, then tongue-fucking me. Howard watched with aroused interest, until a customer walked in the front door. It was exciting to know that there were customers not all that far from where I was getting such a good tongue-lashing. My husband was still busy when Greg brought me to an orgasm that left me dizzy, but he told me later that he could hear me panting and moaning, even though I was trying to be quiet.

After I caught my breath, I moved to return the favor. I unzipped his pants and unleashed his beautiful, very hard love tool. After licking and sucking it for a few minutes, I suggested he lower his pants so I could lay some lovin' on his balls. He had a really good-looking dick, and his balls were a treat, too. (I do love sucking a good cock and licking and sucking a nice set of balls.)

Howard was enjoying watching me work, and I was loving every minute of it. Unfortunately, customers kept interrupting my husband's pleasure, but certainly not Greg's. In short order, he exploded in orgasm, and I felt as if I were gripping a fire hose! The force of his orgasm almost made me come again, and I could feel my juices dripping from my pussy. I swallowed every drop and continued sucking to get it all, then I looked up at him and smiled.

Howard returned to the scene just then, and he was disappointed to discover that he had missed both of our orgasms. He wanted to watch me come with another guy, but that will have to be another story, I guess. Once we locked the doors for the night, however, Howard and I made up for his being left out. He sat my bare ass on one of the counters, threw my legs over his shoulders, and fucked me till I screamed.

—F. F., Kansas

Trade and Show

While working a local trade show, I ran into Barry, an old boyfriend, who was in town on business. He was staying at the hotel connected to the convention center hosting the show, and he invited me to an evening in his room. I couldn't wait!

As I showed my wares that day, my mind drifted to past times with him. Barry had always wanted to have me with another woman, and I started checking out the crowd of possibilities. I had never been with another woman and was enjoying some creative daydreaming while looking for a suitable partner. My visit with Audrey, the petite brunette in the next booth, turned into flirting, and we made plans to have a drink at the hotel when the show closed that night.

Audrey and I sat close to each other while we drank, our legs entwined under the table. I softly rubbed one of her nipples through her blouse. She responded by resting her hand on my leg and stroking the inside of my thigh. Finally, I looked directly into her deep brown eyes, licked my lips slowly, and asked her to join Barry and me in his room. She paid the check, put her lips next to my ear, and whispered, "I want you."

By the time we reached Barry's room, we were both so hot that we barely noticed his presence. We fell into each other's arms as soon as the door was closed behind us. I had no idea that a woman's mouth would taste so sweet or feel so soft. Her tongue gently coaxed mine into her mouth. She sucked softly on my bottom lip, then my top lip, while her hands reached under my sweater. I looked over at Barry. He was sitting on the bed, staring at us. Off came the rest of my clothes, and we joined him, kissing his face, neck, and ears.

Barry told me to remove Audrey's clothing and to suck her brown nipples. First I licked them slowly, alternating between the two. Then I sucked them gently until they both became hard and puckered. As I increased the power of sucking, Audrey threw her head back and moaned. Barry was licking her dripping pussy, holding her thick patch of dark hair out of the way with his fingers. Keeping my fingertips on her firm breasts, I stopped sucking long enough to see him insert the middle fingers of both of his hands into her hot cunt. He pulled them out and let me suck them. My first taste of a woman's pussy juices! I transferred the taste to Audrey's mouth in a long, searching kiss. It felt like my tongue would reach her tonsils. Then I felt Barry's hands stroke my very wet pussy, fingers probing my cunt and massaging my clit. I took a look at the three of us: Audrey and I on our backs, lying across the bed, legs spread wide and dangling; Barry's face in Audrey's pussy, his hand in mine. Audrey reached over and squeezed my round tits, rubbing my big pink nipples with her fingernails. The combination of visual and physical pleasure with the pressure of her nails was too much for me and I came—loudly. Barry pulled his wet hand out of my box and his face out of Audrey's pussy, and smiled up at me. I told him to fuck Audrey while I watched. He mounted her small frame and she guided his rock-hard dick into her hot pussy. What a sight! Barry's big, hairy body bent over this precious, sweet thing, his hard cock going in and out of her cunt. Her hand had moved to my aching pussy.

I moved closer, positioning my hand to rub her clit as his dick slid in and out of my fingers. I kissed Barry and first put my wet fingers in my mouth, then slid them into his mouth, both of us tasting Audrey's juices at the same time. When Barry was about to come, I grabbed his cock and sucked it dry. The taste of both of their juices together sent me over the top again and again.

We spent the night fucking and sucking and watching and, eventually, napping. The next day we met for breakfast wearing our business attire and talking about plans we had for each other for that night. Working our booths, Audrey and I gave each other occasional glances, thinking of what the evening would bring.

—*S. A., Texas*

Quest for Ecstasy

Once again, I have to have it! What started out as a fantasy for my husband and me has turned out to be a never-ending search for that one woman who is as hot and nasty as I can be. Sure, we've had three-ways with other women, and yes, it was fun for me. My husband never complained, but something was always missing.

It was late, the bar was dimly lit and just about empty. I had just about given up all hope for the night when I saw her at a table by herself. I couldn't make out her features, but this feeling I had was overwhelming. I had to have her. Anxiously, I told my husband to stay where he was. I stood up, took a deep breath, and proceeded to fulfill my destiny. My pussy throbbed with every step I took toward her. I could make out her blonde hair and her figure, but still I couldn't see her face. Politely, I asked if I could join her. Without hesitation, she answered yes. Signaling to the waitress to bring more drinks, she admitted that she had hoped I would come over. As I sat down, for the first time I could see her face. The feeling of ecstasy rushed through me. I looked into the eyes of the one woman I knew could give me what I want at the intensity level I've been longing for—because those eyes I was lusting at belonged to none other than porno queen Amber Lynn.

She understood; she knew what I needed. Without words and with a seductive grin, she stood up, grabbed my hand, and led me out of the bar: I had no idea as to where I was going, and I didn't care. She suggested my house, but first we had to stop by her place so that she could pick up a few things. While I was waiting for her, I realized that I'd left my husband at the bar. At that moment, I knew I was in trouble. Not because of my husband; he would understand. I was in trouble because I no longer had control. I was in her power!

As we pulled up to my house, I saw a light go off in the bedroom. Amber did not notice—so I thought. As soon as we entered, we wasted no time pulling each other's clothes off. Quickly, we moved toward the bedroom. I knew if I got her in there, the control would be back. Playfully, I pushed her on the bed. I felt like a pirate who had just found his sunken treasure. I had to taste her. Eagerly, I started licking her pussy while I pinched her nipples. The farther my tongue went in her pussy, the harder I pinched. By the sounds of her moans, it wouldn't be long before her first orgasm filled my mouth with the taste I've been craving. "I'm coming!" she cried. With that, I began sucking up her sweet juices, almost coming myself. She pulled me to her lips. I knew what she wanted, so I let her taste her own juices. Amber softly whispered, "Like surprises? I'll be right back."

As she left the room, I heard a moan from the closet. Quickly, I opened the door to see my husband with his hard cock in his hand.

"You like surprises?" I asked.

With a big smile on his face, he replied, "Oh, yeah."

Quietly, I closed the door and jumped back into bed. When Amber stepped through the doorway, my eyes widened, for she had strapped on a dildo. *This is what was missing,* I thought to myself. I've been with women that almost put me over the edge—that's nothing new—but for a woman to strap on a cock and fuck me like a man, *that* was different.

My pussy was aching with anticipation. Quickly, she grabbed me by my ankles and turned me on my belly. Automatically, my ass rose into the air. I could feel her hot breath as she spread my ass cheeks to expose my pussy. Then she lapped up my pussy like a thirsty dog at a bowl of water. I knew she wanted to please me, which made me even hotter. "Oh God, I'm coming," I moaned. She stopped right in the middle of my orgasm. I felt disappointment only for a split second, until she slipped her latex cock deep into my pussy and started fucking me hard and fast. I spread my cheeks to offer my hot asshole. Reading my thoughts, she wet her finger and began poking my hole. In seconds she had me coming in waves. I love it in my ass!

At the risk of blowing everything, I was going to take it one step further. I turned back to look at her and returned the question she had asked earlier, "Do you like surprises?"

"What do you mean?" she asked. I called out for my husband. Everything rode on her next reaction. After my husband stepped out of his hiding place, she turned to him, looked him up and down, then turned back to me, and asked, "What took you so long?" As she pulled her cock out of my pussy, I instructed my husband to get between us. I offered his cock to her by placing it in her mouth. While she was sucking on his cock, I was licking his balls. After bringing my husband to the edge several times, but not letting him come, we repositioned.

Amber, lying on her back, guided her shaft into my pussy. I started riding like I've never rode before, and at the same time sucking her wonderful breasts. The look I saw from her drove me wild. I pleaded to my husband, "Fuck me in my ass!" He jumped at the invitation—who wouldn't? As soon as I felt his cock in my hot ass. I slid a finger in Amber's beautiful rear with one hand, and a finger in her luscious pussy with the other. With every thrust given me, I gave one back to her. I felt my husband's cock swell, and I knew he was about to fill my ass with his hot come, and by Amber's moans I knew she, too, was very close. Feeling this and being between them started my own climax building. Moments later, all three of us came explosively.

Our three-way lust lasted for several hours but ended with my husband's cock erupting all over her lips and mine. We savored his come as we passionately kissed. I knew my search was over, but the ecstasy had just begun!

—P. P., Arkansas

Sister, Sister

Your article on troilism prompts me to write to you about an experience that started my husband and I off on threesomes.

About a year ago my sister Karen, who is twenty-five and three years younger than my husband and I, came to spend several months with us following the finalization of her divorce. During the course of our conversations about her new life with no man in it, she commented that she was in desperate need of sexual expression, but the thought of going to bed with "just anyone" revolted her.

To keep her mind off her loneliness, my husband. Steve, took Karen everywhere with us. One night after watching a movie with several very explicit love scenes, Karen joked that I had better watch out or she would be making a play for Steve. I carried the joke along and suggested that she sit next to him on the way home.

Suddenly I was intrigued by the idea of my husband and sister making love together and I decided to see what I could do to keep things rolling. I told her that since we were sisters, it would be all in the family and that she could go ahead. As Steve was mixing cocktails in our kitchen, I whispered to him that Karen probably needed a man's touch and suggested that he go into the living room and sit next to her on the couch while I finished making the cocktails. I gave them several minutes alone before bringing in the drinks and mixed several more rounds—each time giving them lengthy periods of privacy.

We were all getting a little high and on an impulse I suggested that we play strip poker. They quickly agreed, and soon we all were nude. As soon as Steve had removed his final item of clothing I could tell Karen was getting desperate, so I said "He's all yours for the night, Sis, I'll just watch."

They didn't have to be told twice. Within minutes, they were engaged in heated lovemaking, while I sipped a drink and watched with fascination. After their climax, I left them alone and went to bed, terribly excited by what I had watched, and eager for Steve to join me. He came in about half an hour later and we made love like we never had before, with the excitement of such an unusual experience still fresh in our minds.

The three of us repeated the scene several times, and on some occasions Karen asked to watch while Steve and I made love. In the ten months or so since Karen moved to another city, Steve and I have had similar experiences with two other girls, and our regular lovemaking alone has reached new heights of passion. Our sex life has taken on a new dimension which we both thoroughly enjoy.

—Mrs. S. J., Milwaukee, Wisconsin

Swing Time

When my husband, Doug, and I finally decided on a vacation, we ended up going to the Caribbean for ten days. We rented a beautiful villa that had its own pool, and we really enjoyed it. Then Doug discovered a nude beach nearby. He wanted to go, but I was reluctant. I'm proud of my body, but parading around in front of strangers just seemed awkward. After several days of his persuasion, I finally agreed. I was both excited about going and a little nervous, but once we got there I realized my anxiety was for all for nothing. There were people of all ages, sizes, and body types.

We found a spot and set up our beach chairs. It

wasn't particularly crowded, and in no time I was totally at ease, not even aware that we were naked. There was a beachside bar and a small outdoor restaurant, where we went to have a drink. All the tables were full, so we sat at the bar and ordered drinks. Everyone in the place was naked; the atmosphere was relaxed and casual.

Soon another couple approached the bar, but since we had taken the last two seats, they stood behind us. Always the gentleman, Doug got up and offered the woman his seat. She thanked him and sat down next to me. She said her name was Sheila and her husband's was Robert. I turned to greet him, and my mouth fell open when I saw the size of his cock. In its flaccid state it had to have been six inches long. I tried not to stare and quickly turned back around.

We chatted with them for about thirty minutes before going back to the beach. Doug said he had noticed my look of amazement when I saw Robert's cock, and naturally I said that it had been difficult not to notice it. Then I said, "I wonder what that monster looks like when it's fully aroused?" Doug asked me if I really wanted to find out. I know it had always been his fantasy for us to make it with another couple, but I would never do it. This time I said, "Sure." Doug suggested we invite them to our place for drinks that night, and he went to find them. He came back smiling and said they would come by around 7 P.M.

The rest of the day I was nervous, but too excited to back out. Robert and Sheila arrived on time. We had a couple of drinks and just talked for a while. Then I excused myself and went to the bathroom. When I came out, Robert was waiting. I said, "I guess you're up next," and started to walk past him.

Robert reached for my hand, and said, "What's the hurry?" Before I could answer, he had wrapped his arms around me and was kissing my neck. When he kissed my lips I started to loosen up, and soon we were in a passionate embrace, our tongues exploring each other's mouths. He was starting to get hard, and I pressed myself into his body and rubbed his ass. Then I pulled back to undo his pants. In a flash they were down around his ankles and his huge cock was free. I led him over to the bed and had him lie on his back. I started licking and sucking his cock and stroking his enormous balls with my hand. I played with them while I teased the tip of his cock with my tongue. I tasted precome and heard his breathing getting faster. I felt him begin to tense up, and then he erupted, shooting such huge amounts of come into my mouth that I could barely swallow it all.

When he finished he undressed me and went down on my pussy. I was so hot I came several times. We lay there, holding and stroking each other, until he began to get hard again. I wanted to fuck him in the worst way. Just thinking about it had me wide open and wetter than I had ever been with Doug. Because of Robert's size, I mounted him and rubbed the head of his cock against my wet pussy. Slowly the head started to go in, and gradually, inch by inch, I rocked his full length inside me. It felt so good to be completely filled that I just stayed still a moment, not moving, until I had truly savored the feeling and committed it to memory for later. I began rocking again in a circular motion, trying to take my time, but his cock felt so good that we were both fucking hard in no time. Then his hands gripped my waist, and it felt as if I were falling. I came over and over again as he pulled me even closer to him, finally exploding deep within me.

We were so involved with each other that we hadn't given our spouses a second thought. When we went back into the living room we were just in time to see Doug fucking Sheila in the ass. Sheila was loving it. Anal sex with oversize Robert was out of the question.

After they left, Doug and I had great fun telling each other what we did. We never saw Doug and Sheila again, but we've since found other married couples who share our interests and enjoy the same kind of good time that we do.

—L. E., Florida

Sex Before the Wedding

My fiancé and I have always been a little crazy, but we didn't expect to throw our own bachelor and bachelorette party, let alone wake up with someone else in bed.

Realizing that the parties our friends had planned for us were pretty lame, Darryl and I decided to take matters into our own hands. We packed up some toys, including my favorite strap-on, and drove north of the border to a Canadian strip club that caters to couples. Darryl was well aware that I've had flings with women, so I knew he wouldn't mind watching me receive a lap dance or two.

We sat at a small table with a gorgeous redhead and her date. The music was pretty loud, so we couldn't talk much, but we could see that the guy was paying a lot more attention to the dancers than his date liked. He would howl and lick between his fingers when they walked by. Okay, so it was a strip club, but you can still have manners.

Despite the guy's obnoxious attitude, Darryl and I were having a great time watching the women gyrate around the stage. I was getting especially horny watching a tall, olive-skinned female strip. When she stepped offstage I caught her attention and asked for a lap dance. I could tell from the grin on Darryl's face that this was just fine with him.

The dancer had jet-black hair, light brown eyes, and large, firm tits. She draped them right across my face as she straddled me, and I could taste her salt on my lips. She didn't waste any time, but unsnapped her panties and grabbed the back of my head, sinking her fingers into my blonde hair and pushing my face into her stomach, forcing my head down until my chin almost touched her silky bush. Darryl started kissing my ear as she turned around, bent over the table, and spread her cheeks wide enough for me to see her little asshole and shaved pussy lips. She twisted and writhed, pushing her ass so close to my face I could feel her heat. I was so wet I just wanted to jam a finger in my pussy and a tongue in hers. The dancer was leaning over the table, wrapping her arms around the cute redhead, and that made my pussy so hot I wanted to tell Darryl just to fuck me right there so the redhead could watch.

When the dance ended, the redhead's boyfriend kept hooting and slapping the table while she tried not to look like she was with him. He said something crude about the bathroom, grabbed his date's tit, and waddled away. She watched him go, then turned to us with a half smile. Darryl and I were ready to leave, but I felt that I should do something because she was in such a bad situation. It was then that I noticed that her nipples were poking at her blouse; she was as turned on as we were. The three of us sat there, looking at one another, waiting for one of us to say what we were all thinking.

A few minutes later all three of us were running up the street to the hotel. In the elevator Darryl asked the redhead if the dancer had got her as horny as she'd got us. Still laughing, the girl said yes. Then she grabbed me and French-kissed me until the doors opened. Once we got to the room there was no talk about what we were going to do. Darryl playfully threw me onto the bed and said to our new friend, "I'm Darryl, and this is Diana."

"I'm Helene," she said, stepping out of her boots.

"Helene," said Darryl, "keep kissing my bride-to-be while I get her out of these jeans."

Helene leapt onto the bed and resumed our long, tongue-twisting kiss. Darryl had my belt open and my fly down. I hoisted up as he pulled my jeans down to my ankles; I was eager to be free of them. Helene's hand quickly found its way into my panties as I tried to get her pants undone. She sat up for a second, whipped off her blouse, and freed her beautiful tits. Darryl was kneeling between my legs, hands on Helene's waist, pulling down her pants and panties as far as he could with her still straddling me. I pulled her tits toward my face and starting sucking, reaching up between her legs to smear her hot pussy juice up and down her crotch.

I knew Darryl would be watching and I knew he'd be rock-hard. Then I felt the bed shift and his cock rub against my hand. I grabbed it and rubbed it against Helene's wet cunt, and she moaned, grinding her hips into my hand. I wanted my man to fuck her and I wanted to watch. I twisted around on the bed so Helene and I were in a sixty-nine position. As I watched her ass coming down toward me I spread my legs open and her tongue slipped into my hole. I groaned and spread her lips with my fingers, licking her clit and opening her up for Darryl's cock. I felt his cock against my lips and I sucked it, leaving it wet and slippery. I tilted my head and let it slide right from my mouth to the red bush above me. Watching that long, slick cock sliding into a pussy was so hot I started coming. Helene groaned into my cunt as Darryl's cock slid in and out, grazing my lips with every stroke. I reached down and pushed Helene's head hard against my cunt as I screamed and fucked her face, grinding my pelvis and smearing her lips with my cunt juice. Hearing my yell, Darryl began to tense up. I pulled her labia wide and wrapped my lips around his cock and her hole. When he came I could feel it pulsing down his shaft. I flicked my tongue around where his cock disappeared into Helene's sweet pussy so that when he pulled out, a flood of his come dripped straight into my mouth.

Helene hadn't come yet, so I pulled her pussy close and sucked her off until she was practically fucking my mouth with her desire. Darryl came around in front of me and started jerking off. There was no way I was going to hold back as Helene stuck three fingers in my cunt. As she finger-fucked my cunt, Darryl jerked himself harder and harder until he arched his back and with a groan shot his load all over my neck and tits. I smeared it around my nipples and wiped it on my cunt. Helene licked it off my fingers. Feeling her lips on my fingers was all I needed, and I exploded again.

I collapsed with a smile and looked at Darryl as he leaned against the headboard, panting. Helene said, "Is this what I think it is?" I turned around and saw her looking at the strap-on dildo, and knew it was going to be the best bachelor or bachelorette party anybody had ever had.

—D. L., New York

In Like Clint

One afternoon I began some on-line flirting with a guy named Clint. This was nothing new for me, but I had never before met any of these contacts in person. Clint was complaining that he needed a back rub. I decided to help him out. I sent him an instant message, asking if he was interested in more than a back rub. With my husband, David, sitting next to me at the computer, I asked Clint if he would be interested in a threesome. He was all for it, and we arranged to meet at a local restaurant.

David and I met Clint outside the restaurant, then went inside to talk for a while. Since he hadn't had a picture to send me on-line, I wasn't sure if I would be attracted to him, or he to me. But once I saw him, any doubts quickly evaporated. A few drinks and an hour later we took Clint back to our house.

I could tell Clint was a little nervous, so I decided to make the first move. I ran my hand up his thigh and began fondling his balls. He leaned over and started kissing me. His cock was already hard when I began rubbing it through his shorts. He started unbuttoning my dress while I undid his shorts and began stroking his cock. I wasn't wearing a bra, so he dived right for my tits and began nibbling my nipples.

Soon he pushed my head down toward his dick. I got down on my knees in front of him and started sucking and licking his cock. David moved behind me and lifted my dress. Then he took off my panties and slid his cock into my wet pussy. I knew Clint was watching me suck his dick, so I looked up at him while I ran my tongue up the entire length of his shaft. I could tell he was really excited at this point, so I suggested we move to the bedroom.

Clint finished taking off my dress in the bedroom. David followed us in, naked, his cock standing at attention. Clint moved behind me. This was a perfect situation. I had David kissing me and fondling my tits, while Clint kissed the back of my neck and pressed his firm cock between my ass cheeks.

Then he motioned for me to bend over the bed. He slid his dick into my already soaked pussy. David maneuvered his way under me so I could suck his dick. I felt Clint playing with my asshole, and I knew he wanted to fuck my ass. The thought thrilled me. Clint's dick slid into my ass like it was meant to be there. David got so excited watching Clint fuck my ass so easily that he soon shot his load into my mouth. Clint continued to pump my ass hard and fast, his balls bouncing on my clit. I moaned in pleasure with multiple orgasms. My pussy was dripping wet by the time he was done.

Clint stretched out on the bed in front of me and I licked the head of his cock while David got down between my legs and started lapping up my pussy juice. Then David began fingering my pussy and my ass while he licked my clit, bringing me to orgasm again. Soon Clint was coming, and I opened my mouth to catch every last bit of his jism. Before Clint left the house he said we would have to do this again. I hope we hear from him soon.

—E. T., Michigan

WOMAN TO WOMAN

Working Out

It was the week before our fifth wedding anniversary, and I wanted to fit into the skintight dress that my husband had loved so much on our honeymoon. There was only one problem—the twenty-year-old body that it had fit so well before had filled out a little. I decided to call a local aerobics instructor and find out when she could fit me into class. She said there were no spots open, but I could pay extra for late private sessions.

The next night I showed up at the club in a leotard, eager to do what it would take. Maggie, the instructor, walked in, and I shivered. She was incredibly beautiful and wearing next to nothing. We got right into the routine, and before long everyone else had left the fitness center. I guess she noticed that I was distracted by her moves, and she came close to assist me with mine. As she stretched my arms up, her hands slowly cupped my firm breasts. My face flushed, as did my peach.

"I know what you want," she purred. Maggie had read my mind. I wanted to smell, feel, and taste her. Her hand flicked my nipple hard as her tongue ran up my neck into my ear. My leotard was wet, and I was hot.

I licked her tongue, and she slid out of her Lycra suit. Then mine came off, our naked bodies moving in perfect rhythm with the flickering of our tongues.

"Oh," she exhaled, as I slid a finger between her thighs. My face followed, and with that, we rode each other's lips. We rolled over and over, giving each other many orgasms. Maggie stood over my glistening body and motioned for me to stay. I fingered my clit as she grabbed a double-ended dildo from her desk.

Before long we were writhing in ecstasy, our perspiring hips slapping together as the dong slid up our holes. The room spun so fast, I came close to passing out, but Maggie was there to keep my full attention. That night we moved from the whirlpool to the sauna to her apartment, where we said good-bye until the next night. Needless to say, "working out" with Maggie for the next four nights fulfilled my ultimate fantasy—and got me into the dress as well.

—M. B., Washington

Working Girls

Brenda and I had been cocktail waitresses at a local club for the past three years, and we'd become very good friends. One night after work, we met for a couple of drinks. At first, naturally, we spoke about the shift we had just put in, but after a few drinks, we changed the subject to sex. As time went by, the conversation became more risqué, and Brenda asked if I had ever been with another woman. I told her that I had thought of it but hadn't actually carried it out. She asked if we could leave and continue talking about this in private.

We decided to take a cab to her house. I was becoming extremely aroused in the backseat, and I felt my pussy begin to moisten. Brenda made it clear that the feeling was mutual, whispering in my ear that she wanted to feel my body next to hers. With that I softly ran my hand up her leg and stared into her eyes.

Once inside, we embraced and kissed for the first time—her face was so smooth. Our lips met, and then our tongues discovered each other. It was delightful, and I couldn't wait for more.

We ran to her bedroom, dropping our clothes on the way. By the time we got there, we were wearing only bras and G-strings. We kissed again and caressed each other. Brenda's hand dropped down and touched my cunt for the first time. She began to rub my clit slowly as I unfastened her bra. Then she removed mine and began to lightly bite my nipples. It was unbelievably erotic having my best friend do this to me.

Soon her fingers began to fuck my pussy. I remained standing, and she lowered herself to the floor and licked my dripping cunt while I rode her face. She knew just what to do. It was unlike any tongue-lashing any man had ever given me. I pulled her up and tasted my own pussy on her lips, licking her fingers as I guided her to the bed. I couldn't wait to lick her delectable pussy.

Her pussy lips were swollen and deep pink. I put my face right on her cunt and began to eat her. *Very sweet,* I thought. Using my fingers, I exposed her button and tongued it at a frantic pace. Her hips rose and soon she was coming all over my face. I must have done a good job, because she pulled me up and licked my face—fresh with her flowing juices—and kissed me passionately.

We lay there for a while, kissing and fingering each other until Brenda asked if I wanted to be fucked. Did I ever! She went to a drawer and put on a strap-on dildo. I told her to fuck me doggie style, grab my tits, and ram me hard. Following my instructions, she pounded me mercilessly. I came in a wave that completely engulfed my body. We lay there embracing and fell asleep in each other's arms.

—R. A., New Jersey

Shop-aholic

It was sort of a dreary, foggy afternoon, and there was nothing else to do, so I decided to go shopping at the local mall. While I was checking out the selection of white pants. I couldn't help but notice the fine-looking woman who was working in the store. Her ass looked so firm and ripe I could feel my pussy getting hot. She was wearing a tight pair of purple spandex panties under a flowing lilac skirt. Her stomach was so tight and tanned, and her breasts looked like perfect mouthfuls. I wondered how big her nipples were under that top.

Just then she spotted me also. She must have caught me checking her out. She walked over to me and asked if I needed any help. Then it was chemistry—and no one was in the store.

We chatted for a few minutes and found out that we were both utterly attracted to each other. Her name was Amy, she was the manager, and she had a beautiful smile. Suddenly, she kissed me, deep and wet, and our tongues were caught up with each other. Then she stopped and said that she'd open up a dressing room for us.

She led me back to the back of the store and I couldn't wait to taste that honey-filled snatch. After all, the mall was empty and the store quiet. As soon as we entered the dressing room I undressed my new babe friend, leaving on only her sexy thong bikini. I spread her legs apart and rubbed her soft thighs. With my three middle fingertips I started to rub her sweet clit. My tongue went straight into her, proceeding to lick and suck nonstop. She shuddered rigidly three times, and her eyes squeezed shut as she climaxed, gasping for breath.

Then it was my turn to come, and did I ever! She started in immediately on my cunt with her thumb and two fingers. I was pinching, twisting, and caressing my nipples—getting very worked up. Her tongue went wild on my snatch, and I soaked her face with my come as I had a massive orgasm. After that we kissed and rubbed each other, softly talking. Then she went down on my tired cunt and made it feel loved and warm. Well, I bought the white pants and I think I'll go shopping again this afternoon.

—N. C., Washington

Picture Perfect

I am a university student who lives in a dorm and shares a room. My boyfriend lives in an apartment nearby, where recently out of curiosity I leafed through his latest issue of *Penthouse.* I found that the women were all very beautiful, and, to my surprise, I couldn't help getting extremely turned on seeing them licking each other. The pictorial featuring two girls made me cream in my panties. I confiscated the magazine to fully enjoy later at my dorm.

When I got home my roommate was out. I took off all of my clothes and started masturbating to the beautiful photos. I dreamed of licking and sucking the models' bodies. I would have done anything to kiss and taste another woman. I started to moan loudly and was reaching an explosive orgasm. Then, right when I was coming, the door opened and my roommate walked in.

I was very embarrassed, and so was she. There I was, lying on the floor completely naked, with the centerfold wide-open. I asked her to excuse me, and she just giggled and told me not to worry about it. I tried to hide the magazine, but was unsuccessful. As she undressed for bed she asked me what had me so turned on. In her half shirt and panties she grabbed it and started to look through it. As she sat at her desk I noticed that her nipples started to become erect.

"No wonder you were so hot. These women are gorgeous," she said. As I sat there blushing I noticed that she started swaying her hips back and forth, her legs spread just enough for me to see the moisture forming between them.

Then she set the magazine down, looked at me, and took off her shirt. Her round, firm tits never looked so good before. She licked her lips and smiled. "What do you think of this body?" With that I crawled over to her—still naked—and told her that I wanted to make love to her right then. "I thought you'd never ask," she said.

Pulling down her now-soaked panties, I smelled the sweet aroma of her pussy. She leaned back on the chair as I began to lick her neatly shaven cunt lips. As I sucked I was amazed at how good she tasted. She began to push my head into her pussy while I rubbed her wetness all over my face. I moved up to her stomach and rock-hard nipples, relishing every inch of her skin. We began to kiss, and I almost came right there.

She suggested that I finger her while riding her face. She wouldn't let go of my pumping until I came in her mouth. We both started to shake and moan, grinding each other into a frenzy. Afterward we just lay on the floor, French-kissing and fondling each other.

Later she confessed that she had always been turned on by me and would try to take showers at the same time just to get a glimpse of my body. This really turned me on, and I told her that she could fuck me anytime. She said that it might be fun to invite my boyfriend into our new relationship. I think he'll be pleasantly surprised, but that's another letter.

—*A. C., Maryland*

From Head to Toe

Last month, in preparation for a meeting the next day, I made an appointment for a manicure at a local nail salon. I was delayed at work and did not get there until 6:30 P.M. A slim, attractive woman, who said her name was Kara, was closing the store. I pleaded with her to stay open. She said that she was the only one left, and that she would take care of me. She closed the shades and shut the lights in the store, then led me in.

I sat down, and she proceeded to do my fingernails. We began talking, and throughout our conversation I admired Kara's natural beauty. She had long, straight black hair, vivacious almond eyes, high cheekbones, and full, sensuous lips. She was so gracious, I was disappointed when she finished. She offered to do a pedicure, and I accepted.

While she was making preparations, I removed my panty hose. I was a little embarrassed when she knelt to soak my feet and my bush was exposed to her gaze. She handed me a folder with loose magazine articles in it. Some of the articles were from Xaviera Hollander's "Call Me Madam" column. I read the first article about foot fetishes, and got really horny when I read the next article about lesbianism.

I felt a tingling sensation in my pussy as Kara massaged my feet. She lifted my right foot to her mouth and began to suck on the big toe, working her way over to the little one. I was shivering with excitement as I felt my cunt juices flowing down my thigh. It was as if the sensation from my foot was directed toward my cunt. Kara kicked the water basin out of the way and squatted in front of me. She yanked my skirt to the floor, then lifted my legs over her shoulders. I was moaning deliriously as I felt Kara's hands on my ass, and I reached down to pull her face toward me. I nearly lost my balance on the chair from writhing and rubbing my snatch against her face. After numerous orgasms, Kara helped me to my feet and embraced me. I was trembling as I tasted my juices on her lips. She sat down on the chair and guided me onto her lap. I rested my head on her shoulder for what seemed to be an eternity. I went to spend the night at Kara's apartment. We didn't sleep much that night. I had the opportunity to please her as she had pleased me earlier. I kissed her from her head to her rosy red toenails. We missed work the next day. Thank you, *Penthouse,* and a special thank-you to Xaviera for stimulating my sex life.

—*J. H., New Jersey*

Alterations

While getting ready for a local beauty pageant, I went to a store where a lady named Sasha did alterations. A few days later, I went to pick up my gown. Standing behind the curtain, I put on the gown. It fit tight and sexy. I walked over to Sasha and saw her eyes going up and down my body. Smiling, she said I looked gorgeous.

Sasha proceeded to feel how tight the gown was on my hips. Her hands moved up, and she tenderly caressed my breast. She gave me a soft kiss, which I returned, and our tongues explored each other's mouths. She began to cover my neck with slow, wet kisses as her hands caressed my body. She whispered in my ear that she loved to eat pussy. "I bet you have the best-tasting pussy of all," she declared. The excitement I was feeling made me very hot and wet.

Sasha pulled the zipper, and the evening gown fell

to the floor. She really loved my lingerie, commenting on its beauty as she unhooked my blue lace bra, noticing that my nipples were hard. She knew just how horny I was, and my knees became weak with the thought of being with another woman.

Next Sasha took each of my big brown tits into her mouth. I moaned with pleasure as she continued to suck and lick. She pulled my panties off and licked my thick golden bush. Standing there in my pink garter belt and black stockings, I let my hair down as I watched Sasha take her clothes off.

We lay down on the carpet, and I spread my legs wide. My clit was hard and throbbing from her lovely fingers, which were going in and out of my hairy pussy. She asked me if I liked what she was doing. "Yes!" I cried. "Oh, yes! Eat me, please! I need it!"

With that Sasha put her face in my hairy cunt, pressing her lips against my pussy. Her tongue was hot and wet as it darted in and out of my juicy pink pussy. The juice was running out of my hole fast and heavy. She lapped it up while she slid one of her long fingers deep inside as she continued sucking my cunt. As she started finger-fucking me, I began to hump my pussy against her face, begging her to fuck me harder as she stuck another finger inside my pussy. I could feel the passion building, and I knew it wouldn't be long until I came. I cried out, "Fuck me! Fuck me! I'm coming!" as I had one great, long-lasting orgasm. Sasha licked my juices from her fingers, then licked my pussy dry.

I began kissing her, tasting my sweet juices on her

pretty face. I wanted this sexy, older woman real bad. I began squeezing her brown tits, sucking them while reaching down to feel the soft, slippery warmth of Sasha's cunt. It was so hot and juicy that my finger slid deep inside her with ease. I pulled her pussy lips apart, my face in her hairy brown snatch, and began to suck her clit. She was loving my tongue as it lapped away at her pussy. She was moaning louder, and I continued to eat her womanhood. Once Sasha had climaxed, I tenderly sucked her free-flowing love juices—licking and swallowing every drop.

That night at the pageant, I saw Sasha and her husband sitting close to the stage. While walking along the stage in my evening gown, smiling to all the people, I looked down to see Sasha running her tongue over her lips. I could feel my nipples getting hard. My pussy was very wet.

Before long I am going to make love to Sasha again, and even have her husband fuck me. When I go back to school, I'm going to have sex with my girlfriends, who are just as beautiful as I am. There's nothing like having sex with a hot, sexy woman.

—*J. R., Iowa*

Envy No More

Although I have always enjoyed sex with my boyfriend, I was envious of the women in your pictorials, who are shown eating pussy and sucking tits. One day last week after looking through *Penthouse*, my wet pussy and I went out in search of a friend for both of us. I went to a local bar and checked out the female clientele. Of the several beauties that made eye contact, one kept staring—a beautiful, big-titted blonde. I sauntered over to her and asked her to come home with me for a drink.

When we got to my house we opened two beers and proceeded to the couch. We talked about our boyfriends for a while and finally came to the conclusion that neither of us had ever had pussy before and we were both a bit nervous. But I decided that one of us was going to have to be the aggressor, so I went to the bedroom, retrieved my ten-inch vibrator, and asked her if maybe a little cock would relax her.

She grinned and pulled her skirt off to reveal beautiful, white-blonde pussy hair and smooth, firm thighs. I reached down and rubbed the vibrator on her clit while she removed the rest of her clothes. I wanted to wait, but when I saw her tits my mouth started watering and I was driven to suck on them immediately. First I gently nibbled on her erect nipples, then deeply sucked her left breast. I instantly forgot about the vibrator. With a soft moan she squeezed her big tits around my face as I kissed and sucked with abandon.

Next she subtly put both of her hands on my shoulders and guided me downward to her cunt. While exploring her creamy thighs and lips I removed my clothes, my pussy now dripping with musky juices. She purred as my tongue darted in and out of her hot hole and my finger worked its way into her crevice. She grew hotter and louder and eventually screamed, "Fuck me harder!"

To meet this request I told her that she'd have to suck my cunt as well. We moved into a sixty-nine and I truly enjoyed her cunt grinding on my face as her ass was shaking above me. She begged me to finger her hard while I ate, and soon she was moaning and pumping out of control. At this point I grabbed the vibrator and shoved it in her twat. To my surprise she took the whole thing, pumped even harder, and cried out, "I want to come all over your face!"

Delighted by this prospect, I got rid of the vibrator again and drove my tongue deep into her folds, causing her to buck and flex like a madwoman. When she was done my face was covered with her sticky juices.

After just seconds of rest she instructed me to get on all fours and let her do the work. I happily complied and she went at it—sucking on my tits, licking my entire body, and mercifully going down on my anxious twat. I was just about to come when the door opened and my boyfriend walked in. Needless to say, we both watched his cock become hard before us. The blonde asked him to join the fun and watch her eat me. She went back to my dripping cunt lips while he removed his clothes and stroked himself. After about three minutes he joined in and rubbed his cock on the blonde's crotch. I rolled on my back so I could see this beautiful girl getting it put to her by my boyfriend.

He shoved his cock hard into her cunt hole but she

never stopped licking me. I started grinding into her, my swollen clit rubbing on her face, while my boyfriend pumped furiously. We came at the same time—my cunt juices on her face and his jism in her cunt.

We all have a lunch date next week at my place. Until then I will just dream of pussies and tits.

—P. G., Washington

Room Service

As I lay down on my stomach, I began to feel slightly aroused. Kimo placed a towel over my ass and began to massage my lower back and shoulders. Her strokes were at times deep, and at others, soft and caressing. The oil she used made her petite hands glide smoothly over my skin. I felt myself drifting, relaxing, and becoming more aroused.

Kimo was making long, slow strokes up and down my thighs. Her strokes were rhythmic, and I was beginning to rock slowly in unison with them. I couldn't control it.

It was then that Kimo asked, "Please. You like special massage?" I couldn't believe myself when I groaned, "Yes." Kimo walked into the bathroom, and I could hear her start the shower. She came back and led me, without eye contact, into the bathroom. Again she said, "Please?" and this time knelt before me and slowly peeled off my soaking panties.

I let the hot water cascade down my back. With my eyes closed, I hovered near delirium. I tried to regain my composure. It was then that I felt Kimo's hands slide around my body, seeking my swollen nipples. This was followed by her now naked body pressing close to mine in the shower. Kimo turned me around to face her, her eyes still not meeting mine. Her body was very petite, with small breasts capped by hard, dark nipples. Her bush was neatly trimmed. Kimo began to lather my body with a sweet, pungent soap. As she reached around to soap my back, our nipples pressed together under the pulsating shower. Her lips brushed my neck. She lathered my body completely, and as her hands slid by my pussy, I moaned again. What little control I had tried to regain I lost. After she rinsed me clean, her tender lips surrounded my nipples with the lightest of kisses. I exploded in an orgasm.

Kimo turned off the shower and began to towel me dry, patting all those places that were now aching for a tongue and fingers. Then she handed me a towel, and said, "Please?" Not really knowing what to do, I let my instincts guide me. Then I kissed another woman's nipples for the first time. We kissed each other deeply, with our bodies pressed close. Kimo put her hands on my ass and ground her pussy into mine.

Then she took my hand and led me back into the bedroom. Again I lay facedown on the bed, but this time completely naked. Kimo climbed over me and straddled my back, facing my feet, and began long, slow strokes of my thighs. This time I spread my legs wide for her and began to rock in unison with her strokes. I could feel Kimo's wet pussy sliding back and forth on my back. This time she didn't stop at the tops of my thighs, and brushed my pussy with her hands at the top of her upstroke, eliciting agonizing moans.

She climbed off, said, "Please?" and rolled me onto my back. Again her lips surrounded my nipples. Her hands stroked my stomach and thighs. Then I guided her head from my nipples, down my stomach to my yearning pussy. The wait was torment as she kissed and licked around my inner thighs, stomach, and pubic mound. My legs were wide apart, and my knees were raised, waiting for her. I almost screamed when her lips reached my slit. Kimo didn't waste any time and began to slide her tongue up and down. Her tongue surrounded and flicked my engorged clitoris as another orgasm came crashing down.

By now I was possessed. I had to taste her and give her the same pleasure she'd given me. I said, "Please?" and began to pull her leg over me so she would be straddling me. At first she resisted, but as I stroked her soaking pussy, she whimpered and let me pull her onto me. Kimo tasted of sweet soap as I licked and sucked her pussy. My tongue entered her deeply as she began to press her pussy against my face. She began to slide herself back and forth in a slow rhythm. I tongued and sucked her clitoris. Kimo groaned loudly as her orgasm rocked her. We collapsed in a heap of sticky-sweet flesh.

We lay together intertwined and exhausted for a long time. Finally, Kimo stirred and kissed me deeply.

She said, "Thank you," and left as quietly as she'd come.

—*L. K., Texas*

Therapy

I find myself becoming excited just thinking about the other day, and I am curious to see if my letter will be printed, if for no other reason than to let that special person know how much I enjoyed her company.

My friend Mary and I were at work the other day, when she noticed that I was rubbing the back of my neck. I explained to her that I had been in a car accident several years ago and that my neck bothers me from time to time. She suggested that since things were so slow at work—we're both physical-therapy techs—we take the rest of the day off and she would give me a neck massage. My neck ached so badly, I couldn't resist the offer and agreed.

Once we got to my house, Mary told me the first thing I should do was to take a long, hot bath, and she would meet me in the bedroom. The water felt wonderful, and I stayed in until it began to grow cold. I put on my bathrobe and found my friend waiting for me on the bed.

She asked when my husband would be home, and I told her not for several hours. She laughed and said that was good, because she didn't want him to walk in on us and get the wrong impression. We both laughed, then she told me to take off my robe and lie facedown on the bed. I thought nothing about being nude in front of her—we have taken showers in front of each other at work—and quickly disrobed. She poured some hot oil on the back of my neck and began to give me the neck rub of my life. Within a few minutes, the pain was completely gone, but I was feeling so good, I didn't even tell her.

After a while, she asked me if I wanted her to massage my back as well. I quickly agreed, and soon her hands were working their magic down my spine to the top of my hips and then back up, but on her return strokes, her hands would move farther down my sides, softly stroking the sides of my breasts. By that time I could feel that something was going to happen, but I didn't care. I had never been so lovingly caressed in my entire life, and I was going to let her massage me in any way she wanted.

Mary stopped just long enough to pour some oil on the small of my back, telling me how soft my skin was, then she began to slowly massage my ass cheeks, gently pushing her fingers farther between them with every stroke. I moaned how wonderful it felt, and that seemed to be all she was waiting to hear.

She gradually pushed my legs apart, and soon I could feel her long fingernails softly stroke the insides of my thighs, then barely caress my cunt lips on the way back up. I don't know what came over me at that point, but I lifted my hips so she could reach whatever part of my pussy she wanted. When she started to stroke my clit with one of her fingers, I lifted my ass as far up as I could and moaned very loudly. Mary stopped and got on her hands and knees behind me. She told me to just relax and let her do all the work. When I felt her part my pussy hair with her hands, I buried my face in the pillow. I knew what was coming next, and since I have always loved having my pussy eaten, I knew I would probably scream. As soon as her tongue flicked out and touched my clit, I let loose with a loud, "Oh my God!" I can only hope that the pillow muffled it enough so the neighbors didn't hear.

That seemed to excite Mary, and she started eating me like I'd never been eaten before. Between licking and sucking my clit, she would snake her tongue so deep inside me, I couldn't believe it. I was bucking and thrashing around on the bed—poor Mary was hanging on to my ass for dear life—until I finally exploded all over her face. She never missed a lick and just kept sucking nectar out of my cunt until I couldn't stand it anymore and pulled away.

When I looked at Mary, I had to laugh. Her short brown hair was a mess, and her face was soaked with my juices, but she had this shit-eating grin on her face and just said, "Oh, my!"

I couldn't resist kissing her, letting my tongue snake down her throat, then licking my juices off her face. I told her to get undressed and to let me do the work for a while. She asked me if I'd ever been with a woman before, and when I said no, she said that I didn't have to do it if I didn't want to. I told her not to be silly—I wanted to taste her in the same way she had just tasted me. She smiled and quickly undressed.

I started kissing and sucking her nipples; they were rock-hard and as big around as the cigar that my husband smokes. When she began to moan and grind her pussy against my thigh, I quickly slid down until the tip of my nose brushed her thick brown curls. Her smell was like an elixir, thick and musky, but very, very sweet. I used my fingers to part her pussy hair and gently placed a kiss on her clit. She ran her fingers through my hair and lifted her hips to my mouth. I started sucking her very swollen clit like it was a tiny cock, and she started to grind her hips against my face very hard. I moved my mouth down until it fit completely over her cunt and pushed my tongue deep inside her, curling it to catch some of her sweet nectar, then bringing it back out again. She started moaning for me to suck her clit hard, and I quickly went back to work on her little button. Soon she began to moan and scream, pulling my face hard against her and grinding her pussy against it. When she finally came, there was so much juice, I had to lick as fast as I could to keep up with the flow. Finally, she arched her back, locked her legs around my face, and just shuddered. After a few seconds, she relaxed and settled back down on the bed. I gently kissed her pussy a couple more times, then scooted up to lie next to her.

—M. M., Michigan

Snowball

This past winter was a nightmare, commuting to work in Manhattan from New Jersey, because of the snow. During the last storm, we had over twelve inches, so I decided to accept an offer from a colleague to spend Friday night at her apartment. I thought it would be easier for me to try to get home on Saturday or Sunday.

I've known Jenna since I started at the firm five years ago. Even though she is in her mid-forties, we are able to communicate with each other freely. I sought her advice when I was having boyfriend problems, and she sought my advice when she was going through a divorce. Since her children left for college, she has been living alone.

We left work early, and Jenna cooked us a delicious dinner. We talked about personal problems and current relationships. I learned that we both had problems and that neither one of us was currently in an ongoing relationship. Jenna revealed that since her divorce three years ago, she'd been on only three dates. She complained that most men do not want to settle down with a woman in her forties. I complained that it is hard for me to keep an ongoing relationship with a man, since the men in my life don't respect my work ethic.

I complimented Jenna that she still looked as young as when I first met her five years ago. She thanked me and complained that her hips are wider, her tits are sagging, and wrinkles are forming on her face. Despite Jenna's complaint, I thought she maintained the same natural beauty she'd had when I first met her. She was the same woman I'd admired for her professionalism, beauty, and elegance. It was getting late, so we decided to go to bed.

As I was reading a magazine in bed, I heard a very faint cry from Jenna's bedroom. I thought she was still despondent, so I went to her room. When I opened the door, I saw Jenna's feet spread apart and resting on top of the headboard. As I walked closer to the bed, I saw Jenna's right hand holding her crotch. She was pushing her middle finger in and out of her cunt. Jenna's face turned completely red with embarrassment when she saw me. I sat on her bed and tried to console her. She was so mortified that her right hand remained on her cunt. I saw strands of pubic hair protruding from either side. I told her that it was nothing to be ashamed of, because we've all done it. I confessed that when I was younger, my best friend and I used to masturbate in front of each other in my bedroom. After we experienced an orgasm from our own hands, we masturbated each other to an orgasm.

To prove my trust to Jenna, I removed my clothes and sat across from her. I wet my fingers and ran them up and down my pubic hair. After teasing myself a few seconds, I spread my lips and rolled my clit between my thumb and index finger. As I rested on my back, I spread my legs apart and lifted my crotch a few inches above the bed to give Jenna a better view of what I was doing. I guess my plan worked, because Jenna overcame her embarrassment and proceeded to mimic me stroke for stroke. We embraced and kissed after we both had an orgasm. I was so horny from feeling her breasts and hairy pussy brushing up against mine.

I guided Jenna to a kneeling position on the bed, then I crawled underneath her to lick her cunt. She was so overwhelmed, she was grinding her twat into my face. As Jenna was hit with another orgasm, I sat up and embraced her thighs from behind. With her ass in front of me, I ran my tongue down the crack of her cheeks to her twat. Holding her ass and thighs for leverage, I slid myself under her legs. Jenna lowered herself until her head was resting on a pillow between my feet. As I continued to ferociously tongue her twat, she grabbed my right foot and sucked my toes. She collapsed on top of me from a thunderous orgasm, but she continued sucking my toes.

We fell asleep in each other's arms that night. I awoke in the morning to Jenna licking me from my toes to my cunt. She refused to let me up until I reached an orgasm, lifting my legs over her shoulders and sucking and licking my cunt for all she was worth. After a roaring orgasm, we shared a sexy bath. Even though it was cold outside, we were naked indoors, generating our own kind of heat and energy. We explored and experimented with various positions and techniques for pleasure. We found that our favorites are sixty-nine, masturbating in front of each other, and kissing each other's wet toes in the tub. I did not go home until Sunday morning to pack a set of emergency clothes to keep in Jenna's apartment. I returned to Jenna by bedtime on Sunday evening. I guess you're never too old to try something new and fulfilling.

—P. M., New Jersey

Vegas Vixen

I'm a twenty-three-year-old flight attendant. My job takes me to a lot of interesting places, where I meet very interesting people. One particular evening I was in Las Vegas, and I decided to take advantage of the diverse opportunities there. That city just screams sex!

My evening began at a large casino right on the strip. I was sitting at the blackjack tables, winning some and losing some. After a few hands, the lady sitting next to me struck up a conversation. We talked for a while and decided to leave the table. We were pretty hungry, so we decided to get something to eat.

In the restaurant I learned that her name was Laura. She was extremely attractive and dressed very well. Her short skirt showed off her luscious long legs. Her tight silk blouse accentuated her beautiful breasts and erect nipples. We finished our meal and talked for a while. I was extremely attracted to her, and I could sense that she was attracted to me. Laura invited me up to her room for a nightcap, and I eagerly agreed.

We arrived at her room, and my pussy was burning with desire for her. She arranged some pillows on the bed and offered me a seat. I sat against the pillows with my legs stretched out. Laura went to the phone and ordered room service—a bottle of champagne and a fruit plate. Then she requested an adult channel for the room. She walked to the television and turned it on. We watched people fucking and sucking like crazy. I thought I would soak the sheets before we could do anything together.

Laura knew that I wanted her badly, but she didn't comply right away. She kept doing little things to drive me crazy. Finally, after room service came, she settled in on the bed with me to watch the fucking on television. I decided I had to take some action. I turned on the light in the bathroom and left the door slightly cracked, then I turned off all the lights in the room. I returned to the bed and clicked off the television.

I said it was very obvious that we wanted each other—she agreed. We kissed passionately for quite some time, then I could feel her hands roaming all over my body. I unbuttoned her shirt until her big, beautiful breasts sprang free. Laura wasn't wearing a bra, providing easy access to her beautiful nipples, which I rolled between my fingers. She began to moan and insert more of her tongue into my mouth. I could feel Laura fumbling with the buttons on my blouse, so I broke away from her. I stood at the edge of the bed and began removing all of my clothes. Laura stared at me intently. She asked me to leave my panties on—I agreed. Then I began to remove the rest of Laura's clothes. She lay back on the bed as I slid her skirt off, discovering she wasn't wearing any panties. After I took off her high heels, I rubbed and caressed her feet. I removed her nylons from the garter that was holding them up and slid them down her firm legs. Laura unhooked her garter and tossed it on the floor. She lay there on the bed entirely naked, waiting for my next move.

I started at her feet, sucking and licking her toes. I worked my way up her legs to the inner parts of her thighs, which I kissed and licked tenderly. I let my hands wander to her beautiful breasts, and my mouth was not far behind. I licked and sucked until she was moaning with ecstasy. I let my tongue slide down her stomach to her clean-shaven pussy. I sucked and licked all over her pussy, making sure I didn't touch her swollen clit: She began to beg me to suck her and fuck her. I let her beg for a while before I parted her pussy lips and inserted my tongue. I licked ever so lightly and teased her until she was bucking, trying to get more of her clit in my mouth. Finally, I sucked her huge clit and pumped her with my fingers. She was screaming for more, but I didn't want her to come yet.

Laura rolled me over and buried her face in my snatch. My panties were soaked with my juices, and she sucked them. She pulled off my wet panties and put her pussy right over my face. She urged me to fuck her and suck her clit, and I was more than happy to. She buried her face in my pussy and began licking and sucking my clit. I pounded her with my fingers and sucked her clit hard, until she spasmed in an orgasm.

Mine came shortly after hers, and I gushed all over her face.

Laura lay back on the bed, breathing heavily. I kissed her passionately and rubbed her erect nipples. She started to pull back, but I held her close and continued stimulating her. She began to moan again. I rubbed her pussy and mine at the same time. I instructed Laura to sit up, then I sat facing her and positioned our pussies so we could grind them together. We fucked each other until we came again.

My night in Vegas was, to say the least, a great success. Now, whenever I'm there, Laura and I get together for lots of hot, steamy fun.

—*K. F., California*

Cabin Fever

My husband and my neighbor were going away for a golf weekend, so Heidi, my neighbor's wife, and I decided to spend the weekend at my husband's family's cabin. It's located on a secluded lake, just a great place to get away and relax.

Heidi is thirty-one years old, blonde, and has a great body. She's a little more petite than me, but she has the type of breasts that make most women jealous—very firm and very large.

One night while having dinner, the topic of sex came up. The conversation became rather intimate, and we revealed all our latest sexual adventures. We were quite surprised at the similarities in our sex lives, right down to the fact that our husbands insist that we shave our pussies. We soon became too horny to continue our talk. "I don't know about you, but I've got to do something to cool down," said Heidi as she waved her hand in front of her face. I suggested a late-night swim and sauna to help us relax before bed.

We quickly discovered that the water was quite cold, so it wasn't long before we were sitting in the lakeside sauna, warming up. We joked about skinny-dipping, and suddenly, our swimsuits were on the dock and we were back in the lake, swimming in the nude.

Feeling a little mischievous, I got out of the water, grabbed the swimsuits, and ran to the sauna, with Heidi close behind. I had never seen Heidi nude before, so I tried to be discreet as I looked at her body. Her nakedness, combined with the glow of the sauna's red light, made me strangely aroused. I became increasingly aware of her body and how sexy she looked as the water trickled down her skin. She has extremely long nipples, and I watched as the water ran down her breasts and then slowly dripped from her hard pink points. Her pussy was almost totally shaved and its lips were thick and full, like petals on a rose.

I became even more turned on when I saw her eyes drop down and give my clean-shaven snatch a long, lingering look. I went to get some champagne, and I remember walking into the cabin, totally nude, and feeling very naughty.

When I came back, Heidi smiled at me, a really delicious smile. When I popped the champagne, I purposely sent a spray of foaming bubbles cascading all over Heidi's naked body. She shrieked as she held her glass against her skin in an effort to save some of the liquid. It was such an erotic sight. She quickly grabbed the bottle, shook it, and sprayed me. The feeling of the cold liquid splashing all over my nude body was excruciatingly sexy.

We took a few sips, not saying anything, just looking at each other. We were going down a path that neither of us had been down before, but it was as if we knew we had to follow it. Finally, she slowly leaned forward and kissed my cheek. A feeling like an electric shock ran straight to my cunt.

Our first kiss was tentative—we just brushed lips as if we were testing the waters. Slowly, our explorations grew more bold, and it wasn't long before our tongues began a dance of unbridled lust and discovery. It was like nothing I had ever experienced before. Her mouth was so soft, wet, and inviting. The feel of her velvety, moist tongue in my mouth had me aching with desire. She sucked on my tongue and moaned, her body trembling lustfully.

The sensation of kissing Heidi was indescribable. It was so sensual, so erotically overpowering, and the prospect of exploring further had my pussy gushing with anticipation. I slowly made my way down her neck with gentle kisses and a darting tongue. She arched her back and lifted her breasts to my mouth.

Her nipples were huge and hard as I bathed them with my tongue. I gently bit them and sent her into a frenzy. Heidi's moans implored me to go on. I spent a long time giving her tits loving attention while she touched her dripping snatch. I was so overcome with pure animal lust, I slowly kissed my way down her flat belly and gently licked the insides of her thighs while her finger teased her engorged clit. I slowly slipped her finger into my mouth. Looking into her eyes, I could see she wanted more. I tenderly began to lick around her sopping pussy, my tongue delicately probing her most intimate places.

She began to gently rock her hips back and forth as I teased her with my tongue. I felt her hand on my head pulling me forward, guiding me to her dampness. The whole atmosphere, the pure sensuality of it, overcame me, and I began to eat her like a starving animal. "Oh God, yes!" she screamed as my tongue worked its magic on her gash. My face was buried in her sex; she had both hands on the back of my head, pulling me toward her. My tongue found her clit, and I sucked and licked it as I slid a finger, then two, into her drenched cunt. She began to wail, "Oh, fuck . . . I'm coming. . . . Yes, yes!" Her orgasm started somewhere deep inside her and came in waves as she furiously bucked her crotch against my face and hand. A flood of pussy juice gushed from her as she came, and I could feel her pussy contracting around my fingers.

She pulled me up to her and kissed my pussy-soaked face as she sat me down. Without any hesitation, she went right for my cunt and began her own exploration. It was like nothing I had ever felt before, much different from a man. She tongued the folds of my snatch, sending bolts of sexual energy coursing through my body. Her tongue found its way to my clit and she lovingly lingered there, treating me to the best cunnilingus I had ever had. "Fuck me with your tongue," was all I could say, and she responded by plunging her tongue into me. It felt almost like a cock as she passionately thrust it into me. I began to finger my clit, her moans of approval driving me forward, and it wasn't long before I had a huge, pulsating orgasm.

We kissed again, a long, very tender kiss, as we basked in the afterglow of our experience. That weekend was the start of a very special, very erotic, and very sensual relationship.

—C. H., Ontario

Winona

My husband Wilson and I rented a luxurious beachfront house for a week of vacation. Our place was nice, but it was nothing compared to the one next door. It was two stories high, with a strongly reinforced hot tub on the second-story deck and a sweeping view of the beach.

The couple staying next door was very friendly and very attractive. The husband, Vic, was in his late forties, tall, and slender. His wife, Winona, was in her mid-thirties and a natural blonde with beautiful eyes and a great figure.

One evening they joined us for a barbecue. After dinner, Wilson and Vic decided to go into town and have a beer and watch a ballgame on the big-screen TV at the tavern. Winona suggested that I come over around sundown and enjoy the view from the hot tub. She winked when she said, "No swimsuits allowed."

Near sundown I put a beach robe over my sunburned body and went next door. Winona was just fixing a pitcher of icy pina coladas. We went upstairs to the hot tub. The view was spectacular. As the sun set, a full moon glimmered on the water. Winona removed her robe and reclined on a lounge chair. I was more modest, slipping into the tub as soon as I removed my covering.

The hot water did not feel good on my sunburn. I quickly got out of the tub and started to put on my robe. Winona stopped me, saying she had an excellent lotion for my tender skin.

She placed a large beach towel on a lounge chair and instructed me to lie on my stomach. She gently rubbed the lotion into my back and arms. When she rubbed my back, her fingers slid around to the sides of my breasts.

She moved down to my legs, starting at my ankles and working her way up to my ass. Even though my butt wasn't sunburned, she began applying the lotion to my cheeks, rubbing and squeezing.

She told me to turn over. I was a little embarrassed, because her massage had turned me on. I naively didn't know what to expect next.

Winona continued applying the lotion, starting with my upper chest and shoulders. When she touched my breasts, she cupped each one—one at a time—with both hands, her fingers playing with my nipples. I was nervous but excited when she leaned over and sucked my nipples. They were firm and protruding, and she alternately flicked them with her tongue and kept sucking.

She sat up and shifted the short stool she was sitting on, so she was sitting near my knees. She slowly pushed my legs apart and placed my feet on the deck. She put a firm pillow under my hips.

Winona ran a finger between my pussy lips, almost but not quite entering my cunt. She continued teasing me, squeezing my lips and rubbing her finger from my pussy to my ass.

I sat up in a panic when I heard a car door slamming and Wilson's and Vic's voices as they entered the house. Winona pushed me back to a reclining position and told me to relax. She placed a beach towel across my body, covering me from mid-thigh to my neck.

Wilson and Vic came out onto the deck and poured themselves a cold pina colada. When they sat down, Winona stared into Wilson's eyes, and said, "I was about to make love to your wife. You can stay and watch or take her home." Wilson looked at me, and he could see that I was embarrassed, but also that I hadn't been resisting. I could see that he was admiring Winona's beautiful naked body.

She reached under the towel and caressed my breasts and squeezed my nipples. She slowly pulled the towel down to my waist and played with my breasts to relax and excite me. Then she removed the towel completely and turned her attention back to my pussy. Again she parted my knees, putting my feet on the floor.

As she gently spread my cunt lips, she leaned down and ran her tongue slowly up and down between my parted lips. She inserted a finger into my cunt and moved it in and out while her tongue circled and teased my clit. As my arousal increased, I raised my hips, and her soft lips and tongue continued to bring me closer to climax.

As I reached my climax, she placed her hands under my hips, holding my pussy up to her mouth. When I was through, she covered my exhausted body with the beach towel, then she and her husband walked quietly into their bedroom, closing the door behind them.

Wilson and I returned to our place and spent several hours making love.

—L. A., Washington

Sexy Setup

I've always enjoyed erotica with my husband—especially woman-on-woman. We've also talked about me getting it on with another woman. Although it made my pussy wet to think about it, I still was a little shy.

About two weeks ago, he suggested that I stay with a mutual friend of ours, Jodi, while he went on an overnight fishing trip. I agreed, not knowing that my husband had set me up.

It was a normal evening, until Jodi suggested we get into our pajamas and go to bed. I had no idea what she had in mind. I slipped out of my clothes and put on an oversize T-shirt. I turned to see that Jodi had returned to my doorway. I was amazed! She was wearing nothing but a white mesh bodysuit. Her long red hair barely covered her hard nipples as they poked out through the mesh holes. Her pussy hair was framed perfectly between two great legs. I turned away from her, embarrassed that the sight of her had turned me on so much. I heard her walk up behind me, felt her hands encircle my body and slowly come up under my shirt to cup my tits. It felt so good with her hard nipples rubbing on my back. I said, "Jodi, what are you doing?"

"Relax and enjoy it," she said. "Let me teach you." After pulling my shirt up over my head, she told me to remain standing as she lowered herself to the floor. She firmly grabbed the top of my panties and slid them off. I jumped as I felt her head come up between my legs, pushing them far apart. Her wet mouth quickly found my equally wet pussy. I rubbed my tits as she licked and fucked my cunt with her tongue. I thought I would explode. She gently pinched my clit between her fingers with great expertise. She pulled me down to the floor with her, and guided my mouth to her waiting cunt. I had never tasted anything so sweet and wet. I licked her clit like a lollipop. She pulled my head up and rubbed our crotches together, back and forth. It was amazing. She reached out and grabbed my nipples, sending us both over the edge. We both creamed from pure pleasure as our cunts overflowed with juice. She bent over and lapped mine like a cat drinking milk. Soon we were both asleep from exhaustion.

I felt I had to confess my night of pleasure to my husband the next morning. He chuckled, and said, "I know all about it." I could have smacked him. Instead, I grabbed his cock and suggested we invite Jodi over for dinner. I was excited to show him what I learned, and he was more than happy to see it all.

—K. M., Maryland

Coffee Clutch

I have been married for many years and have two kids. Sex in our marriage is wonderfully fulfilling and varied. Jed and I have been swinging for the last several years with other couples. Occasionally, we invite males and females into our bedroom.

I had been mysteriously drawn to our friend, Dahlia, and felt a strong desire for close contact with her whenever I thought of her. When my husband and I were with her and her husband, Wilson, about once a month or so, I had increasingly concentrated on touching her. I finally expressed my feelings to her one day over a cup of coffee. With a radiant smile, she leaned over and put her soft lips on mine. Her warm, wet, velvet touch shot like lightning through my body. Blood surged to my brain and awakened a sweet, powerful desire. I opened my mouth, and our tongues met and danced a delicate ballet of love. Dahlia's natural sweetness overwhelmed me, and I felt weak. When I finally broke the kiss, I gasped, "Darling, you make me feel mushy and *soo* good."

We resumed our kissing for an eternity. Then she whispered, "Let's go to the bedroom." We undressed each other slowly, our lips glued together all the while. We finally lay naked, side by side, arms around each other. Our bodies touched lightly, Dahlia's voluptuous breasts weighing against mine. I gently reached around her back and very slowly traced my hand lower until my fingers felt the cleavage of her bottom. I continued more slowly, and finally reached the silky hair and her swollen pussy lips. They were wet, and with ease I slipped my middle finger between those lips. Her head moved away, just a few inches from mine. Her eyes were closed, her mouth open and wet, her breathing heavy and fast. I increased the pressure inside of her as she responded, meeting my movements with quick thrusts of her pelvis. She finally locked her arms around me and screamed her familiar, hoarse orgasmic cries.

After a short break, she kissed me again, more vigorously than before. And then she went down on me. Oh, did she go down on me! No man has ever matched the excruciatingly sensitive touching of all the love nerves of my sex like my friend Dahlia. She breathed kisses all around my pussy without actually touching the lips. She started licking around my anus and the space that led to my cunt. I felt the air on the inside of my open, swollen love hole. Then for the first time, I felt the tip of her tongue caressing the outer lips.

All my feelings were in turmoil. I know I love men more than anything. I adore cock. I open up to the touch of a man, and I feel consumed with passion when a man's tool hammers my inside. But now I was with a woman who elicited the most exquisite feelings I have ever felt. My body was tense, and at the same time open and relaxed. The silky touch of her mouth and tongue had brought me to the delicious brink of an orgasm. She penetrated deeper into me. Then she sucked alternately on my cunt lips. The mix of our juices ran copiously. One of her fingers touched my asshole and slowly pushed inside, and then with broad strokes, she lapped my sex with her tongue while she rubbed my clit with the other hand. I thought I would die. I completely gave myself to an all-consuming climax.

For a long time, we lay in each other's arms before I came to my senses. I asked my friend, "Does this mean we're bi?"

"Does it matter?" she asked in return. And it really did not matter. We enjoyed each other again and again. And when we put on a show for our husbands that night, they applauded us and fucked us with great vigor.

—*T. W., California*

Transfixed

On my third visit to my new health club, I noticed an attractive young woman in the locker room with me. She had just stepped out of the shower and was only wearing a towel. I was amazed at how beautiful she was. I could not keep my eyes off her. She strode to the lockers and passed by me. She smiled and let her towel fall to the floor. I was so transfixed by her that I had not noticed how wet my pussy was.

I began my workout, but all I could think about was this gorgeous creature from the locker room. I wanted to touch her. I wanted to taste her. I knew that I had to say something to her. I hoped that she would accept a come-on from a woman. I wanted to bring her home as a third partner for my boyfriend and me in bed. We'd had sex with another guy, but I wanted her to be our first woman.

I walked up to her and introduced myself. She said that her name was Jamie, we made small talk for a little while, and I asked her to join me for a drink right there at the club. She said yes without blinking an eye, and I was psyched.

After a few drinks I asked her to come home with me. "I'd love to," she said, and we drove to my apartment and sat in my living room for a while. She went to use the bathroom, and when she returned, she put a hand on my thigh, the other on the back of my head, and pulled me to her. Our lips touched, and we kissed passionately for several minutes. Jamie sucked my tongue and licked the top of my mouth. She pulled each of my lips into her mouth and her tongue caressed my teeth, then slid to the far depths of my throat.

My hands could not resist touching her. I massaged her left breast through her T-shirt. Her braless boob felt soft and it filled my hand completely. I slid my hand under her shirt to feel her bare skin, and my heart raced when I squeezed her boob and felt her ripe nipple harden between my fingers. Her breathing quickened as I tugged on her nipple and rubbed her tiny bumps.

Within moments both of our tops were off. Jamie's warm hands felt wonderful on my tits. She bent her head down and took one of my breasts into her mouth. She wrapped her arms around my waist and continued to suck me. Across my nipples her dancing tongue and nibbling teeth made me tingle all over.

Next she crawled down on the floor between my

legs and began to kiss my bare thighs. She started at my knees and worked her way up, kissing and licking my ever-spreading legs. I slipped off my shorts and panties, and soon Jamie had her face in my pussy. I moaned out loud when her warm breath ran across my moist lips.

She brought her hand down to my pussy and spread my lips with her fingers, driving her tongue into my wetness. My back arched and I grabbed her head as she buried her face in my open box. She inserted her tongue deeper into my hole and licked my inner walls. Then she pulled each of my cunt lips into her mouth. My body started to quiver when she reached my clit. First she rolled it between her fingers like a marble. When her tongue flicked over it, it was more than I could take, and I was soon bucking and humping her face in orgasmic pleasure.

For several minutes—which seemed like hours—I lay limp on the sofa. Jamie's head rested on my thigh. I could still feel her breath on my pussy. I opened my eyes to find her watching me, smiling. Her face was slick and shiny with my juices.

Without saying a word, we changed positions. I was a bit hesitant at first, since I had never licked a pussy before. My fears, however, soon subsided as I began to eat her sweet box. She tasted wonderful and aromatic. I ran my tongue up and down her lips. I inserted two fingers into her box and sucked her pink clit. Jamie was moaning with great pleasure as I worked her sopping pussy. She then told me to stop for a moment. "Eat me from behind," she requested as she got on her hands and knees on the sofa and raised her ass high in the air. I rubbed her round bottom and spread her cheeks so that I could bury my face in her twat.

I licked her pussy all over and reached under her to massage her swaying boobs. I continued to tongue her pussy from behind when she started to have a very loud and wet orgasm. The amount of pussy juice she produced literally covered my face and ran down onto my tits.

When she was finished I crawled up onto the sofa with her and we nestled in each other's arms, kissing gently. About an hour later my boyfriend came home to find his girlfriend with another woman, naked on the sofa. I guess it didn't bother him too much. We had a wonderful night of sex. I watched him fuck Jamie. I watched him eat her. I watched her give him one of the best blowjobs ever . . . and I loved every minute of it.

—*T. Y., Oregon*

Less Is More

I am a shapely twenty-three-year-old with green eyes and what is considered to be a very sexy body. Although I had never been with another woman, I'd always fantasized about it, and my boyfriend, Greg, encourages my fantasies. Greg has always liked women with short hair, and because I lost some stupid bet we'd made, I had to get my hair cut short.

My girlfriend Sandy owns an upscale beauty salon. She was working by herself when I arrived for the last appointment of the day. Sandy greeted me, and while she went to lock up, I got to admire her shoulder-length auburn hair, 35-22-36 figure, and green eyes that make men—and even me—melt with desire. Sandy was wearing a skintight pullover top and the cutest little red miniskirt I'd ever seen. Watching her tight ass and long legs made my nipples hard and my pussy tingle.

I explained to Sandy that I wanted my hair cut short. I took one last look at all my beautiful, long blonde hair as she took up the scissors and slowly began snipping away. As she was cutting my hair, I noticed that I was becoming aroused. She had cut my hair to about shoulder length, but at that point a fire seemed to be ripping through my body. I looked into her green eyes, then closely into the mirror, and decided I wanted it shorter.

Sandy took the scissors again and started snipping more long strands away. There seemed to be an erotic current going through the two of us. Sandy kept clipping until there were only a few inches left. It's difficult to describe the strange erotic sensation I felt as my blonde locks fell into my lap and then onto the floor. Sandy left me with a crew cut and a wet pussy. I was horny as hell, but she wasn't finished yet. She turned on a pair of electric clippers and finished cropping my hair. I started to come while she spread shaving cream over my head and proceeded to shave it bald. I couldn't believe how good it felt.

Suddenly, Sandy began kissing my neck and fondling my breasts—the sensation was unbelievable. While we undressed each other, she nibbled on my ear and asked me to give her a haircut. After a long, passionate kiss, she handed me a pair of clippers and sat in the chair. I ran the clippers over Sandy's head and, after a few minutes, all her hair lay on the floor. Then I lathered her head with shaving cream and shaved it as smooth as mine.

At that point my panties were soaking wet, and I realized I needed this woman—now. We began kissing, our tongues lashing against each other. I was sucking on her tongue and inhaling her scent. We undressed and embraced in a long, sloppy kiss. Our nipples touched, hard as little pebbles, and rubbed together. I loved the feel of her breasts against mine. We fell back on the floor, Sandy on top of me. I could feel her fingers reaching down between my legs to caress my pussy. I told her that I wanted her tongue inside me.

Sandy started to lick my body. She worked her hot tongue into my begging cunt and hungrily lapped up my juices as I came in an intense orgasm. She kissed me long and hard, giving me my first taste of pussy—my own. Sandy pushed my shaved head to her pussy, and I kissed her clit and drank up her juices. She bucked wildly against my face, and we came together.

We repeated this later at my place with Greg, but only after we shaved his head. Needless to say, he was pleased.

—*G. S., Minnesota*

Something about Sylvia

Last Valentine's Day I ordered a subscription to *Penthouse* for my husband. We enjoy reading it together, and since we have three children, it's one of the few adult activities we can still share. Kyle and I have been married twelve years, have maintained a healthy sex life, and stay in shape. We do a lot of things together, but when I received a wedding invitation from my best friend, Janine, Kyle and I realized that we couldn't both afford to make the trip. He knew Janine and I had been like sisters in college, so he said I should go, insisting that he and the kids would be fine. At first I felt guilty about leaving them for four days, but soon I was looking forward to the trip.

I arrived in San Francisco late on a Thursday evening, and was met at the airport by Janine and two of her friends, Chris, her supervisor, and Sylvia, a college intern who was working in Janine's office the summer before senior year. Chris was a friendly redhead with a smile that wouldn't quit. Sylvia was very petite with very long brown hair, dark eyes, and a strikingly tiny waist.

After I checked in at the hotel, we went to the lounge for a snack and drinks. I hadn't seen Janine in about two years, and it was fun catching up. Chris and Sylvia were wonderful too.

The bachelorette party was held on Friday night, and by this time the four of us were like old friends. Chris had organized the party and asked each of us to contribute $50 toward food and entertainment. It seemed like a lot of money, but Chris assured us that we would get our money's worth and more.

When I arrived around eight music was playing and there were already about fifteen other women there. A nice buffet was laid out on the bar and one of the girls was fixing drinks. There was a sunken living-room area with a fireplace, and several of the participants were sitting on the couch and chairs. Chris met me at the door with a hug and a smile and directed me to the bar. Janine introduced me to the other guests. I found a stool near the bar and picked up a glass of champagne.

Sylvia was sitting with some of the other women by the fireplace. When she saw me, she smiled, stood up, and headed toward me. She was wearing a black-silk blouse that was just short enough for me to see her pierced navel, and just sheer enough for me to tell she was braless. Her breasts were small and jiggled slightly with each step, her tiny nipples poking against the fabric. Her black-leather skirt was incredibly short, barely covering her butt. She wore black stockings, and as she stepped forward from the fireplace, I caught a glimpse of white skin and lacy black garters.

I found myself admiring her body in the same way I have admired the models in your magazine. While I had never had an experience with another woman, I'd wondered what it might be like—and how Sylvia's body would look. As she reached me, she stood on her tiptoes and gave me a hug. Her perfume was musky and filled my head. I returned the hug, enjoying the way her body felt against mine and her soft hair against my face.

She ordered a drink and sat on the barstool next to mine, crossing her lovely legs. As we talked, I kept trying to steal discreet glances at those legs. Her skirt kept riding up enough for me to see the skin above her stockings, and this was getting me very excited. Feeling a little flushed, I took a second glass of champagne.

Before I had the chance to embarrass myself further, the doorbell rang. Chris went to the door and stepped outside for a moment. When she came back in, she asked for everyone's attention and announced that the entertainment had arrived. She put a tape in the sound system and dimmed the lights. Through the door came two young men dressed in business suits. They were tanned and appeared to be very well built.

The first young man walked to the center of the room while the second waited his turn. One by one, they put on a high-energy strip show as we all hooted, whistled, and generally misbehaved. Eventually, each of the guys was down to a G-string. Eager hands stuffed money into their elastic waistbands.

When the men were finished they slipped into the bedroom to dress while we girls cheered wildly. Chris took up a collection for tips and handed it to them as they left. On the way out, they each stopped to give Janine a deep kiss that left us all weak-kneed.

Sylvia and I continued to talk for a while, but I soon became aware that being with her was making me feel uncomfortable—not in a bad way, but giddyish. I was pretty worked up by the show we'd just seen, and Sylvia's outfit wasn't helping a bit, so I smiled, stood up, and excused myself, saying that I was going to mingle a little.

I was standing behind a large couch talking with one of Janine's coworkers when the doorbell rang again. Chris went to it once more and then announced that the second act had arrived. Again the lights went down and the music began. This time, however, the two dancers who entered were beautiful women. They wore tight-fitting short dresses, stockings, and heels. The music was slow, and they danced together for a long time, almost touching but not quite.

I was feeling very excited, not knowing what was going to happen next. Slowly, the two dancers came together in an embrace, and then kissed each other deeply. Some of the onlookers gasped, if only for a moment, but most continued to watch in silent amazement.

I was really getting turned on now. I wished I could just reach down and rub myself, because I could feel my juices beginning to soak my panties. I moved next to the couch so that I could lean slightly forward and press my pussy against the back cushion. As the two dancers began slowly to undress each other, I gently rolled my hips, humping myself against the couch.

The girls put on an incredible show. For fifteen minutes they touched, stroked, and kissed each other, removing clothing one agonizing piece at a time until they were totally naked. Wrapped in each other's arms, they slid down to the carpeted floor in front of the fire as the soft music continued to play. We were all mesmerized.

Suddenly I was startled by the light touch of a hand on the small of my back. I turned and saw Sylvia at my side, squeezing herself between me and the wall. She delicately pressed against me from behind, pushing my crotch against the corner of the couch. The feeling of her body against me and the pressure on my pussy was almost enough to make me have an orgasm right there. I reached for the couch to steady myself so my knees wouldn't buckle.

As the two beautiful women continued to kiss and caress, I felt Sylvia pull me closer until I could feel the soft leather of her skirt against the back of my hand. I couldn't stand this much more. I pressed myself harder against the couch, slowly turned my hand, and let my fingertips stray over her silky leg. I was trembling so hard, I'm sure she could feel it. I delicately worked my fingers up until I could feel one of those garters. Hooking one finger into it, I tugged playfully just to see if Sylvia would react. Did she ever.

She slid her hands up *my* legs and gripped my waist. She pushed me forward slowly but firmly into the corner of the couch, and suddenly I realized that she knew what I had been doing all along. My nipples started tingling and my fingers began to seek out the soft flesh of her thigh. When the tip of my index finger touched bare skin, I could feel her jump slightly, and she leaned into me just a little. My hand traveled up her leg slowly until, almost unexpectedly, I felt moistness tickling the back of my fingers. She wasn't wearing panties.

I froze for a second, not sure what to do next. On the floor, one of the dancers had the other's nipple in her mouth and was feasting on it. I turned my shaking hand palm up and eased it against Sylvia's mound. She was very wet and had almost no pubic hair. I held my hand tightly against her pussy, and she started to move her torso, causing my middle finger to slide back and forth between her lips. I don't know where I got the courage, but I slowly started to curl my middle finger. She was so wet that it easily slipped inside her, and I could feel her warmth surrounding it.

I was now humping the sofa. Sylvia was fucking herself on my hand, and the two dancers were engaged in what appeared to be a realistic session of mutual oral sex. It's a good thing their moans were so genuine-sounding; otherwise, my own gasping would have given away what we were up to in the darkened corner. Sylvia pushed herself down against my finger, and it slid all the way into her.

I had never touched another woman's pussy before, and the sensations were incredible. Her juices were all over my hand, and I could feel her muscles gripping my finger, trying to pull it in deeper.

Suddenly the whole scene caught up with me. The sights, sounds, and now even the smells burned themselves into me. I could smell a combination of Sylvia's perfume and her sex. It seemed that everyone had an orgasm at the same time. The girls on the floor did a very convincing job of squealing and moaning as they humped each other's faces. Sylvia gripped my waist and flooded my fingers with her hot, sticky juice. I came so hard that I almost fell over the couch. I bit my lip to keep from crying out, and Sylvia's hands kept me on my feet.

The rest of the lights went out for about thirty seconds, and when they came back on the two dancers were wearing white robes, standing side by side in front of the fireplace, smiling broadly. I took advantage of the darkness to slip my hand out of Sylvia's crotch, and she moved to stand beside me. After a moment of stunned silence, we began to applaud. The dancers took a bow and headed to the bedroom to get dressed.

As I applauded, I could smell Sylvia's sweet scent on my fingers. I looked down at her, and she gave me an innocent smile. Making sure no one was looking, I slipped my middle finger into my mouth and sucked in her sweet honey. It was delicious. Sylvia blushed deeply and giggled.

The party broke up shortly after the dancers left.

Everyone was whispering about how wonderful the show had been. I said my good-byes and headed for the door. Sylvia was leaning against the wall with a drink. She glowed as if she had just finished making love, and I guess she had.

We smiled at each other and hugged. I whispered in her ear that she was welcome to visit my room for a nightcap. Sadly, she had to stay behind and help Janine make final preparations for the next day. I returned to my room and soaked in the bathtub for a long time, fantasizing that Sylvia had chosen to join me.

The wedding went as planned. At the reception, Sylvia and I spent a lot of time together. When it was time to go, she took my hand, pulled me into the coat closet, and kissed me long and hard. After all that had happened the night before, this was my very first kiss with a woman. I promised to look her up on my next trip to San Francisco. We exchanged phone numbers and addresses. It just might be Sylvia and not Janine who will be the reason for my next visit.

—R. G., Idaho

While John's Away . . .

One day after I came home from work I picked up the mail and ran inside to get out of the rain. Changing into some dry clothes, I sat on the couch with the mail and spotted a letter from my boyfriend John. He's in the Navy and is sometimes gone for weeks at a time. I was so excited to see anything from him. I always write him about the adventures that my friend Judy and I get into, and he writes back telling me what he's going to do to me and Judy when he gets home. As I continued to read his letter I got so horny, I found myself rubbing my pussy. Suddenly in the mood, I popped my favorite porn tape into the VCR. I like to watch two guys and a girl get it on. It gets me so hot.

A couple of minutes into the flick I had to take off my sweatpants. I reached down and touched my wet, aching pussy, then brought my fingers to my lips so I could taste the sweet juices. I opened the drawer to our end table and pulled out my vibrator, a set of vibrating beads, and some lubricant. I quickly lubed the beads, turned them on, and started plunging them into my ass. The vibrator was next. It began to buzz as I moved it around my clit, occasionally dipping into my pussy.

I was just about to come when the doorbell rang. I popped the vibrator into the drawer, hit the POWER button on the remote, grabbed my sweats, ran to the bedroom, put on a robe, and came out to answer the door. It was Judy. I told her to come in out of the rain. Knowing that John had been gone for three weeks, she asked me how I was doing. I said I was okay but that I couldn't wait for John to get back. Then she saw that I was wearing only a robe. "Did I come at a bad time?" she asked.

I said, "No. You came just in time."

I grabbed her hands and put them on my hips. She

jerked backward, and said, "What the hell was that?" What she felt was the anal beads still vibrating inside me. I told her to go sit on the couch and I'd show her. She sat down, and I stood with my back to her. I dropped my robe and bent over, exposing my vibrating crevice. She was fascinated, staring at the control switch that dangled in the air. Her eyes slowly moved up the wire until the wire disappeared into my ass. She asked me how it felt, and I told her it felt wonderful. She reached up and gave a little pull on the wire until one of the beads popped out. I told her to go ahead and pull them all out. As she pulled them out one by one, I was getting hornier.

When the last one came out, I pulled another set of beads from the drawer and told her to try them out. She was quickly out of her clothes and sitting next to me on the couch. With beads in hand, she asked me for some help, and I was happy to assist her. I sat in front of the couch as she leaned back and spread her legs. I put a little lube on the beads, turned them on, and gently slipped the first one into her rectum. She laughed and said it tickled a bit. I inserted the other three beads and asked how they felt. She gave another laugh and said, "Pretty good." Then I kissed her inner thigh, inching my way up to her love box. I glanced up at her, and she gave me a big smile as my tongue roamed around her semiwet pussy. I continued to lick, concentrating on her swollen clit. She started to moan. Then she screamed, "Fuck me!" I reached up and shoved three fingers into her beckoning hole, and she moaned with relief.

It didn't take long for her to come. When she did, my mouth was filled with her sweet-tasting juices. Then we both lay on our sides, I between her legs and she between mine. I reinserted my own beads into my ass and we started to grind our pussies together. After about ten minutes I came full force, with Judy not far behind me. We both lay on the couch talking about past and future adventures, occasionally kissing and rubbing each other, until this cuddling quickly escalated into another pussy-eating feast.

—E. I., California

Nurse on Call

Her name was Katrina, and we met a year ago at my doctor's office when I went for my annual physical. I had been seeing the same doctor for years and was familiar with his staff, but when Katrina greeted me in the reception area it was a pleasant surprise. She was about forty years old, had a voluptuous figure and an inviting twinkle in her eyes. I have been married for more than twenty years and my husband, Paul, and I have an open marriage. We have tasted almost the entire repertoire of sexual pleasures, including threesomes with both men and women, and spouse swapping. Occasionally I have engaged in woman-on-woman encounters, sometimes alone or with my husband watching and participating. Since I am a very erotic being and open up quickly to sexual overtures, something about Nurse Katrina struck a carnal nerve in me.

In the examination room, she asked me some general questions about my health and did her examining most delicately. She touched me softly—and just slightly more than necessary. While I disrobed, she eagerly helped me and complimented me on my perfect body. More than once her soft fingers touched my skin. When my doctor walked in, Katrina stayed in the room and watched the entire time as he did his examination. On my way out, I scribbled my telephone number on a piece of paper and handed it to her.

Katrina called me that evening, and we had a long conversation about our sexual lifestyles. She'd been married for a few years, and divorced after she discovered her interest in women. Paul overheard our conversation and demonstratively licked his lips. I invited Katrina to our house the next day. Physically we hit it off right away. We embraced and kissed. Her full lips felt soft and velvety. We looked at each other and laughed and kissed again. This time she gently opened her mouth and cupped my lips. The tip of her tongue lightly brushed back and forth. Soon we were French-kissing and exploring each other's mouths with slow, loving strokes.

The lower part of my body turned into quivering jelly as my pussy heated up and became increasingly wet. Katrina's hands explored my back and finally seized my butt cheeks, pulling my pelvis into hers. I gently disengaged myself, and asked, "Bedroom?" Katrina nodded and followed me down the hallway. Sitting on the king-size bed we undressed each other, kissing and fondling. Her luscious breasts were white as snow, with light brown large, firm nipples. I lowered my head to lick and suck them.

"Suck hard," she moaned. With one hand she kneaded my own globes and with the other she searched between my legs. When I spread my thighs to give her access, my slit was already very wet and open. I felt the cool air and then the touch of her finger. She lightly rubbed the outer lips, sending shivers of delight through my body. With her wet finger she stroked lower over the bridge between my vagina and anus and back across the pouting lips. Then farther down, she rimmed my puckered asshole. I was hot and ready to explode into nirvana. Her tongue was still deeply exploring my mouth when suddenly she inserted two fingers into my cunt, and with her thumb on my clit, pushed me over the edge into another world. I came in waves of delicious emotions.

Wanting to repay Katrina's sweetness, I pushed her onto her back on the bed, knelt, and started to caress her thighs with my hands and tongue, licking my way up to the central part of her sex. With broad strokes I lapped up her flowing juices, evoking a sigh every time I touched her clit. Then she pulled her legs up into the air, spread wide open, and wiggled her body up and down, meeting my tongue thrusts. I increased the pressure until finally she let out a long, hoarse wail.

We embraced and relaxed. While she caressed me, I asked if she would stay until evening and meet Paul. Mischievously she asked, "For an encore?"

She helped me cook dinner and was the most gracious guest ever to dine at our table. Paul was enamored of her; I could see the lust in his eyes. After the meal we agreed to "play." What a show Katrina and I put on for Paul. When at last we engaged in a hot sixty-nine, Paul could wait no longer. He maneuvered himself into position and entered me from behind while Katrina was still licking my pussy and clitoris. With firm, steady strokes he fucked me until we both climaxed with joyous cries. Katrina, we found, was not completely averse to men. She let Paul fuck her repeatedly. It was a night full of ecstatic sex all around. Since that day, Katrina has become our frequent bedroom partner and companion.

—S. V., California

Tanning with Sandi

A few months ago I had the most amazing experience. After spending last summer with my relatives in California and being on the beach almost every day playing volleyball and working out, when it was time to go home to get ready for my last semester in college, all I could think about was leaving that great weather and losing the tan I had worked so hard to get.

I'd been home a couple of weeks when I decided it was time to try out a tanning shop near campus. One evening after class I put on my new bikini, under a sweatshirt and pants, and walked down to the tanning shop. The woman at the counter was very friendly. She was about thirty, very attractive, and about five-foot-eight, with long red hair and nails and a beautiful tan. I couldn't help noticing that her ample breasts were straining against her T-shirt, and her nipples were clearly visible. Her name read "Sandra," but she insisted that I call her Sandi.

Sandi gave me a tour of the shop. Then we settled down in one of the tanning rooms. She said we had to figure out my skin type so I would know what setting to use on the tanning bed. When she asked me to remove my sweatshirt I hesitated for a moment. Sandi smiled and put her hand on my knee, saying, "It's okay, honey. I do this every day."

I pulled my sweatshirt over my head and dropped it on the massage table. Sandi smiled and started to hold some photos up against me, one at a time. She told me about how careful people with sensitive skin have to be in a tanning bed. "Here, look at this one," she said, holding a photo of freckled skin next to her chest. I could see her own freckles as they disappeared into her cleavage. "Redheads like me can do only a couple minutes at a time."

Finally, she had me narrowed down to two skin types. "Let's see your tan lines," she said. "That will help me figure this out." Slowly, I stood up and began to remove my sweatpants. As I struggled to pull them over my sneakers, I noticed that Sandi was watching very closely. I turned around to put my pants on the massage table, and as I started to turn back, she put a hand on my hip, and said, "Hold it. This is just what I wanted to see." She held one of the photos up against my bottom and gently ran a long red fingernail along the tan lines. "Hmm," she said, putting the photos down and gently placing a hand on each cheek, "I think this is just right."

She scratched, squeezed, rubbed, and gently pinched every inch of each of my mostly bare cheeks. I stood perfectly still, afraid to move, almost afraid to breathe. Then Sandi hooked one finger in the back of my G-string and gently but firmly pulled it tight. A shiver ran through my entire body as the thin fabric snuggled into my crotch. My knees felt weak and I had to bend over and lean on the massage table to keep from falling. I felt Sandi's hands on my hips, and as she held me her nails dug slightly into my thighs. Her breath and lips on my bottom soon canceled any apprehension I might have had.

Her fingers worked their way under the sides of my bikini bottom, and as she kissed and nibbled my butt cheeks, she slowly slid off my thong. Then she turned me around and sat me on the massage table. Now we were face-to-face, and the lust in her eyes must have matched my own. She leaned closer and kissed me. Not one of those tentative first-date kisses. Sandi covered my mouth with hers and drove her tongue in until it seemed to wrap around mine. Our arms went around each other. I held on as much to keep from collapsing as with desire. I could feel her pillowlike breasts squeezed tightly against my own.

I didn't even notice it, but somehow her fingers had unsnapped my bikini top. The small triangles of fabric and string fell away, exposing my tiny tits. To my surprise, my nipples were bigger and redder than I had ever seen them. Immediately, Sandi's mouth covered my entire left breast while her devilishly red nails went to work on my right. She pinched and bit and sucked and lavished my breasts like no boyfriend had ever done. She knew what a girl likes to feel. My head fell back, and I had a small orgasm. I heard myself moan as goose bumps popped up all over my body.

Sandi's kisses began to travel lower. She licked, kissed, and gently scratched the insides of my thighs, then lifted my legs so that my sneakers were flat on the massage table and my knees in front of my face. She leaned forward until I felt her hot breath between my legs as her hands grabbed my ass. Her nose gently roamed through my curly bush, which I had trimmed that day so I could wear the tiny bikini that was now somewhere on the floor. Softly, she kissed my pussy lips, and I could feel them swelling and pulsing with excitement. I couldn't control my breathing now. It came in short gasps with each lick. She pointed her tongue between my lips and pushed. Sparks began to go off inside me as she licked and sucked my most sensitive places. She found my little button and began to concentrate all of her energy on it.

I grabbed my knees and pulled, trying to open myself up wider. This also gave me a better view of what Sandi was doing. She stopped for just a second and put one of her fingers in her mouth. She slowly drew it out glistening with her saliva. The long red nail toyed with my moist lips for a moment, then started to wriggle its way between them. It felt so good that I thought I would explode. Sandi looked up at me and smiled, her face wet from the treatment she had been giving me, then her mouth went to work on me in earnest. The slurping sounds were audible now, as her long tongue drilled into me and her finger pumped back and forth. My legs quivered, and my stomach muscles started to spasm as I began to shake all over.

This was Sandi's signal really to go for it. She started to devour me, consuming me with her mouth. She alternated licking, sucking, and stabbing my throbbing little button with her tongue. That was it. I couldn't stand any more. A devastating orgasm tore through me. In the distance I could hear Sandi's muffled moans as I gushed into her mouth.

As the tremors began to subside, she stood up and began to kiss my neck and chest. I could smell myself on her face as she drew nearer and kissed me deeply. The taste of my own sex on her lips gave me another, smaller orgasm. She felt it, and it made her giggle. We cuddled for a few minutes, then I asked if she wanted me to try to do the same thing for her. She gazed deep into my eyes and hugged me tightly again, mashing her breasts against mine.

Suddenly we were startled by the sound of the bell on the front door, announcing that a customer had just entered the shop. Sandi jumped up, straightened her shirt, and frowned. "I have a customer." She sighed. But, she added, "You enjoy your tanning session. We'll work out a schedule for your future visits." She smiled, blew me a kiss, and hurried out of the room.

I collapsed onto the tanning bed for a few moments, trying to comprehend everything that had just happened. I felt as though I had just been run over by a train loaded with orgasms. Still shaking, I dressed and tried to sneak out of the shop, certain that anyone there would be able to tell what had happened just by looking at me. Sandi, who was talking with a customer, caught my eye, and I blushed again.

Sandi and I got together at the shop one or twice more, and once at her apartment. She taught me a great deal about how to please a woman, but then her ex-husband started calling her and she said that maybe we shouldn't see each other anymore. I still have a very nice tan, though, and always blush and get a warm smile whenever I visit the shop. I often fantasize about my trips to the tanning shop. The possibility of this letter appearing in "Forum" really excites me too.

—U. T., Idaho

DREAMS AND DIVERSIONS

Wet Dreaming

I've always had wet dreams, and I love them. I awake right afterward and enjoy the sexual, sensual feeling that comes with my fantasies. Sometimes I dream about sex with a complete stranger or with one of my husband's friends—particularly one friend.

Recently, I had the opportunity to be alone with him at his house. His wife had to go out, and left us alone. It started out innocently enough—we were sitting on the couch, watching television and talking. Our conversation turned to the subject of dreams, especially wet dreams. I confessed that I had dreams about him. He asked me to tell him what they were about. I could see that as I was describing what happened to us in my dreams, he was getting turned on.

He had an enormous bulge in his shorts. Being brave I reached out and gently began to stroke his cock through his shorts. It didn't take long for him to take them off. Slowly, I moved between his legs and wrapped my lips around the glistening head of his penis. Sucking and licking it was like one of my dreams, but much better.

After I had sucked him dry, he had me stand up and spread my legs. I had on a miniskirt and was not wearing panties. He pulled my skirt over my tight ass so he could see my engorged clit. I trim my bush very close, so it was very visible. I was dripping with juices, I was so horny. Starting on the inside of my thighs, he licked his way up my body. I was almost screaming by the time he finally reached my clit. He had a *wonderful* tongue. As he nibbled on my clit, he slowly inserted his fingers into my vagina. All I could think about was having his cock inside me. That's all it took—I came and came. It was most enjoyable. Afterward, we both had silly little grins on our face, like two kids who had their face in the candy jar and got away with it. Needless to say, I doubt if his dreams, or mine, will ever be the same.

—*J. B., Georgia*

A Real Dream

Last night I had this dream. We were on the Harley, driving down the coast. I had on a pair of thigh-high black boots, black-leather shorts, and my black-leather jacket—nothing else.

We decided to take a little break at a secluded cove along the shore. I had to have you. I asked you if you would unzip my jacket for me. As you did you kissed my nipples so hard they ached. You slipped off my jacket and started to undo my shorts, but I stopped you. It was my turn.

Your jacket was already off, so I started kissing you and unbuttoning your shirt at the same time. I ran my fingers up and down your chest and back. I started licking right after that, and I made your nipples as hard as mine. But I wouldn't let you touch me. I just wanted to touch you.

As I unbuttoned your pants, I could feel something inside getting harder with every move I made. I wanted you. As I slipped your pants to the ground, I took your huge cock in my mouth just to get it a little wet. But I was the one who was getting a little wet. You were turning me on so much—just by letting me touch, kiss, and love you.

I started playing with your cock in my mouth—rolling it around with my tongue, gently sucking it. My hands were touching your nipples and caressing them with my long, painted nails. You were moaning ever so slightly. I was doing something right.

I began to suck just a little harder on your cock. It got so hard going down my throat. I could just taste your juices getting ready to explode. You said you couldn't wait any longer. You just had to shoot off in my mouth. With my lips around your cock, you started to let every ounce of come explode down my throat, and I opened my mouth just enough to let some of it wet my lips. It tasted so sweet, just like candy. I licked all of your come from your cock and rolled it around on my tongue. That really turned me into a raging female. I wanted to have you put your cock into me. I never got to . . . that's when I woke up. Between my legs my underwear was very sticky.

But when it's three in the morning and there's an empty space next to you in bed where the one you love should be, you do the best you can. So I got out the baby oil.

I warmed it in my hands before I moved them to caress it all over my nipples. I got them so hard, they stood straight up. I wished you were lying next to me, just watching. The thought of that turned me on even more.

I put more baby oil on my hands and moved them down between my legs. I could smell the combination of my own juices and the oil ever so slightly. My fingers felt cold because my body was so hot. I just started thrusting my fingers in and out of my vagina—but that's not what makes me come. I need to have my sweet spot gently rolled around, just a little harder with each touch. It felt so good to have my hot body being touched, with the oil helping me feel the pleasure. I came with my own hands deep inside me, feeling the waves of every thrust coming from within. I had to lie there for a few more minutes. I still had waves of pleasure washing over me. There really is no feeling like it.

When I washed my hands, I got out of bed and

started to phone you . . . but calling at three o'clock in the morning would have been very rude of me. Do dreams ever really come true?

—B. L., California

Fantasize

Recently I met my biggest challenge—a very sexy male friend who I had dreamed about fucking ever since I laid eyes on him. We had been good friends for several months and enjoyed partying together, but, surprisingly, we never fucked. I had tried coming on to him by grabbing his perfectly curved ass, and I would undress him with my eyes whenever he looked at me. Every night I would fantasize about fucking him. My sex-filled dreams became so explicit and erotic, I woke up one morning in a puddle of pussy juice with my fingers soaked from masturbating during my dream the night before. As I licked the juices off my fingers, I decided that my sex life would remain incomplete unless I fulfilled this fantasy.

One night, while at a party, I left a sexually explicit poetic message on his answering machine. When he arrived at the party, I sweet-talked him into taking me back to his place. He played the message, which said:

Fantasize getting high,
Stripped black lace in your face. . . .
Fantasize naked thighs spread out wide,

Tongue inside . . .
Fantasize . . . lick your cock,
Hard as rock,
Balls knock . . .
Fantasize . . .
Pussy wet,
Bodies sweat,
Don't come yet . . .
Fantasize seducing eyes. . . .
Fuck all night,
Feels so right. . . .
Fantasize me and you
Fantasy coming true.

As he listened to my voice begging for sex on the answering machine, I stripped out of my clothes to expose my body—barely covered in black-lace lingerie. When the message ended, he wrapped my spread legs around his waist and carried me into his bedroom. He lay me down on my back and fed his hard, horny cock to my anxious tongue and lips. I rolled his balls around in my mouth as he stripped the lingerie from my body. When he freed my hands, I sucked his hard cock harder and harder. For the next three hours, he maneuvered my body into the most erotic positions, and we licked every inch of each other's flesh.

My fantasy came true that night, and now I not only enjoy sharing my body with him, but we both feel an erotic high when I seduce him with my sexually explicit poetry.

—A. L., Nebraska

The Natural

Arriving at the bus station in New York City, I'm surprised by the number of people rushing about. I make my way out to the heart of the city. I'm knocked somewhat off-balance—my suitcase and my purse are snatched out of my hands. I'm left in a daze. I can't believe this could happen to me within the first hour of my adventure.

Gradually, reality settles in. I accept the fact that I have been robbed, and I'm thankful that I still have my carry-on bag in my possession—makeup, hair products, toothbrush, black-lace bra and panties, but nothing else.

At this point I spot a coffee shop across the street from the office building in which I had sought shelter. Immediately, knowing I have a few dollars left in my pocket, I make a mad dash toward the street. Suddenly, I collide with someone, sending him down on top of me.

Looking upward, I am engulfed in the most mesmerizing set of blue eyes I have ever seen. They're so full of sparkle and life! I hear a voice—it breaks through my unconscious state, and I am drawn to focus on a face . . . *Robert Redford's* face! I am also aware of a throbbing sensation in my right ankle, my head hurts, and, shit, I broke a nail, too!

"Robbie" sees that I'm injured. . . . He wants to take me to the hospital. I refuse, saying it throbs but there's nothing broken but my nail. He laughs warmly.

Getting up, he lifts me into his arms and carries me to his car, insisting that I be a guest at his apartment until I feel that my injuries are healed. I tell him about my grand adventure to the Big Apple.

I am entrusted to the care of his housekeeper and a doctor friend, who appraises the situation—a very badly sprained ankle, possibly torn ligaments, a mild concussion, and, of course, a broken nail.

After a few days, I'm feeling better. I take a shower, dress in my bra and panties, and look for something to wear over my undergarments. Finding a shirt—*his* shirt—I put it on and set out to investigate my surroundings. (Although it had been wonderful to lie in bed and get flowers every night when he came home.) I am overwhelmed by the size and warmth of his apartment—everything is so beautiful and soothing.

"Nice shirt," I suddenly hear behind me. I am startled to hear Robbie's voice. He doesn't seem to mind that I've borrowed something to wear. He just looks at me with an amused grin. . . . Provocative undertones can be seen in his eyes. My pulse quickens.

After a nice, relaxing dinner together, Robbie sets off into another room, then there is this beautiful, romantic music playing. Reappearing, he asks me to dance. Looking at my ankle, I tell him that I can't dance very well. He offers to teach me.

In his arms I am nervous, excited, and out of breath! He holds me just close enough so that I am comfortable—close enough to feel the heat of his body without feeling its strength, close enough to smell his warm breath laced with a hint of alcohol from the wine we shared.

I can feel an electrifying numbness overtake my body. I'm entranced. I feel light-headed. My legs are weak and shaking somewhat. My sex is warm and wet. He gathers me up into his arms and carries me to his bed.

Laying me down, he begins to massage my neck, then he slowly moves down toward the buttons of the shirt and opens them. Then he begins to caress my lace-covered breasts. He removes my apparel with such skill.

Still caressing my breasts, he moves in a downward direction, over my stomach and around my navel. Expertly finding my clitoris, he magically strokes me to an earth-shattering climax. Licking his fingers, he moves his head between my thighs and begins to suck my hot juices long and hard, thus sending me into orbit with my second orgasmic moment.

Sliding his way back over my body, he guides his manhood into my waiting canal of love. At first it is painstakingly slow and lingering, then the rhythm begins to increase in intensity. He fondles the right cheek of my ass while gently sucking my left nipple. It feels so good! My body begins to feel feverish. It progresses into a blazing fire desperately seeking release. At last, with a final thrust, Robbie and I reach the same orgasmic plane together.

My loins are numb with ecstasy, my vulva drips with the sweet juices of our lovemaking. This moment never ends . . . we are married shortly after.

—G. J., Massachusetts

Ghostly Lover (Halloween Special)

I had never put much stock in the stories I read in *Penthouse* until recently, after my husband and I moved into our house. We were doing some renovation work in one of the bedroom closets, when I found an old watch and set it. It still worked, and with a little leather conditioner, it looked brand-new. I put it on, and after putting on my nightgown, I went to bed.

Later that night I awoke for no apparent reason. My husband was sleeping beside me, undisturbed. I got up and walked down the hall to the bedroom we had been working in. I thought we had left the closet light on, and I went to shut it off. I opened the door and found a man standing in the corner, looking out the window. I was terrified, but then something else took over. I stepped into the room and closed the door.

It was as if something or someone else was guiding my hand as I turned the key in the lock. With that the person turned and I saw that he was a black man, about twenty-five years old or so, but he seemed older somehow, like his clothes were sort of outdated or something. I tried to scream but I couldn't. He walked across the room and stood in front of me. I couldn't believe it when I felt my pussy start to tingle. I tried to stop, but instead I began to slip off my nightgown. He smiled and put his arms around me to help with my nightie.

At that point I was so horny, I quit trying to resist and gave myself over to this dream, or whatever it was.

I reached down and unbuttoned his pants, releasing his thick, stiff cock. He put his hands on my shoulders and I slid to my knees in front of him, taking his dark member between my lips. I began sucking—slowly at first, gradually increasing the pressure—until I was slurping away with abandon. I couldn't believe how good his cock tasted. I ran my hands around his waist and pulled down his pants. I had never been with a black man before, and the very thought of him fucking me drove me wild. He ran his hands through my hair and behind my head so he could pump his cock in and out of my mouth. Before he came he pulled me to my feet and guided me back onto the bed. He took one of my ankles in each hand and raised my legs straight up over the edge of the bed. His grip was like steel. I watched as he positioned the head of his thick cock against my slit. My pussy was very wet, and I couldn't wait for him to satisfy me.

He eased the head of his penis between my lips, causing me to moan with pleasure. For a moment I hoped my husband hadn't heard, but then another wave of lust swept over me.

Slowly, he increased the tempo as I gasped and moaned, until I came with a huge gushing orgasm, which seemed to trigger his, as I felt a warm flood fill me.

That is all I remember about that night. The next morning I awoke in bed with my husband. There have been other such incidents that always take place when I'm wearing that old watch. I am convinced that I have a ghostly lover who is somehow connected to the watch. Now, every time I put it on, I feel a twinge of excitement, wondering if he will come.

—S. W., Texas

Imagine

As a woman who enjoys *Penthouse* as much as any man, I thought I would share some of my most vivid masturbation fantasies with your other readers. My husband enjoys hearing about my solo sex life, and after I tell him my dreams, we always have the craziest sex ever.

I like to start with my ankles together and my legs up in the air. I can feel the air on the back of my legs, and I start to get warm. I trace my fingers over the outside of my thighs, toward the inside, up and down. I can feel the goose bumps starting to form on my legs, and soon after my cunt starts to throb, but I don't touch myself—not yet.

Sometimes I imagine that I am on a glass platform and there are men standing under me. There is oil on the table, and I look down at the men and start moving my whole body slowly. I put my pussy straight down on the glass and move my ass from side to side.

The room is dark, spacious, and quiet. Next I imagine that the men start to take off their clothes, and I know they want me. Somehow the men lower the platform so they can have their way with me. I lie there with my knees apart just imagining the sucking of a tongue—an expert tongue—licking my pussy with a sweet tickle. The sucking isn't hard, but gently firm. The tongue pushes softly around and slowly into my clit, matching the rhythm of my throbbing cunt. Then a finger is pushing inside of my slit, and the mouth continues its magic on my lips and clit. The fingering stops and the hand moves to my bottom, exploring and stroking until my sighs become moans.

A new hand is working on my pussy now, also moving back to my butt to send shivers through my whole body. I groan with the feeling of my pussy gushing as a little wetness drips out onto my leg.

This man has a beautiful, straight hard-on with a delicious purple head—I want it. I put my legs up and wiggle around, but he just touches me. He pushes his finger slowly in and out of my pussy. I lift my legs up higher, so I am completely exposed. I need it so badly! But he puts my legs down and straightens me out. He starts to lick my nipples, nibbling just a little bit and then sucking firmly. He lies down on top of me. I can feel his swollen cock pressed into my stomach. He kisses me with his perfect tongue, wet and succulent.

Another strong, naked man joins in. I know they want me at the same time. He lies down next to us, and they turn me on my side. I wiggle my pelvis around because I'm so hot. Behind me the new man's skin is touching the entire length of my body. After putting their hands in the oil, they both stroke every inch of me. I bring my legs forward a little because I want to be touched from behind. He puts his hands on my ass and squeezes it—I like that. I push it out toward him to let him know that I want more. He starts to rub the head of his cock against my crack, and another deep moan escapes my lips.

Then they roll me onto my back and one of the men pushes my legs up in the air, gets his cock just right, and starts pushing it into me very slowly, making me plead for more. It feels so good. Another man walks over and eases his dick into my mouth. I put my hands around his cock and suck hard while the man inside of me is now up to full, forceful strokes in my twat. I move back and forth with loud and erotic moans as I taste sweet precome and smell my own juices. I can't stop screaming—the sensations are too intense. One by one we stiffen and flex in passionate climax. The lights go very dim, I imagine.

—O. L., Virginia

Your Force

I can see you sitting there—almost close enough to touch, but just out of reach. You look at me with that wanting look in your eyes—a look I've seen many times. You know how hard it is for me to resist you. Your eyes plead for me to come closer. The incredible power you have over me makes me move toward you.

Like steel to a magnet, I'm attracted to you—your force pulls me in.

As I draw closer, I imagine your arms around me, holding me close. I can feel your warm breath on my neck, sending shivers down my spine and making my hair stand on end. Your hands explore my body.

I run my fingers up the back of your neck and through your hair. I bury my face in your strong chest as you place tender kisses on the side of my neck. When I lift my head to look into your eyes, our lips finally meet. Your kiss is slow, tender, and filled with passion. As we stand there kissing, my mind fills with the thought of making love to you.

When I come back to reality, you are slowly unbuttoning my blouse and anointing my neck and shoulders with warm, wet kisses. I want you more now than I ever have in the past. My body is consumed by lust, and I urge you to continue your seduction.

As we slowly undress, you turn to light a candle, and my gaze wanders up and down your perfect body. The candle starts to flicker, and I see you sitting there, the glimmering light casting shadows against your skin—you look so beautiful. I look into your eyes and see the love, passion, and desire you have within you.

We sink to the floor and begin to touch each other, exploring each other's bodies as if it is the first time we are making love. Your solid shoulders and firm body feels so good pressed up against mine. My thighs start to tingle with anticipation as we begin our lovemaking adventure.

I press my body even closer to yours, trying to make myself one with you. You nibble your way down my body until you reach my pleasure pit. You use your tongue to take me to heaven before bringing me back down to earth.

I flip you over and return the favor, working my way slowly up and down your body. When I reach your mouth, you kiss me, place me on my back, and enter me. You move slowly at first, almost timidly, as if it is my first time. I urge you to pick up the pace, wanting to feel every powerful thrust of your hips. You whisper in my ear how much you want me, driving even deeper into my soul.

I rotate my hips to meet yours with every pulsating thrust, wanting to please you. You speed up, your pelvis grinding against mine. I am moaning with delight.

You give one final push and I feel your love flow into me. Our juices mix, overflow, and run down my legs. You kiss me, telling me how wonderful our love-making was, and I return your kiss with the same declaration.

As we lie together, bathed in the dim light of the morning, the candle having gone out hours before, you stroke my hair. I fall asleep in your arms just as the sun begins to rise.

—D. D., California

My Awakening

The Greek god Eros was the god of desire. It was said that when he cast his eyes and placed his touch upon any mortal woman, she would be overwhelmed and consumed with an insatiable desire for him and only him.

All my life I had waited for someone to arouse the desire that I could feel smoldering inside me. I graduated with honors, I was captain of my cheerleading team, and I was voted "best-looking" and "most likely to succeed" by my peers. I've met and dated many handsome, powerful, and wealthy men, including a famous movie star. No one stirred me. When I married I was a virgin, and even after my divorce, my passions still seemed asleep . . . until I met him.

The very first time I was with him, I felt an immediate trust, and we talked as if we had known one another for years. We went out for a business dinner, and I felt an immediate alliance which I did not question—an alliance that would become intimate and pleasurable. The first night we were together, I cried, fearing my lack of sexual experience would matter. But learning to please him mattered above all else. Words could never describe all that he does to me.

There was something in his eyes and smile that touched my very soul. His eyes held me spellbound and seemed to look through to my most hidden thoughts. His body was hard and beautiful. His smile made me quiver with a hot longing that claimed every part of my body. When his lips touched mine, he was in complete command, I could deny him nothing. I would obey his every whim. I wanted to tell him how very much I wanted him, but his mouth still had possession of me. He touched me as no one ever had before. His lips and fingers allowed no words. My body tingled and throbbed with an indescribable ecstasy that I never wanted to end. When his cock stroked deep and hard inside me, I thought that was where I wanted him most. But suddenly I realized I wanted to feel his smooth, hard cock fill my mouth, and I wanted to taste him more and more. But I had never taken anyone in my mouth before . . . not even my former husband. The more we made love, the hotter I became for him. I was obsessed with his lips, his touch . . . and his cock—it was so incredible to me, I asked him if I could name it.

When I think of him, my pulse races madly, and when I close my eyes, I can feel him. My nipples become hard, and my pussy is so wet I can easily slip my fingers inside me. His lips on my breasts set my whole body on fire, his muscled chest and hard legs pressed against me bring me within a hairbreadth of coming. His mouth and tongue tasted me, and passion took me over the edge of ecstasy more times than I can remember. When he parted my thighs, his fingers found my button of sensuality. I heard moaning coming from me that I never thought possible.

I knew that it was time to take part of him into me. I slowly traced his stomach with my tongue and teasingly licked his cock very lightly. My tongue went between his thighs as I hungrily caressed his balls and, finally, took him into my mouth. The more I sucked him, the more I wanted to . . . I could feel his fingers in my hair, pulling me closer and closer until his hard cock filled my mouth. The excitement was consuming every fiber of my being, and I sucked him until he exploded in my mouth. The taste of him made me drunk with desire as I swallowed every drop of his sweet elixir. It was then that I knew I had found my own Greek god and that I had been deliciously overwhelmed and consumed.

—T. P., New York

A Star Is Porn

My biggest fantasy is to play with myself in front of the camera and go all the way to orgasm. It would be such a turn-on getting the guys so horny. I start out on all fours on the bed, the camera pointed at my behind, and I squeeze my ass so it's closed tight, and keep my thighs pressed firmly together. As the camera lingers on me, I slowly relax my rear end and gradually let my legs move apart. All the while, my face is turned toward the camera and I'm looking right into it—like I know a man is watching me. As the camera closes in, my legs open even more, so the viewer starts to see my pussy and between my cheeks. Then I slowly reach up between my legs and let my fingers gently caress both my openings.

Next, I turn and lie on my side, keeping my legs apart. I start to let myself go and I feel my juices start to flow. With one hand, I rub and pinch my nipples so they stand up stiff, and I bring the other hand down to spread my pussy open. I know the guys can see up inside my hole and I can't believe how sexy and feminine it makes me feel, knowing their cocks are getting thick and hard and how much they want to stick them deep inside me. I moisten the lips of my mouth, while my lips down below get wetter and wetter, and my fingers pull my ass cheeks apart to reveal my asshole. I'm tingling there, too, and gently touch it, my most private opening, even letting one finger go a little inside. All the time I'm looking right into the camera, knowing my face shows just how horny I'm getting. I continue stroking myself and I can't help letting out some little moans.

Now I move onto my back, put my hands on my knees, and slowly spread my legs open all the way. I keep gently touching my breasts and nipples, but most of my attention is on the sweet spot between my legs. With one hand touching my pussy, I smile a sexy, lustful smile into the camera, watching as it focuses on my fingers. I let my nails gently run over my crotch and notice how smooth my mound is, because I keep my pussy hair trimmed and partly shaved. Doing this has an incredible effect on my clitoris, and I feel it start to shoot right out. I bring my hand down over my cunt and squeeze my clit between my second and third fingers, letting it peek out so the camera can focus right on it. I'm so glad this is all being shot in color, because I know what a vivid pink my clitoris is, and I love knowing the men can see it. I squeeze its little tip and lift up my bottom off the bed so you can see even more of me! I know the camera shows how very wet I am, and I can feel my juices pouring out, soaking my crotch and my asshole, too. I wish I could feel a tongue down there, licking both my openings, sliding over the folds, going deep inside. I know I smell *so* good down there. I rub and stroke myself, then bring my hand up to my nose to breathe in the heavenly wetness. It smells so good and sexy, my eyes roll way back in my head. Then I put my fingers into my mouth and taste my sweet girl juice. It's delicious, and I have to have more, so I move my hand back down to my crotch. Closing my eyes, I touch my little clitoris again. It is throbbing now, driving me crazy. I need to slow down, or I'll explode. My fingers touch the cleft, gently pressing my soft, pillowy lips, working their way inside until my middle finger finds the moist center. I slowly let it work its way in, feeling how warm I am there, each touch seeming to make more moisture flow inside me. I put my finger all the way up into my tight, sweet pussy, twisting it, bringing myself closer to the brink.

Now I let my index finger join its friend inside me and the two fingers rub and stroke, exploring every inch of my female place. I almost forget the camera is watching all this, and when I open my eyes, I look surprised—even a little shy and embarrassed. But I'm so unbelievably aroused that I spread my pussy lips open wide, so you can see even deeper inside of me. My breathing is fast and heavy now, and I begin to grind my hips, my fingers finding their way inside again. I begin to thrust them over and over up into my creaming snatch. I look down and see my fingers glistening with my sweet juices, then bring them back up to my mouth to lick them, savoring my heady girl flavor once again. I'm even wetter than before, and the taste and aroma of my sweet little cunt is intoxicating.

I imagine what it would be like to have a man's long, thick cock shoving itself into my tight hole, touching every part of me inside, stretching me, and I know it's going to burst and fill me up with sweet come. Then I think about how good it would be to have that cock in my mouth, to wrap my lips around it and suck up and down the shaft. I imagine what it's like to have it swell up and to taste it, teasing the head with my tongue, nipping it gently with my teeth. I hold the thickness in my hand and take it out to admire it. I look at the huge manhood and squeeze and caress it with my hand, feeling its weight. I begin to pump it, knowing that soon it's going to happen. I hear my man groan, telling me he's going to come, and I put the huge organ back in my mouth. I feel it start to jerk and feel that first spurt of sweet, male liquid. Then there's another and another, and I feel the cream filling my mouth. I taste it on my tongue and hold it until there's so much I have to swallow some. This turns me on so much I can hardly believe it. I want to see him now, so I take his cock out and pump it more and more. He has lots left, and it shoots out onto my face in big, beautiful wads. I love watching it and bring my hand up to catch some of his sweet come in my palm. I dip my tongue into the warm liquid, letting the come already in my mouth pour out and mix with it. There's so much I can't believe it, and I press my hand to my mouth and suck up the creamy white jism, tasting its sweet-salty flavor. I bring my hand to my face and rub it all over, smelling it, feeling the big drops of come coating my skin. I finally swallow a huge mouthful of his load, then bring my fingers back and lick up every last drop like a cat, all the while gazing deep into his eyes.

Fantasizing this way makes my groaning get stronger and louder as I continue to finger myself. I bite my lip in sweet ecstasy, and my nostrils begin to flare with overwhelming excitement. I look deep into the camera, imagining my man poised between my legs, ready to eat my pussy. He goes down on me, taking my clitoris between his lips, rolling it around, just nipping at it, sucking it gently. I take it myself between my fingers and bring my other hand down to join in the pleasure. While I gently massage the clit, my other hand rubs my pussy and opens my bottom to touch my asshole. I know I'm going to explode soon now, and I put my thumb deep inside my cunt while my middle finger works its way into my tight little asshole. This is too much, and I feel myself start to come in an incredible wave. My entire body is shaking, and I feel myself scream out, flicking my clit again and again. I'm so wet now that my fingers slip easily in and out of both silky-smooth openings. I bite my shoulder in ecstasy as my orgasm begins to overwhelm me, and I think about how the camera is capturing every detail. I feel the lens focused on my hands as they rub and caress my sex, watching as the creamy female juice pours out of me, soaking my hands. I cry out, "Mm . . . Oh, God, it's so good; oh, my pussy!" Knowing that the words will excite my viewers even more, I pinch my little clit one more time, and it makes me erupt. I come again, then again, and finally a long, incredible climax explodes through my body, and I scream out with pleasure. I want it to last forever, and it seems to.

When it finally begins to subside, I keep gently fondling my private parts, knowing the camera is still watching, showing how wet and swollen my little pussy still is, how warm and wet my asshole is, and how my fingers are soaking wet from all my orgasms. It is so incredible, knowing what a girl's body can do, knowing how she can get herself so excited, and how hot she can get a man by letting him watch her play with herself.

—L. R., New Jersey

Long Time No See

"How would you like to meet me at the bar for a drink?" I say softly over the phone. "I'm wearing a long black coat, black boots, black-leather gloves, and a black cowboy hat. Later you'll find out what's underneath."

At the bar our seats are pulled close together so our knees touch. I see the bulge in your jeans grow larger—the anticipation shows in your eyes. We barely touch our drinks before I suggest we go to my house.

I have a blanket laid out on the living-room floor, soft rock on the stereo, and candles flickering around the room. "How about another drink?" I ask. Standing behind me, rubbing my shoulders, you lean down, and whisper, "Yes," in my ear. Over our glasses we look into each other's eyes, and I realize how long it has been since I saw you last. I put your glass aside, and demand, "Kiss me."

Kissing me, you throw my hat and coat to the floor, revealing what I'm wearing underneath—a black bra, a thong, and stockings. With fire in your eyes, you tell me how much you like it.

"You want me, don't you?" I inquire. You moan a yes as I take your clothes off. I ask you to lie facedown on the blanket. "Relax and feel everything I do," I whisper. I rub your tanned body and lick your ear with my hot tongue. You squirm and moan, rubbing your hardness against the floor. With strong hands I rub your muscles with a gentle motion. "Kneel for me," I command.

I rub my nipples against your ass as I lean over you from behind. Reaching in front of you to grasp your cock, I kiss and bite your back. With my tongue I trace a line down your spine. "Doesn't my tongue feel good on your back?" I ask. I follow the curves farther to lick your warm, soft sac as I gently stroke your shaft. You moan and gasp as I run my nails over your ass and thighs.

"Close your eyes," I tell you firmly. I kiss your lips and run my tongue down your arm and chest and along your side. "Are you ticklish?" I ask. You breathe a "Yes" as I bite and nibble your stomach and nuzzle the soft fur that surrounds your cock. I lick the wetness off the head of your cock and gently tease your testicles with my nails. "Does that feel good?"

You can't take it anymore and call to me to suck it. "How deep do you want me to suck it?" Pumping your hips, you force your cock deep into my throat and tell me, "This deep."

I suck it to the base and back to the head, twisting and turning my hand around the shaft with every in-and-out motion. You moan loudly and passionately call my name. "Oh, Sandra, yes, that feels good."

"Do you want me?" I ask, already knowing the answer. I glide a hand moistened with lubricant over your waiting shaft. Straddled over you, I slide your hardness into my cunt. "I want you to watch me come," I tell you.

You raise your hips to meet me as I reach down to rub my pussy. It's more than either of us can take, and we explode together. My twitching muscles milk every last drop of come into my cunt. Hot and breathless, I whisper, "I'm not done yet." I lead you to the shower, saying, "I want to feel your wet body against mine."

I suck your soapy cock back to life while you rub my body gently with your warm hands. "I want to feel you inside my pussy again." I face the wall and bend over. With your hands on my hips, you fuck me from behind. I can hear myself moan loudly over the din of the shower. "Fuck me." Pushing against the wall, forcing my body into yours, we pump and moan together. I tighten my pussy and pump harder. "Do you want to come?" I ask. You moan and grab your cock. I turn to catch the sweet come in my mouth. "Mmm, you taste good."

We finish showering, washing each other's tired bodies. Snuggling in the blanket on the living-room floor, we listen to the music, taking in the night and finishing the drinks we'd started hours ago.

—S. C., California

SURPRISE PARTY

Make a Wish

As the date of my twenty-second birthday approached, I was looking forward to it, but I wasn't expecting anything out of the ordinary. Little did I know that was exactly what was in store for me. The night before my birthday, my boyfriend called me. "Come on over," he said. "Your birthday begins at 12 A.M. sharp, and we don't want to waste any time." He refused to tell me what was going on. He would only say that it would be a birthday I would never forget.

When I arrived at his house, I immediately noticed that mischievous smile on his face. "Happy birthday," he whispered in my ear. "What are you going to wish for?" I thought I would try to shock him with my answer, so I replied, "Oh, I don't know. How about one orgasm for each of my birthdays." Without the slightest hesitation, my boyfriend replied, "Well, I think that can be arranged." Then he handed me a package and said, "I think this will help make your wish come true." I proceeded to open the box, and soon discovered that I was the proud owner of a beautiful, new, state-of-the-art vibrator! It was made of soft, flexible rubber, and the base of the phallus was filled with rotating multi-colored beads that—according to the owner's manual—were designed to stimulate the G-spot like nothing else could. The most curious feature of my new toy, however, was the rabbit's head that, when the shaft was inserted, tickled the clitoris. As my initial shock wore off (I was a vibrator virgin), I became highly aroused by this complex piece of equipment. I looked up at my boyfriend, and said, "What a lovely gift. Shall we give Mr. Rabbit a try?"

After we entered the bedroom, my boyfriend started to kiss me all over my face, neck, and ears. He started to nibble and suck on my earlobes, which he knows drives me absolutely wild. By the time he laid me down on the bed, I was pushing his face down toward my breasts, dying for him to lick and kiss my nipples. He slowly began to unbutton my blouse, but I was too impatient and ripped it off for him. "Suck my tits, please," I whispered in his ear. As his tongue swirled around my nipple and flicked from one breast to the other, his hand traveled down to caress my inner thighs. By this time I was going wild and soon had the rest of my clothes off. When I reached out to take his clothes off, too, he stopped me. "Not yet," he said with a smile. His tongue continued its workout, moving down my body to finally reach my soaking-wet pussy. I moaned with relief as he began to send me into delirium with short, even strokes. "Make me come!" I screamed out, unable to contain myself any longer.

He paused long enough to flash me a wicked grin, then began to give me a true tongue-lashing. As he expertly sucked and licked my clit, I started to buck my hips up to drive his tongue deeper into my pulsating cunt. Suddenly I let out a howl as waves of orgasm flashed through my body. Before the last contraction had even ended, my boyfriend had Mr. Rabbit fired up and ready to go. He inserted the huge rubber cock into my hungry box, and the strong electric vibrations immediately made me cry with pleasure. He pushed the device in farther, and I could feel the rotating beads pressing against my G-spot. I had never before experienced such a sensation, and I felt as if I were coming in buckets. The combination of the gyrating beads and the rabbit ears swirling over my clit was sending me into orgasm after orgasm, each one stronger than the last.

Finally, after what seemed like hours of endless orgasms, my boyfriend said to me, "It seems as though your birthday wish is about to come true after all." I could only answer, "Not yet," as I reached out to pull his completely hard cock out of his pants. I ran my tongue down the length of his shaft and flicked my tongue over his balls. He let out a soft moan, and I sucked him with gusto. I brought him to the brink, and felt his body tense with impending orgasm. Then he pulled away from me and said, "I'm going to make sure your twenty-second birthday is the one you will never forget." He flipped me over onto all fours and entered me from behind. As I felt his steel rod slide into me, I gasped and started to grind against him. We were soon fucking like two wild animals, and just as I started to feel the most intense orgasm of the evening, his rock-hard cock exploded inside me, rocking my body with an earth-shattering finale.

We continued our escapade for many hours, and my birthday wish more than came true that night. In fact, I had over sixty orgasms that night, making me a golden girl! Needless to say, this birthday gift will keep on giving.

—S. A., California

Big Tippers

I'm a thirty-five-year-old divorcee. One afternoon a coworker and I had lunch at a very chic restaurant and were served by the most gorgeous waiter either of us had ever seen. We tried to get to know him better, but he was as cold as ice. It took a year of lunches for us to begin to break through, but he finally agreed to let us buy him dinner for his twenty-third birthday.

We thought he was really shy at heart, so we plotted to build up our birthday boy's self-esteem. We sat him between us in a booth in the most elegant restaurant in town. Somehow, my girlfriend turned the conversation around to blowjobs while I nibbled provocatively on some berries and cream. We had promised to deliver him back to his apartment after dinner, and so we did. Not surprisingly, he invited us in.

The moment the door closed, we guided him right down onto the soft carpet and took turns licking down his stomach to his throbbing cock. Then we both took turns kissing and caressing our prize. I stared intently into his eyes, running my fingers over his chest, as my girlfriend's red mane bobbed up and down on his engorged cock. He came without a sound.

He kissed us both shyly, then said he had to get dressed to work the night shift. We lay there, hot and wet but without complaint. The next time we had lunch at his restaurant, our waiter was as cold as ever! Why were we surprised? Oh well, the obsession goes on!

—H. L., California

Making My Mark

This is for all the men out there who dream about threesomes, especially the ones who will never get to experience one. But mainly, this is for my husband, Eddie. One of his fantasies is now a wonderful memory, and I hope he gets as excited while reading about it as he did while experiencing it for the first time.

A good friend of ours, Mark, and I set this up as a

nice surprise for Eddie's birthday. We started out with some beers and a porno movie, which we had never done before.

A few minutes into the video, Mark came over and sat right next to me on the couch. He casually unbuttoned my blouse and played with my boobs very slowly and gently. After thirty seconds of this, I was ready for anything. I reached over and tickled his member through his jeans. It immediately jumped up. We continued this for a few minutes, then slowly undressed each other.

Mark started sucking my right nipple and fingering "Hilda"—my pussy—which was by that time real wet. Eddie decided to join in on the fun and started sucking my left nipple. I reached over and played with his already enlarged toy. All this went on while I alternated kissing one, then the other. This was heaven on earth. Shortly thereafter, Mark moved between my legs. His tongue went in and out of my pussy while he tickled the insides of my thighs with his fingertips. All this time Eddie was still sucking and licking my nipples. What a wonderful feeling!

I whispered in Eddie's ear that I wanted to suck him off. He got into position so I could. I ran my tongue up and down his shaft and around the head. He was larger than ever before and filled my entire mouth. I slowly moved my mouth up and down and tickled his balls with my fingers. He was still playing with my tits and getting really excited watching Mark between my legs.

I started teasing his crack with my fingers, and he shot a huge load into my mouth. Even after doing that, he was still rock-hard.

At about that time, I exploded. He came up for air, my juices all over his face and his member still waiting for attention. Mark sat on the couch with his legs outstretched. I immediately got into position to return the favor. As I was sucking his cock and lightly pinching his nipples, Eddie knelt behind me and started pumping me from behind. Both guys enjoyed watching each other get their rocks off with me in the middle. And I loved every minute of the attention.

We never did finish watching the porno movie, but we had such a good time that we have repeated the scene many times since then—with Mark and with other people. So wait for the next episode—I'll write again soon!

—C. P., Illinois

People Fucking

I am going to tell you a true story of what I did for my husband's birthday last year. Let's preface this by saying that we have the most wild, crazy, lustful, wonderful sex life that any couple could want.

Last year on Marty's birthday, I told him that he was not to come home from work until 7:30 P.M. I had arranged for two people to help celebrate his night with me, Lori and Mabel. Both ladies are erotic dancers who work in a club in L.A. Lori was to arrive first, and Mabel was supposed to come at about nine o'clock. Lori had performed for my husband on two previous occasions—for his best friend's and his own bachelor parties. (I helped arrange his bachelor party, too, but that's another story.) Lori is a voluptuous strawberry blonde, and she's very much to the point when it comes to entertaining men. She goes for it all, and, as my husband put it, "She's hot."

She showed up at the house all dolled up and ready for Marty and me. Lori likes both women and men, and she doesn't try to hide it. It definitely made for an interesting time. She started by taking off her clothes for my husband and putting her tits in his face as I watched. Then she began to get down and horny. She rubbed her body all over Marty, and she made me sit down next to him so she could get to both of us. The part I remember best was when she sat down and made Marty get up and take his clothes off. She spread her legs and wanted him to eat her, which he did in no time. Marty eats pussy like an expert. He laps your pussy with his whole tongue—it is so soft and wet—and his busy hands finger you and rub your tits. Every woman should experience this once in her lifetime. I loved watching him eat her—it made my pussy so wet and hot. As he continued to eat her pussy, I crawled underneath him, between her legs, and began to suck and lick his dick and balls. I love licking and sucking on his dick, and feeling him get hard in my mouth.

Finally, he made her come so good that she screamed—so loud I thought the neighbors would hear. Then we switched positions, and I started licking her pussy while Marty got behind me and fucked me doggie style. It was evident that he was incredibly excited, because he came so quickly inside my cunt (he normally lasts for an hour or so). We had fantasized about this for a long time, and actually to see it was far better than I had imagined. I also remember leaving the room after I ate her (we took turns doing what we wanted with her) and returning to see Lori lying on the floor with a bottle of honey and a spoon, and Marty laying on top of her, licking it off wherever she applied it on her body—her tits, her stomach, her pussy, et cetera. This was great, and I loved watching them. But I wanted to eat her again, so I stuck my head between their legs and started licking her pussy. She tasted so good I couldn't get enough of her. After she came in my mouth, we were all still horny. But knew that she had to leave, and that Mabel was due to arrive any minute. We all agreed that we would have to get together again sometime. She told us to enjoy Mabel, and from the way she said it, it was clear that *she* had.

Marty had never met Mabel before. I had attended two of her "Strip for Your Lover" classes, and had wanted her ever since I had first seen her. This woman is the most erotic person I have ever met. She is so incredibly sensual. She arrived at the house at exactly nine o'clock and wanted to go straight into the bedroom to change. She asked me to come with her. When

I did, she asked me what I thought he would like to see her dressed in. I said anything black, perhaps what she had worn to teach the class to strip (a short, tight black skirt, a black-leather jacket, black fishnet stockings, and black six-inch heels). She wanted me to watch her change and help her get into the outfit. This made me very hot as I brushed up against her, stroking her body and fondling her breasts. I wanted to continue feeling her all over, but I thought we'd better stop for now and go see how Marty was doing. When she was ready, we both went to the living room to see how he was handling the waiting. We could both tell that he was more than ready to begin, so she told him to put on some music for her, sit down, and then let go and enjoy it. You cannot imagine how erotic this woman is. I knew that he was going to enjoy watching her.

She started taking off her clothes so very slowly, and she kept incredible eye contact with my husband. She had him help take off her fishnet hose, and spread her legs for him. When she had stripped, she got up, went over to Marty, and slowly rubbed her body down his, breathing heavily on his neck and ears and driving him crazy. She lay on her back and teased him, raising her legs in the air—first closed, then spreading them wide open for him to see her hot little pussy. Then she got up and got some baby oil and a sheet. She laid the sheet on the floor and poured oil all over her body. She had a long string of pearls, and she turned around so her ass was facing him and slowly pulled the pearls up through her pussy and ass. Marty loved it. She was very sexy in her movements, and she loved rubbing up against him.

When she was completely oiled up, she came over to me and asked if I would mind if she lay on top of him, breathing on his neck and getting all of us very aroused. Marty had on his shorts, and I wish he had taken them off. I wanted to see him all oily with Mabel, and see his dick rub all over her body. She stood up over him and danced so that he could see her pussy right above his head. She made my pussy so wet. I loved watching them. When she was finished dancing, she asked me to come to the bedroom with her, and she told me that her pussy was so hot and wet. She said that Marty was so sexy and his hands were so soft and big. She made me feel between her legs to make sure she wasn't lying about her pussy. She was dripping wet. I left my hand there for a few minutes and played with her wet cunt. She was loving it. I wanted so badly to get on my knees and lick her cunt, but she had another appointment, and I knew she had to leave soon.

Instead, I just kept playing with her. After a few minutes, I bent my head and sucked on her nipples. That was enough for her, and she instantly came on my hand. I pulled my hand up and she watched me as I licked her come off each of my fingers. She had come so much, it was all over my hand and in between my fingers. She tasted so good. I wish Marty had seen it, because he would have come on the spot. When she left, she told me to call her so that perhaps we could go shopping for some sexy, sleazy clothing to wear, and she would give me a personal lesson on stripping.

She winked at me, and we left the bedroom. When she left, Marty and I decided that Mabel was the hottest, most erotic woman we both had ever seen, and I guess we both knew that she would be a part of our lovemaking and fantasizing from then on. We both love to fantasize about her and think about what will happen the next time one of us invites her over for a dance. The next time we'll make sure that she doesn't have another appointment on the same night. Or maybe one night, we'll both surprise her at the club where she dances. Either way, I'm sure I'll have another story for *Penthouse.*

—L. M., New York

Private Stag

I am a forty-one-year-old woman who became involved with a fifty-one-year-old man several months ago. He was already engaged to another woman, but I found him exciting and irresistible, and had to have him. We have carried on an affair for the past several months. Recently, he married his lucky fiancée.

A few days before his wedding, I gave him a private bachelor party. I explained that many bachelor parties have a whore, so I was his whore. I told him he should tell me what I do that he wants more of, what I do that I should stop, and what I should do, but have not.

He began by kissing me with those deep, forceful, tender kisses that drive me crazy. As I undressed him, I saw his cock had already risen to the occasion. We continued kissing and sucking and licking tits. My pussy was quickly wet, and he began to finger-fuck me ever so teasingly. I could feel the juices oozing out of my pussy, and I was ready to come already. But this was his party, and I was there to please him.

I made him lie down in the center of the bed. I began kissing him and slowly moved down to his nipples—I enjoy sucking them and rubbing them with my fingers. I flicked my tongue down his chest to his stomach and darted it in and out of his navel, and down to his cock. But being in a teasing mood, and knowing I had not even begun to carry out my plan, I avoided his cock, and tongued my way down his legs and back up to his balls. After kissing and sucking his balls, I let my tongue slide up his cock, over the head, and back up his stomach and chest. His cock was hard and ready, so I was ready to begin.

First I danced an ostrich feather across his chest, lingering at each nipple, which stood erect in response. I repeated the same pattern with the feather as I had with my tongue. It moved slowly and lightly down his chest, stomach, and legs, and then up between his legs onto his balls, and over his cock. The feather danced up and down his body several times. As it moved up his cock, I followed it with the tip of my tongue. His cock responded by moving up to greet my tongue, on its head. When I felt he could endure no more of the feather, I moved into phase two of my desire to please him—serious cocksucking.

I am always searching for new ideas in cocksucking, so this pleasure trip had three stages. When I drink Greek ouzo, it warms my mouth and all the way down to my stomach. I took a mouthful of ouzo, held it, and went down on his cock—careful not to let the ouzo drip out of my mouth while I took in his full cock. The heated sensation drove him wild. He said his cock felt like it was on fire, creating that fine line between pleasure and pain. After swallowing all the ouzo, I rubbed hot massage oil all over his cock and began again. This time I had to breathe on the oiled cock while tasting it, to initiate the heated sensation. Once again, after tonguing his cock and balls, I took him in my mouth and began the up-and-down motion, working toward deep-throating him. By now he was ready to explode, but I held his cock, with pressure, to subdue him, and told him it was time to cool down. This time I filled my mouth with crushed ice and went down on him once more. He was ready to fuck, but I refused, even though I desperately wanted his big cock inside my pussy.

I left him lying there throbbing and told him to think about what he wanted to do next. I returned in a couple of minutes and he wanted more ouzo. After I repeated the mouthful of ouzo on his throbbing cock, he begged me to cool it down again, which I did, obediently. By now almost one and a half hours of licking, sucking, teasing, and eating had passed, and it was time to fuck. As he mounted me, I raised my legs into the air so his cock could penetrate deeply into my pussy. We fucked furiously. But all good things must end, and we both had to return to work after this extended lunch hour. I never did find out what he did not like.

—S. J., New Jersey

Birthday Bash

My husband, Harold, had had this fantasy of seeing me with another woman for a couple of years. Last June he finally was able to fulfill this fantasy, and it was even better than he could have imagined. Ever since he told me about this dream of his, I had been pondering the idea of having sexual relations with another woman. In May I started going to bars and nightclubs, searching for the perfect woman for a one-night stand. I didn't tell my husband about my quest, so that it would be a surprise to him, perhaps a birthday present. A week or so before my husband's birthday, I happened to meet Eva. I met the blonde beauty in what is commonly referred to as a lesbian bar. I asked the stunningly large-breasted twenty-one-year-old if she would mind coming over to our house on the night of June 5, about 5:45 P.M. The gorgeous blonde arrived perfectly on schedule, and immediately things started happening. When I opened the door, I saw that she had on a trench coat. She took it off, and I saw the sexiest lingerie ever made. I could see her huge tits right through the lingerie, and that made me horny enough. She walked right in, grabbing one of my breasts as she went by. She walked into the kitchen and cleared off the table with one swipe. She told me to lie down on the table, so I did.

I was only a rookie, under the spell of this seasoned veteran. I couldn't believe I was having sex with such an attractive girl! She slowly stripped me, starting from the top. She began kissing me deeply, then moved down my neck. She slid the straps off my shoulders, and as she pulled my dress down she licked every inch of the way. At this point, I began to feel bad about letting her do all the work, so I pushed her off of me and mounted her. Taking off her lingerie, I started with a mouthful of her mammoth-size breasts. Then I licked my way down to her waiting, hungry snatch. I darted my tongue in and out as fast as I could, licking up her tasty juices. After getting my lips (and hers) wet, I got up, turned around, and slipped into an absolutely vicious sixty-nine. It was right about then that I felt Harold's rock-hard eight-incher sliding in and out of me at an incredibly fast rate. I knew that he had been watching for a while, because his member was already covered in his own precome when it entered me. Eva rolled out from under me and stood up. I rolled over and watched Harold play with her enlarged nipples. It was driving all of us wild. Then I got up and gave Harold one of the best blowjobs ever. As he was taking it, he lay down and Eva sat on his face. He must have done well, because Eva's groans became screams as she came to her first climax. She proceeded to roll off Harold and take a breather. Harold stood and picked me up off the table. Then he positioned me properly and did me doggie style until we came wonderfully. Then the three of us lay down on the table and caressed one another's bodies as we kissed French style. This is now a regular occurrence around our house, and sometimes we even go to Eva's apartment. Harold thinks that this was the best birthday present ever, and I happen to agree.

—J. S., Ontario

Winter Wonderland

I couldn't quite decide what to do for my boyfriend's upcoming birthday. It would be difficult to top the previous year's champagne bubble bath. We were in a full-size, outdoor Jacuzzi, mirrored all around, with candles in the corners and an ample supply of bubbly. I scrubbed him from the top of his head—with a lengthy stop at his *other* head—to the tip of his toes. We kept dipping in and out of the tub, grabbing bursts of the cold North Dakota air. Most people don't believe it, but we made passionate love seven times that evening. So you see why he was so anxious about this year's surprise.

He picked me up on a Friday night, and we went for a casual dinner at one of our favorite restaurants. After dinner I suggested we go for a little drive. I led him along my predetermined path to the state's large national forest. Unbeknownst to him, I had loaded all our ice-fishing gear and clothing into the back of the pickup truck. He had no idea of our destination until we came upon a log cabin, which was to be our love nest for the weekend. After unloading, setting up some tunes, and exploring our surroundings, we had a wild and loud fuck session in front of the large picture window, which had a view of the frozen lake. One of our long-standing birthday traditions is that he puts his perfectly greased, stiff shaft in my cunt from behind and rides me until one of us passes out from pleasure. I'll never forget the feeling of my big nipples rubbing on the white bearskin rug as he rammed my beckoning hole.

The next morning we got up early and drove out onto the lake for some fishing excitement. He had no idea just how exciting it was going to get! We were all alone on this northern lake, surrounded only by abandoned cabins and cold wind. After our holes were dug and the poles positioned just right, I lay my man out on the ice. The look of excitement in his eyes was priceless. I unzipped his snowsuit and very slowly pulled out his beautiful pink prick. I maneuvered myself around so I could take the whole shaft in my mouth and then proceeded to suck him until he was spinning. Every time he was about to come, I would shut him down by squeezing his large, firm balls and removing my mouth. This went on for a good half hour. By then we could hear snowmobiles buzzing around the lake, but the thought of getting caught only added to our excitement. Finally, when I knew he couldn't take it anymore, I let him shoot his load to the back of my throat. He let out a loud scream, which echoed through the thick woods. As I removed my mouth from his rocket, I noticed that it was steaming. Vapor just kept rolling off his wonderful dick. The weekend continued for another day and a half, but now I find myself unable to continue this letter. I'm going to go find this terrific man and let him have his way with me. Or maybe I'll have my way with him. Either way, it's pure ecstasy!

—C. V., North Dakota

FUN AND FETISH

Let Your Fingers Do the Walking

My boyfriend Jeff and I live eight hundred miles apart, and although we get together as often as we can, there's still considerable time between visits during which we get very horny. We usually tell each other when we've masturbated for relief. One Monday night when Jeff called he asked me if I was in bed. I said no. He said that he was and told me to get naked and crawl between the sheets. Although I was puzzled, I was also very intrigued and did as I was told.

When I told him that I was in bed, he told me to imagine that he was there with me, squeezing my tits and sucking on my long, hard nipples. Lying there in bed listening to him; my nipples immediately became erect and began aching for his touch. Before I knew it my free hand was massaging my breast and rubbing my nipples between my thumb and finger. It felt so good!

Then he told me to imagine that his tongue was working its way down my stomach to my navel and passed then on to my dark, clipped bush, stopping just long enough to give my swollen clit a flick of the tongue before he was off lightly to suck and nip the insides of my thighs. By then I was totally caught up in what he was saying, my juices were flowing, my pussy was soaked, my clit was throbbing, and my hand was following Jeff's instructions as closely as possible.

Next, Jeff said to imagine that he was now working his masterful tongue back up the inside of my thigh to the sensitive skin between my thigh and my box. My hand was right there, stroking in place of his tongue. Then he said his tongue was thrusting into my cunt, lapping up my sweet nectar and working its way up my swollen lips to my clit. Then he said I should imagine that his hot, probing tongue was wrapping around my clit and pulling it gently between his lips.

At that point my fingers were trailing up my soaking pussy and, finding my clit, all I had to do was just gently rub it to have one of the most glorious orgasms ever, with Jeff softly saying on the phone, "Come, baby. Come."

He said that was just the beginning, and I should remember one afternoon when we were out fishing—I got on my hands and knees, and he rammed his great rod into my snatch up to the hilt, filling me up while he leaned over and squeezed my aching tits. Remembering this from our last time together and recalling the feel of his come shooting into my cunt, my pussy was overflowing with nectar. My hand stroked up to my clit and before I knew it I was having another mind-blowing orgasm.

I was so ecstatic by this long-distance method of making love that as soon as I caught my breath, I told him to lie back and think of me sitting on top of him with his magnificent shaft nestled between my hot, juicy nether lips. Then I am sliding down, kissing his wonderful body, his now wet, glistening rod sliding up my stomach to my tits, where I rub it across my erect, waiting nipples. Then he could imagine me going down a little farther so that his beautiful, hard cock is waiting, poised just below my breathless, parted lips.

I told him to imagine me swirling my tongue around the head and dipping it into his hole for that first savory taste of his come. Then I am opening my mouth wider to let his whole magnificent rod slide into the back of my throat as far as it can go. Then I close my mouth tighter and let his pole slide out while sucking on it until I am at the tip again. Imagine, I said, that I have a hold of it with both hands and I'm working my tongue down the shaft to your balls, which I take into my mouth, roll them around and tongue them one after the other. At this point, I realized that my boyfriend was as excited as I had once again become, my cunt throbbing and my juices flowing. My hand crept down to give what aid it could.

I told Jeff to imagine that I was again running my tongue up the rock-hard shaft of his cock and taking the head gently between my teeth and nibbling it. I could hear the moan that always told me that he was just about to come, and so I told him to think of me sliding his magnificent member as far into my mouth as I could while he shot his load into my eagerly swallowing throat. As I was saying this, I heard him moaning that he was coming, and as he was my hand was at my clit, bringing me to another screaming orgasm.

While it will never replace our being together, the telephone has definitely become the next best thing to being there.

—E. C., Oregon

Party Favor

My husband, Jeremy, and I have been together for ten years. I was nineteen when I met him, and I was definitely not a virgin, but I'd never had experiences with other guys like I've had with him. We've done the train, plane, and automobile quickies, but a few months ago we experienced something a little more out of the ordinary.

We were at a party for an acquaintance, which started out to be fun but became pretty boring after a while. Jeremy promised me a little surprise if things got dull. We would have left early, but had driven there with some friends who had no other way home.

Jeremy was deep in conversation with some buddies of his when I slunk over to him in my very tight, very low-cut, short black dress. He was sitting down, and I leaned over him to whisper in his ear. Needless to say, his buddies got quite a view of my cavernous cleavage, and made no point of hiding the fact that they were enjoying this. I smiled and asked Jeremy when we could go and *really* have some fun. He said, "Follow me, I've got a surprise for you."

He led me to the men's room, but not before getting us a couple of drinks from the bar. The sneaky smile on his face left me very curious. I felt uncomfortable going into the men's room, but he assured me he'd check to see that it was empty. He returned to say it was empty, and his surprise was in there. Well, we entered and he pulled out a package of edible his-and-her panties as he led me into one of the stalls. It was almost immediately that I felt that familiar wetness begin to emerge between my legs. "So, this is the surprise!"

Jeremy kissed me, our tongues meshing with the anticipation of what was to come. I unbuttoned his silk shirt, running my fingers down his soft chest hair, and when I reached his pants I became obsessed with unzipping them as soon as I could. My kisses then ran all the way down his muscular chest and nipples, my hands running down his back, until I reached his throbbing-hard dick with my mouth. I teased him for a few seconds while concentrating on his balls, then knelt on the floor, kissing him gently until I had his huge, pounding cock in my wet and hungry mouth. After sucking him for a pleasurable while, I told him I wanted him to try on the edible pants before he ejaculated. He obliged, quickly slipping into them, and I licked away until the sweet cherry taste dissolved in my moist mouth. I figured it was now my turn.

I asked Jeremy to unzip the back of my very sweaty dress, which he did while kissing my neck and back. Then I turned around in the small space, sat on the closed toilet seat, and pulled down my panty hose. Jeremy helped me slip on my version of the panties, which were grape-flavored. In a matter of seconds, it seemed, my panties were eaten away. I spread my thighs wide, and Jeremy ate me out while I tilted my head back in extreme pleasure. He told me how good I tasted, especially with remnants of grape flavor on his hungry tongue. He sucked me hard, fluttering his well-rehearsed lips and tongue all around my clit until I had to place my hand over my own mouth to keep from screaming when I came. Then I took off my dress and bra and got up, still drenched between my legs. I turned around to the sink and grabbed the edges, my nipples just inches from the faucet while Jeremy ran his fingers all over my huge, erect tits.

His fingers wandered down my tight body until he screamed, "Wow!" at how wet I was down below. When I'm horny, it's like a spigot down there. Jeremy gently opened my legs and entered me from behind, his thrusting bringing me constant pleasure. My giant, hard tits were flopping all over the place, in tune with his movements. After a couple of minutes, we heard noises just outside the door. I hesitated, and we both kept quiet while we waited for whoever was there to get out! The devilish smiles on our faces were soon replaced by sultry, hot panting when we realized our "company" had left. By now, Jeremy was going in and out of me with a fast-paced rhythm, and he was fingering my clit to no end. It felt so incredible, I couldn't help but scream and squeeze the edges of the sink when I came for a second time. I must've screamed fairly loud, because I felt Jeremy's other hand over my mouth. Just then he came, his sweet come oozing into my snatch with full force and heat. He pulsed inside me for a few seconds, then reluctantly pulled out.

When we finally emerged from the bathroom, Jeremy checked again to see if anyone was around. When the coast was clear, we made our way back to the party.

—L. K., Pennsylvania

The Husbandly Hard-on

Many years ago, I found I was playing second fiddle to a beautiful and buxom neighbor in the important wifely function of building my man's hard-ons. Our marriage had started much like most. We met at a college dance back in the days when you danced cheek to cheek and belly to belly, holding your partner close as your legs slid together to romantic music in a dimly lit hall. He had a terrific erection that was soon boring against my girlish vulva. For once I didn't pull away or pretend to ignore it, but I decided to grind back as lewdly as I knew how at the age of nineteen. I whispered in his ear that he felt "just marvelous and so big." Naturally, he asked me for a date the next night. I gave him my address, and I also told him that I hoped he would bring his "big friend."

He did just that, and though we went to a movie, we were soon petting intensely. We left the movie early and drove to a lover's lane, where we had sex with each other for the first time almost as soon as we arrived. When we came up for air, I began to giggle at my boldness of the night before. My wandering hands began petting him again until he had another hard-on, and then we had even better sex. This was a definite change from my usual pattern of behavior. I was not a virgin, but I had never taken such overt actions.

We married two and a half months later. Our honeymoon was sex, sex, sex day and night. I would greet him at the door with a French kiss, and I'd unzip his fly so I could stroke his penis and feel it jump to life in my fingers, even if we didn't fall into bed immediately. This idyllic period lasted a year and a half, until he graduated. Then we moved to another city. Our relations were heavenly whenever we had them, but the frequency was far less. We rarely did it two nights in a row, and sometimes we would go almost a week without finding the time or the inclination.

Two things happened to open my eyes. First, my sister and I overheard our husbands talking to each other when they didn't know we were around. The men were on our apartment balcony when our neighbor came out wearing a sunsuit. She was a really stunning gal, a few years older than I, a redhead (dyed, but a good job), with a pair of forty-inch honeydews straining her thin cotton halter almost to splitting, as well as practically spilling out of the deep-cut neckline. I heard my husband tell my brother-in-law that this neighbor was always giving him a hard-on. My sister's husband replied that he was a tit man, too. He asked my guy if he had ever gotten a "piece of that," and my husband said no, but he would like to. He grumbled that I almost never gave him a hard-on anymore. My brother-in-law said that my sister was "getting too settled down" and was always "acting like a wife." Were we girls surprised and mad! We sneaked out of the house and went for a long ride to talk things over.

While thinking about how I had failed to remain sexy, I began to realize that my husband and I were doing so many things for the community and the church, we weren't leaving time for a decent sex life. I knew the next move was up to me. I dispensed with girdles, which I hadn't really needed, and I began buying sexy French undies from mail-order houses. I bought dozens of naughty panties, wicked bras with holes for my nipples to poke through, and tiny, beribboned garter belts. I would give him a show at least once a week. My new nighties were for wearing around the house, not for in bed. I would wear just a sheer slip to cook dinner in, to keep his interest up—and his penis, too.

I am careful to tell my man if another guy gets hard looking at me, and this always pleases and stiffens him. I also smooch him shamelessly at movies, cocktail parties, even in lover's lanes once in a while, and I don't give a damn who knows it or thinks I am making a fool of myself. I like what he has in his pants, and that's what I am a fool about. I have even taken hula- and belly-dancing lessons so I can keep him erect. I have bought him girlie magazines, and I've sent away for nude photos and porno films. I introduced *him* to *Penthouse*. I watch for sexy things to call to his attention. If I see a well-stacked woman coming along, I nudge him and point out the jiggling yummies with a manly, ribald comment.

Many women tell me that they envy my sex life and wish they could get away with my lack of inhibition, enthusiastic emphasis on bedroom activity, and determination to monopolize my husband erotically. I tell them to let themselves go, and I am quite sure some of them have done so, even after years of lukewarm, married sex.

—Name and address withheld

Blindman's Buff

Here is what I think is a great party game, one that we students at a good Arizona college originated. It was a sultry evening, and we had a party at a male student's apartment. As it was the beginning of the term, we didn't know one another too well. There was one boy who had great physical attraction for me, but it was impossible to get to know him, what with a full curriculum and sports activities, and he seemed to care little for females. I'd begun fantasizing about him, but that night was my chance.

The game goes like this: Each boy or girl can cross the line and kiss someone of his (or her) choice, then follow it up with one minute of mild petting. Then the boys are sent out of the room while the girls undress. Each participant must wear a paper bag with eyeholes over his or her head to blind them and to make facial recognition impossible. The boys, fully clothed with paper bags over their heads, now enter. They grope for the object of their desire and hopefully, after much manhandling, recognize her through how they imagined she would feel like. After each boy thinks he has found who he was looking for, he puts a label with his name on it on her behind. Now the boys undress, and the girls try to identify the boys of their desire by running their hands all over each one. I imagined my fellow to be fairly well endowed, with hair on his chest and some on his belly. After about five or six explorations, during which I gauged for height, muscle tone, penis size, and hairiness, I found him—only he was smooth-skinned, had a lovely muscle tone, and what a straightforward erection! I was so sure it was him, I tried to kiss him, but then I remembered that big shopping bag on his head. I put a label with my signature on one of his hard ass cheeks.

When we took those silly bags off our heads, there was great rejoicing. I inspected the label on my ass, and lo and behold, there was my name on it with his signature.

The prize for mutual recognition was a nearby motel room, prepaid. Now Freddy lives with me.

—Name and address withheld

For a Better Head . . .

My boyfriend sure enjoys his blowjobs, and I usually don't mind giving them, but several weeks ago, he asked me to go down on him when I had a terrible cold. I didn't feel like it, but after a little persuasion, I went and did it. I did not take the mentholated cough drop out of my mouth, and he said it added a special tingle to the head of his cock. In no time at all, he was coming like mad! He said that it was so good, we should share it with the public.

—Name and address withheld

A Pearl of an Idea

Last Valentine's eve was a night I'll never forget. George gave me the sexiest teddy I'd ever seen, and I just had to try it on right away while he opened a bottle of wine. We started to play cards, which then turned into strip poker. But since I was only wearing one article of clothing, we had to change the rules. The winner of each round was granted a sexual favor by the other. I was feeling good, wearing this little teddy, and George was ready . . . but rules are rules. Unfortunately, I was not very successful at the game, and George started the requests.

The first was for me to fuck him in my favorite position. Well, I have lots of favorites. We became really hot as we explored new favorites. . . .

His second request was that I masturbate in front of him. I had never done that before, but nothing would stop me that night. I began rubbing myself and putting my fingers in my crotch, feeling good all over. I was moaning very loudly. George stood next to me, watching as he stroked the biggest, hardest cock a girl could want. Seeing him, I fingered myself faster until I was about to come. Then I jumped on top of him, and we fucked until we both exploded. I was shaking.

George pulled out a copy of *Penthouse* that was next to the bed, and I started reading the "Forum" letters aloud. We both got really horny from this, and my voice started cracking. That was when I announced it was my turn for a request. I stated that we would act out the next letter we read. He couldn't believe it, because some of them are really wild!

While George went to the kitchen for more wine, I read the next letter and prepared myself accordingly.

When he returned I asked him to read the letter. After he finished he turned to me and asked if I had a pearl necklace. I smiled and guided him down to my crotch. He went crazy when he saw the pearl sticking out. He pulled the rest out with his teeth, really slow. The letter was right—it felt as good coming out as it did going in. George and I spent the rest of the night playing our new game.

His last request was that I write to *Penthouse* and tell you how much we enjoy the letters.

—G. Y., New York

Porch Swinging

After my husband and I had enjoyed a leisurely dinner of barbecued steaks and a bottle of wine, things began to heat up. Sitting on the porch swing, we began to fondle each other and were soon tugging at our clothes and petting each other frantically. Ed pulled my shorts off, got on his knees, and plowed into my wet crotch with his tongue. As I massaged my hard nipples, he licked and tickled my erect clitoris. I moaned and squirmed as my breathing became out of control. I begged Ed to fill my aching hole with his enormous hard-on.

He stood up just long enough to pull his shorts down, then he lay down on his back on the porch and I eagerly slipped my soaking pussy over the head of his cock, slamming it down on his shaft. We bounced and moaned, gyrated, and eventually screamed as we came together. We stayed on the floor for about ten minutes holding each other, then went into the house to fuck again.

We were just about to get in the shower when the doorbell rang. Ed's hard-on was at full height again, so I put on my robe and went to the door. Our neighbor Doug was there with his girlfriend Stacy. Doug smiled widely, said he knew he was interrupting something, and began waving the videocassette he was holding.

By the time we all got to the living room, Doug had the VCR and TV ready to go. The tape started out with shots of his other neighbor's garage roof, the shingles going in and out of focus. Sensing our growing anger, Doug quickly told us to keep watching because the good stuff was just about to start.

I noticed then that Stacy was gently massaging Doug's crotch. Just as I thought *Oh no. He wouldn't,* I saw our porch come into focus. And sure enough, there I was with my shirt pushed up over my breasts and Ed's head bobbing between my thighs. We just sat there with our mouths hanging open as the camera zoomed in on Ed's tongue darting about in my crotch.

When I turned around, Doug and Stacy were groping each other passionately and pulling off their clothes. I watched in amazement as they quickly disrobed and began licking and sucking each other everywhere. I noticed that Ed's reaction to all this was to masturbate under his robe. Without another thought, I flopped down to the floor and began to suck that great big hard-on. As I licked up and down, I could feel my crotch getting wet. I felt someone's hands pull my robe up off my bottom, then a tongue licking my soaked crotch. When I looked around, I was surprised—and very excited—to discover that it was Stacy who was so expertly licking my twat.

I could hear Doug moaning and I knew he had mounted Stacy and was having the ride of his life. I bobbed my head over Ed's thrusting hardness while Stacy ate away at my hot snatch and Doug pounded her from behind. The room was filled with shouts of ecstasy and the smell of sex as Doug's moans told us that he was about to come. At this signal Ed began eagerly humping my mouth, and Stacy's excitement was beginning to improve her agility in licking my sopping pussy. We all came in one shattering orgasmic wave from Doug to Ed.

Of course, the evening didn't stop there, and we have the videos to prove it!

—H. W., Wisconsin

A Different Approach

Most men are so sweet and gullible. I have yet to meet a member of the opposite sex who would refuse to have sex with me. Occasionally, about twice a year, I take risks. I drive to a neighboring town and go to a supermarket. I look for the perfect stranger, walk up to him, introduce myself, and ask him to give me an hour of his time. I immediately follow up with the simple statement: "I'd like to have sex with you."

The reactions vary only in form. All men so far have followed me to a motel. I make it clear from the beginning that I am not a hooker and I only want them to pay for the room. After wild, uninhibited sex (always using condoms) I dismiss them before I take a long, hot bath. Over the years I have targeted older gentlemen. The leisurely, relaxed pace for foreplay and fucking of men in their fifties and sixties is far superior to the frantic impatience of younger males. Surprising, also, is the wonderful strong libido of these men who are supposed to be past their prime.

I spent a most beautiful afternoon with Frank, sixty-six, who was also the only one I saw more than once and whom I finally introduced to my husband and into our bedroom for threesomes. Dave and I have an open marriage and never deny each other the extracurricular carnal experience.

I saw Frank at the produce counter, squeezing tomatoes. He answered my smile with a big grin. After my introduction and statement of intent, he followed me to the motel. I was dressed for the occasion in black-lace garters and panties under my skirt and blouse. I proceeded with a salacious striptease, dropping my skirt, unbuttoning my blouse.

A warm rush of anticipation permeated my body as I freed my breasts and massaged them. Frank helped me unhook my stockings. I bent down to wiggle my ass just inches from his face. He kissed my buttocks, and slowly stripped the hose down my legs. I moistened from the excitement, and between my legs I noticed the wetness through my panties. I took Frank's hand and placed it squarely on my sex. He gently rubbed my pussy through the fabric, and I told him how good it felt. Then he stripped down my panties. His hands now went on a trip to all the most intimate parts of my body. They tenderly traveled up my thighs, to the inside, back over my ass cheeks, up my spine, under my arms, over my shoulders, along my neck behind my ears—I shuddered in delight. His fingertips felt the outline of my face. I turned toward him. His hands wandered to my tits, and caressed them ever so gently. My nipples were hard and begged to be touched. He caressed them and leaned down to kiss them. Meanwhile, my arousal reached a high pitch. I wanted him so much now that I opened his shirt, revealing the mat of gray hair on his chest. I burrowed my head into it and licked his nipples. His trousers came down. So did his shorts. His cannon was loose, but rock-hard.

I marveled at this old young man's equipment and its readiness. I enjoyed the sight of it, its scent, its touch. I pushed him onto his back and climbed on top of him in the classic sixty-nine. On my knees, my pelvis over his face, he had all my charms to see, and he murmured his appreciation of them.

I slowly deep-throated him while he touched my pussy. My tits dangled to make contact. Oh, how delicious were his tongue and lips. The vibration of his deep moans exquisitely titillated my cunt, and I squealed in the transport of an intense orgasm. Frank knew, and he let up in his ministrations so I could recover my senses. He waited until the supersensitivity between my legs subsided.

It did not take long until I felt raunchy again. I turned, pressed my sex upon his pole, guiding it with my hands into my pussy. He looked at me and smiled. I leaned over and kissed him deeply, smelling my juices on his face. I slowly rose and fell, creating the perfect friction between us. He urgently met my movements. Then he held on to me tightly, rolled on top, and commenced some vigorous fucking. Oh, how I loved it. His pubic bone hit my clit powerfully. My climax began to rise, and I told him so. With a loud groan, his body jerked violently. I came and came as he trembled all over and spilled his come into me.

Frank has become a good friend, and we are delighted to have him come to our bedroom. He is sensuously considerate. He is sixty-seven years old now, and his sexual energy and drive are amazing.

—T. W., California

Brief Encounter

I am a twenty-five-year-old, well-built woman who enjoys reading "Forum," especially with my man looking over my shoulder. I think a pair of bikini panties on a man is a fantastic turn-on, especially when he has a body like my man does. Just seeing that line across his rear through a pair of tight jeans makes me want to grab his cheeks. The front is better yet, because there's always a beautiful bulge just aching to be caressed. My lover first introduced me to his panty fetish about a year and a half ago, and we have shared some wonderful experiences ever since. I've never felt anything as exciting as a man's balls and hard prick through a pair of soft, sheer panties, and the more I caress him, the larger he grows, until his prick begins to grow out of the lacy edge and we are ready to make love.

One evening, he came over and asked me to undress him, so I slipped my hand into his jeans and felt his cute little cheeks through the soft nylon. I couldn't wait to get his pants off. To my delighted surprise, he didn't have one pair of daring little panties on, but five—each more daring than the one before. First I slowly removed a print pair, caressing his balls as I slipped them off, only to reveal a pair of black, wet-look string bikinis that by now held only his balls, for his prick had grown quite large. As I took those off, his hand slipped into my lace panties and began exploring my already very wet pussy, making me want him even more. The next pair left almost nothing to the imagination—they were beautifully sheer and pink and gave me a fantastic view of his throbbing organ. I stripped him of those dainty things, only to see that he had adorned his body with two pairs of crotchless panties. We left the last pair on, for they were slit from front to back and trimmed with a little black lace—just to tease. I was so hot, I knew that as soon as he entered me, I would come, and I did—not once, but several times, until we both exploded together in a fantastic climax. My lover has more than a hundred pairs of panties, many of which I have given him—he loves the way they feel on his body, and so do I.

—Name and address withheld

Bathing-Cap Trap

I am thirty years old and men have told me I'm attractive, yet I don't consider myself overly sexy. A few months ago, when my husband and I decided to take separate vacations, I opted for the sunny beaches of Acapulco, where I was lucky enough to meet a handsome young man who appeared to enjoy some affluence.

While we were swimming one day, my new boyfriend embraced me from behind, tightly cupping my breasts. I could feel him becoming hard, and I reached behind me, pulled his rock-hard penis out of his bathing suit, and placed it between my legs. He climaxed rather quickly as I flexed my thigh muscles. As he came he put both of his hands on my head and began to kiss and lick my rubber swim cap. Having read *Penthouse,* I am tolerant of fetishes and thought nothing of it.

Of course, we became lovers that afternoon. I brought him to my suite, where he asked me to wear my swim cap during our lovemaking. He seemed particularly to like holding my rubber cap as I sucked his cock.

I must say that he reciprocated and gave me the best oral love I have ever had. After his first orgasm, he went down on me forty-five minutes at least, making me very happy indeed.

The next day he took me to a leather shop and bought me a red-leather minidress, a black-leather coat, and high boots. We then returned to the hotel, and he asked me to wear combinations of the new gear as we made love. I really turned him on. I had one of those clear vinyl raincoats in my closet, and when he saw that, he asked me to wear it with nothing on underneath except my boots. He began to get hard and masturbate. I didn't want him to do that, so I climbed on top of him and fucked him like a wild woman! It turned me on like nothing had before, and I had a fantastic orgasm!

We had a wonderful two weeks together and had the most fantastic sex, although sometimes it seemed that he was more interested in what I wore than in me. But I didn't care, because I was getting a lot of his hard cock. I think we screwed more often in those two weeks than my husband and I have in five years of marriage. When I came home, I modeled the leather garments for my husband, but he didn't seem at all interested. However, when I wore the gear on a shopping trip downtown, I noticed many men staring at me in a very horny way, which excited me.

In crowds, many men would brush up against me with their hands, feeling the smooth leather. In an elevator, one man put his hand on my bottom. As we got out, I turned to him, and said, "Like my outfit?" He stammered and nodded. I suggested that we go somewhere where he could really enjoy it. He said he couldn't afford it, and I explained that I wasn't a professional. We went to the enclosed parking lot and to my car, where we had a sensational fucking and sucking session. This man, too, loved to caress my leather as we screwed.

Now, whenever I'm horny, I put on my "fucking clothes," and I have my pick of most men on the streets. I can be very selective. I just wait until I get an admiring glance from someone who looks good to me. I especially love rainy days. I bought some vinyl and thigh-high boots like some of your *Penthouse* girls wear. I wear my red-leather minidress and my clear vinyl raincoat. It's my most successful outfit!

—Name and address withheld

If the Shoe Fits . . .

I am taking the liberty of writing to you in regard to a high-heel fetish. I am just twenty years old, four-foot-ten, and weigh ninety-six pounds. But my figure is considered very good, and I've been told I have beautiful legs. I've been married for eleven months. When I was sixteen, I purchased my first pair of high heels. The heels were four inches, and I enjoyed them very much, as they made me appear tall. Since I am short my feet are also very small, so I still wear the same size. I never did know what a high-heel fetish was until I met my husband, two years ago.

He asked me if I could wear higher heels, and I told him that a four-inch heel was the highest I could purchase, and that since my feet are very small, I did not think I could wear higher heels. About two weeks later, while out on a date, he parked his car and from the trunk brought out three new pairs of shoes in my size. They all had five-inch heels. He said he ordered them from Frederick's of Hollywood. It was a little difficult at first being raised another inch in height, but in no time at all I was used to wearing them constantly. But a month later, he again said that he would love to see me in higher heels. I argued that it wouldn't be possible. Then the following week we visited a custom shoe builder in Pittsburgh, who, after looking at my high instep and the arch of my feet, insisted with my boyfriend that I could easily wear a six-inch heel. At this point I really was scared. I felt that it would be impossible to wear shoes with heels that height, but again I had no say in the matter, and I love my boyfriend.

So both of my feet were measured very carefully,

and my boyfriend ordered two pairs of shoes, both pairs with ankle straps to help hold the shoe on my foot. I thought the shoes would be mailed to my boyfriend, but no, we had to go back for the final fitting. The shoes fit wonderfully, but after ten minutes, I got a cramp in both calves of my legs, and had to remove both shoes. The man then put a small piece of cork under the ball of each foot, and slipped the shoes back on my feet. The cramp was gone, and did not come back. Amazing as it was, my boyfriend was thrilled as I walked around Pittsburgh for better than an hour. But that night when I got home, my legs, from the ankles up to my hips, throbbed something fierce. Again, I got really used to wearing the six-inch heels and got a special thrill in wearing them—to say nothing of how much my boyfriend enjoyed seeing me walk around in them.

Right after we were married, once again he said how he would love to see me "perched" (that's the word he used) on even higher heels. I said no way was it possible to wear higher heels, and that's what I thought. Two weeks later I was wearing shoes with eight-inch heels (but with two-inch platform soles). And a few weeks later, I had shoes with nine-inch heels and three-inch platforms! And believe it or not, I am getting to be quite an expert at wearing them.

Some of my good friends tell me that some people call me the "high-heel freak," but that doesn't bother me, as I love my husband, and I know he loves me.

That's what is important to me. Three months ago my husband came up with an idea that perhaps I could wear a ballet type of shoe. It would have no vamp, my toes would be pointed straight down with a separate leather loop for each toe, and the tips of my toes would rest on heavy cotton padding. Well, I have the shoes now. They are black patent leather, and they lace onto my foot at the instep. They also have heavy ankle straps, and are very light in weight. These shoes have a full ten-inch heel.

I have been wearing them every night in our bedroom for my husband's pleasure, but it was a week before I could stand in them, and it took a good month of practice before I could actually walk in them. Now every night I walk around our bedroom wearing these shoes for nearly twenty minutes before our marital relations. It drives my husband crazy, and I myself really enjoy wearing these out-of-this-world shoes. It has made our marriage a very, very happy one.

My husband would love to have me wear these shoes in public, and I said I would after I get used to wearing them for about two hours. I must admit, it requires a lot of stamina to wear this type of shoe, but for my husband's love, I would stop at nothing as long as it makes him happy. I realize how dangerous these shoes can be if I should fall, as I have read of quite a few people falling off their shoes and breaking bones. But I guess I have been very fortunate.

—*Name and address withheld*

Bridge Club

My friend since high school, Liz, and I and two other girls have been very close for years—we would go on vacations together, play cards, go to the theater and movies, double-date, and so forth. Then Liz got married, while the other three of us stayed single (we range in age from nineteen to twenty-two). But the four of us have still remained close friends, and Liz's husband, Bob, has sort of become part of the group, too. The fella she married is extremely good-looking, well built, and a very nice guy. And I must say that whatever resentment there was among the remaining three of us when she got married—it was mostly jealousy—soon passed as we go to know him better, and as we found our group was not splitting up. When Liz was not there, the three of us often joked about how well hung he must be (especially after being at the beach with them, or seeing him in short cutoffs) and speculated about their sex life . . . but not in her presence.

But one day Liz and I and one of the other girls were in Liz's house, looking over some magazines with male nudes and comparing the qualities of the various men pictured. Liz was pretty quiet until she burst out that her husband was better than any of those pictured—even one of the pictures we were drooling over. We kind of put her down when she walked out of the room (we thought she was mad), but she returned with a box of photos. Were we surprised to see that they were all of Bob in some fantastic nude poses—quite a few with a hard-on. Liz was in a few of the pictures herself (the camera had a self-timer, she told us), but she was dressed or partially dressed. For example, she would be standing behind him, holding or stretching his hard-on. We knew that she was an avid photographer from the various trips we'd been on together, and that she had expensive photo equipment, but this really caught us by surprise. Also, we got really turned on by looking at these photos (much more than by the magazines, since he really was better-looking and better built). Since she was being so open with us, we admitted how we often talked and fantasized about Bob.

The next time we had our monthly bridge game at her house (our fourth friend was there this time), Liz had quite a surprise for us. Bob, who usually talked with us for a while and then disappeared, stayed around the whole time, and was extremely friendly and talkative. After about an hour of playing, Liz asked if we'd like to watch a photo session with Bob. Of course, none of us protested, although we weren't quite sure what she had in mind. We were in the family room in the basement of their home, and she brought out her photo equipment and lights while Bob set up the backdrop and some other props. He left the room and returned in a robe. When Liz was ready, he got in position and threw off his robe. The three of us let out an audible gasp as we saw him completely nude. He's really quite a man—beautifully proportioned, just the right amount of body hair and muscles for my taste, small, tight ass, nice legs, and best of all, a thick penis, which was about four inches, in its soft stage at that point. Liz took several poses before she invited each of us to get in the photos. We all made believe we wanted the others to go first, but I finally started. I stood next to him, behind him, et cetera, but didn't touch him with my hands. When the next one went, Liz posed her and Bob more precisely and told the girl to touch him on the hips and chest in some rather sexy poses. Finally, when the fourth girl went in, Liz told Bob she wanted a hard-on for this one and then asked Ann if she wanted to help. Without further instructions, Ann grabbed his penis, and he was hard in an instant. We all gasped as his penis grew and grew and grew. (Later we all measured it at about eight inches long and six inches around.) Although we had seen it before in the pictures, it was much more exciting in the flesh. Ann continued posing with Bob, stroking his penis, balls, and ass. She and Bob (and the rest of us) got really worked up. When I got a second chance to pose with him, I knew I wanted to take some of my clothes off and get groped in return, but I didn't want to turn this into an orgy without Liz's okay. None of us had ever engaged in any kind of group sex—certainly not within *our* group. Finally, Liz said she wanted a picture of Bob coming. She told me to hold his penis very tight and pull way back on it, from behind, so his penis was stretched real tight—and not to pump it at all. This was unusual for me (I'd jerked boys off before, but never like this, and I didn't think it was possible for them to come without any motion). I held his penis for about two minutes like this, squeezing harder all the time. I could feel it throbbing and contracting in my hand. He made a few back-and-forth movements, and finally he squirted—at least three feet. Liz got every bit of that in the photograph (which we saw a few days later).

After that, Bob left the room, and Liz cleaned up and—believe it or not—asked us to play some more bridge.

Where all this will lead is anyone's guess, although let me say for myself, it's gotten me real horny—to the point where I masturbate at home much more often. In addition, I've gotten much bolder and more aggressive with my dates and the fellas I go out with. On several dates I've had recently (once even on a first date), I began groping and undressing them before they did anything except kiss me.

—Name and address withheld

What a Show-off!

My husband and I have been married two years, and about a year ago he started bringing home *Penthouse*—rather furtively at first, I must admit, as I suppose he didn't know what my reaction would be. Anyway, one night I caught him avidly admiring one of your Pets and as it obviously pleased him, I naturally felt a little jealous. We talked it over, and when I realized that the poses of the girls really turned him on, I began to think seriously about it: I certainly wasn't going to take second place to a photograph, however beautiful the girl (and may I say that your models are lovely).

As it happened, for our holiday this year we went to Copenhagen. We both became a little tiddly one night and ended up at a sex show in one of the less reputable areas of the city. Surprisingly enough, I thoroughly enjoyed it, though it is generally held that women are not excited by visual stimuli as men are. The girls (and men) were all attractive with good physiques, and I think it was their honest enjoyment of sex that led me to overcome inhibition and watch with fascination. We saw strippers, lesbian couples masturbating each other with vibrators, coitus and cunnilingus in many different positions. After a while I noticed that my husband was very aroused, and I teased him about it, saying that I could do better than any of the girls when we got back to our hotel. That night we made love with more enthusiasm than for a long time—and that's saying something!

As it was our anniversary the next day, I decided to give him something special, and the next morning, under the pretext of going to the hairdresser, I went to a sex shop and bought some rather erotic lingerie—a purple-satin open bra and matching briefs that were crotchless. When I returned my husband was out, so I spent a pleasant half hour trying on my purchases and adopting different poses in front of the bedroom mirror. I remember thinking to myself, "God, if this doesn't give him the biggest hard-on of his life, nothing will." It all seemed such a childish game at the time.

That evening after dinner I suggested an early night, and while my husband was getting undressed I went into the bathroom and "dressed to kill," so to speak. I'll always remember the look of rapture on his face as I came into the bedroom—I had on the bra and briefs plus a tight white sweater which emphasized my figure, and a wide leather belt. I consider myself not bad-looking for thirty-one and I certainly did full justice to the sweater, which was a size too small anyway. As the liqueurs after dinner had inflamed us both, and I had been feeling not a little randy for some time, inhibition was scarcely a problem. I paraded round for a few minutes wiggling my hips and cupping my breasts in my hands, while all he could do was to stare in pleasurable amazement. Then I proceeded to grind my hips, standing by the bed just out of his reach, and slowly pulled off my sweater. By now I was enjoying it almost as much as he was, and the sight of his erection standing up like a harbor bollard told me I was doing all right. I then knelt on the bed and held out my breasts for his admiration, using a few four-letter words by way of encouragement. When I took off my bra and draped it round his penis, I thought he was going to come there and then. Anyway, to cut a long story short, it led to the longest and most excruciatingly pleasurable lovemaking of my life.

I have never felt so much of a woman as that first night I "gave him a show," though we have done it many times since. I'm convinced that if more wives would let themselves go in this way, even once in a while, prostitutes would be out of business. I can certainly recommend it to any married couple, and the sensation the wife experiences in arousing her husband like this is a pleasure in itself, not to mention the tumultuous lovemaking it's bound to provoke. If you print this we'll both be looking forward to reading other wives' comments and their suggestions. Need I say where we're going for our holiday next year?

—Mrs. L. D., Newcastle-upon-Tyne, England

Art and Amputees

Being an amputee myself, I have been intrigued by the recent correspondence advocating one-legged Pets and recounting what great sex objects we are. Actually, it's a lot less enthralling and more mundane to be without a leg than your correspondents would have us believe, particularly the one who spends her time gliding from one Boston bar to another on her aluminum crutches, picking up men by letting the end of her stump poke out a bit below her skirt. It's true that some guys are turned on by our dangling modifiers, but they are outnumbered by those who find the whole idea repulsive and would no more be seen with a one-legged girl than with a rosy-cheeked baboon. And given the American fetish for apparent perfection and success, it's understandable.

Our supposed sexual desirability is more myth than reality. If anything, the loss of a limb creates a barrier, making it harder to meet people in spite of whatever charms and talents we may otherwise possess. Too often, what at first appears to be interest in us proves to be nothing more than a search for novelty and cheap thrills. That is not to say that we are damned by our flaws to a life of celibacy—far from it—but it is an added burden that I would rather do without. It gets tedious being stared at and deferred to, not to mention having to rely on mechanical contrivances that won't go quite everywhere to get about.

To be perfectly honest, being minus much of my left leg is not exactly the greatest thing that ever happened to me, but after a while one comes to terms with it and learns to get by. It gives my husband something to play with—an ironic dividend. Not that that has much to do with us or why he married me. He would have preferred me complete, but neither of us had much choice in the matter.

—Mrs. S. F., Pittsburgh, Pennsylvania

Monopede Mania

Several weeks ago my roommate was given a copy of *Penthouse* magazine with readers' letters entitled

Monopede Mania. Since we are both amputees, she called and told me about it. I was able to acquire several back issues and was quite interested in your readers' comments on this subject. Then I decided to write about my own experiences.

I lost both feet in an accident some time ago and, as can be imagined, was terribly depressed; doubly so since I was a professional dancer. However, life must go on and mine did. I was fitted with artificial feet and went to work with a large insurance firm. I shared an apartment with a coworker and gradually became very content with my new work. An advantage that a foot amputee has over other types of amputees is that we can walk on our stumps, and this I learned to do well.

I had formed the habit of removing my artificial feet when I got home from work if there were no visitors. One evening I was alone when the doorbell rang. I was wearing hot pants and an old shirt, so the man at the door, who was a salesman, couldn't help seeing my legs. When he noticed my bare stumps, he got an immediate and obvious erection. He became flustered and quickly left. I was perplexed by his behavior but didn't think too much more about it until a similar incident occurred several weeks later.

During that time I had been dating a friend of my roommate's boyfriend and decided to see what his reaction to my stumps would be. Several days later we had dinner alone in the apartment. After the meal I mixed some drinks, excused myself, and went into the bedroom to change. I removed my feet and put on a very short skirt and sexy blouse, and then padded back into the living room on my stumps. His eyes bugged out when he saw me and he couldn't take them off my legs. I sat on the far end of the couch and stretched my legs out so that they touched his thigh. He began stroking my stumps, and we both became very aroused. I reached over and unzipped his fly and gently massaged his penis with the tips of my stumps. This was more than he could stand, and he took me into the bedroom for a very passionate evening of lovemaking.

I have discussed this with other women amputees and have found that sexual attraction for amputated limbs is almost universal. Most commonly, men say they are attracted to women for the usual reasons, but that a stump is extremely sexy, and being with a woman with an amputated leg heightens their sexual enjoyment. I am no longer sensitive about my feet and sometimes emphasize not having any. I had a pair of boots made that have small walking surfaces similar to flat ice-skate blades. When I wear these, it is certainly obvious that I don't have any feet. I also have a pair of boots that end in wide, round wooden pegs. And a man once gave me a pair of shoes with six-inch stiletto heels and I had special feet made so that I could wear them. I would not try to walk far in them but can get around well enough, and men enjoy seeing me wear them.

We are hoping that *Penthouse* will begin printing photos of amputee girls. It would have great appeal to men, and would be a tremendous morale booster to amputee women everywhere, who would learn that their amputations are a sexual advantage.

—K. A., Venice, California

The Iceman Cometh

I've been seeing a really great guy for about a year now. I'll call him The Iceman. Not only does he love to suck on ice, but he can do wonders with an ice cube. He can hold a cube in his mouth while tracing it along every sensitive area on my body. After letting it melt he licks every last bit of water from my body.

We are always looking for new sexual experiences to try with one another. One night we decided to rent a room in a motel and meet there for the evening. It was wonderful, to say the least. From the moment The Iceman showed up at the door until he left, my whole body was in total bliss. When he came in I was lying in the middle of the bed wearing a skimpy white top, the tiniest of panties, and a big smile. As soon as he crawled up onto the bed with me I knew I was in for several hours of the best kind of hot, mind-blowing sex.

He started kissing me so softly at first, then began to slide his tongue farther and farther down my throat. He took his hands and rubbed them up and down the length of my body, gently caressing me and holding me close in his arms. He knows this relaxes me and really gets me in the mood for making love. He kept rubbing my body, then slowly caressed my hips and ass.

Finally, he slid his hand underneath my panties and slowly rubbed his fingers across my mound, causing a rush throughout my entire body. Then his fingers teased their way across my opening, touching just enough to make me squirm closer to his hand. The deliberate slowness of his touch made my body crave him even more.

Soon, his magical digits were moving easily in the wetness of my now dripping pussy. Just as his tongue met mine, his fingers slid deep into my pussy, causing me to have one of the most intense orgasms ever.

From that first climax until the final one, The Iceman never hurried. He took his time making me come over and over until I thought I'd go crazy if he didn't stop. After I calmed down from his wonderful foreplay, we undressed completely. Then I took his hot, throbbing dick in my mouth and sucked on him until he was almost ready to blow. Whenever he gets to the point where he is just about to come he stops me. He knows I have to have him inside of me when he comes.

Then he began rubbing the head of his dick right near my wet opening, teasing me with his hardness until, without warning, his cock gradually and completely filled my dripping box. He took his time entering me, and the sensation was unimaginable. I couldn't help but scream out his name before my body began a new series of orgasms. The Iceman doesn't just slide in, pull back, and start the normal routine of fucking. He slides all the way in very slowly, then just holds still and waits. He knows that if he is patient, I will come several times. I always do.

Then he slowly moved back and forth a few times before casually brushing his fingers across my clit, knowing this would send me into orbit. After my next wave of orgasms, he repositioned himself so that the head of his cock went deep before he began pounding my pussy. Before long I was crying out his name over and over again while trying to concentrate on his satisfaction. The Iceman is always so in control of the situation that sometimes it is hard for me to remember his needs. Then he looked deep into my eyes and knew that he had been doing a superlative job of making love to me. He was ready for his own release.

The instant his hot come began shooting deep within me, I exploded again with the most satisfiying climax of all. I felt his massive load filling my pussy and his hard tool throbbing deep within my box. It was the ultimate fuck. He didn't just stop and roll off me—he slowly brought me back down to earth and kissed me one last time, long and hard, making this session of lovemaking another work of art. I rested, thinking about round two and hoping the ice machine down the hall was in working order.

—R. C., Georgia

FAST FOOD

Orgasmic Orgy

My boyfriend and I were watching television when several of his buddies came over. All they talked about was sex and having an orgy. They talked and talked and talked, hinting subtly about having one—with me. Now, normally I'm not into kinky things, but lately my boyfriend and I have been getting into some pretty unusual stuff, like doing it outside on the wet, slushy, muddy ground and having what I call "salad sex"—when we use various items such as celery, cucumbers, carrots, and sometimes salad dressing (our favorite is Italian).

Without giving it another minute's thought, I stood up and stripped in front of them all, going very slowly and dancing seductively. My breasts heaved at the sight of the men hastily stripping off their clothing and sheepishly looking at one another. They had me sit in a chair and asked me to close my eyes. As I did so, I could feel my body becoming hot, and my pussy becoming wet.

My boyfriend talked to me in a deep, husky voice as he slid a cold cucumber up my pussy, laughing as I moaned at the pleasure the succulent vegetable gave me. I licked my lips as they poured Italian dressing over my sweating body. I was so horny, sitting still was becoming very difficult. Someone rubbed his dick across the dressing that was running down my body, and brought it up to my lips. I lavishly licked and sucked the enlarged penis. He withdrew, and started sucking and teasing my tits with his tongue. I groaned with delight, hearing others groaning around me.

I arched my back when another began rubbing me down, very gently at first, then harder and faster. He inserted his wet hand inside me and slowly worked in and out of my cunt. Before I knew it, my body was heaving in orgasm. My boyfriend told me to open my eyes, and when I did, not only were the guys still there, but some women had joined them as well. The girls quickly stripped and we fucked on the floor of my apartment for the rest of the evening, with and without the addition of Italian dressing. Now every Friday night we have an orgy, and I can't eat a salad without thinking about it!

—W. T., Texas

Dinner Is Served

I was pissed! Every time Tim and I wanted to get in some good fucking, something got in the way. First it was his job, then I was sick, then his sister arrived unexpectedly for a visit. It had been over two weeks since we'd fucked, and we were horny as hell. So here we were in our favorite restaurant. Tim had to go back to the office right after dinner, and I was truly ticked off.

As I played with my salad, all I could think about was his big cock, swollen and purple with a drop of jism plugging its eye. I wanted that prick so much it hurt. Finally, I'd had enough. Reaching under the tablecloth, I placed my palm on his crotch. Sure enough, it was as hard as an iron rod.

"This is not the place," he grumbled between pants.

"It's going to be the place," I said, sliding under the tablecloth onto the floor. Kneeling between his legs, I unzipped his pants, reached in, and pulled his large member through the slit in his boxers. He was so stiff with passion that it took a real effort to bend his prick forward, then down.

I grasped his cock with my hand, massaging it with palm and fingers. The fat, bulbous tip pushed and shuddered against the smooth skin of my palm. I could hear Tim panting above me. My mouth was level with his cock. Licking my lips, I leaned forward and ran the tip of my tongue up and across his balls and along his prick's length to the head. The taste of his flesh shot a ribbon of fire through my cunt, my clit pulsating to the thrusting and throbbing of his dick.

I licked up, over, and around the whole head, relishing the taste of his cockflesh and musky sweat. I could feel my snatch becoming soaked with my own lust juices. With my free hand, I pushed aside my panties and felt for my clit. It was slippery wet with cunt juices, and as I rolled it between my fingers, waves of pleasure washed through my body.

Suddenly Tim began thrusting more forcefully. I moved my head to his rhythm as his dick slid back and forth, distending my cheeks with its movement. I wanted to take his whole length in my mouth and down my throat. It had been so long since I'd tasted Tim's come, I was going to make sure that he shot his load in my mouth.

Pumping furiously, I fondled his taut nuts with my free hand while bobbing my head up and down on his slick shaft. With a muffled moan, he blasted warm, salty jism into my mouth. It flooded so fast, I couldn't swallow quickly enough. Some of it gushed around his cock and my mouth, through my lips and down my chin. This blast of jism and my clit-diddling fingers triggered an intense climax, my cunt contracting as I quaked with a violent release.

"Your main course, sir," came the voice of our waiter. I heard the clatter of plates and retreating footsteps. I slipped back up to my seat, wiped my chin, and began to eat my rare steak. It was good, but not as good as Tim's raw meat.

—G. W., South Carolina

Strawberry Monday

It was a typical Monday morning. Bob had gone to work, and I was straightening up the apartment. Around midmorning, it began to pour outside. Bob appeared in the kitchen doorway and announced that he was going to take the rest of the day off. After a weekend of sipping wine and fucking it was hard to believe that we were going to have another day of it. I was already getting warm just thinking about it. Bob went to the store while I pulled out the sleeper sofa and made it up. He returned shortly with a bottle of champagne and a basket of fresh strawberries.

Little did I know that what was ahead was to be the most romantic, erotic experience of my life. As we sat on the sofa bed feeding each other strawberries and sipping champagne, the ceiling fan above felt like a cool summer breeze on our naked bodies. Bob moved to the opposite end of the bed. His blue eyes took in every inch of my body, and I wanted him to do anything to me. He crept up the inside of my legs with his tongue, up to my thighs, teasingly licking his way to my anxious pussy. Earlier, while he was at the store, I had massaged a bit of strawberry oil between my legs and onto the outer lips of my pussy for some added excitement—and excite me it did!

Bob took a strawberry and rubbed it on my clit as he ran his hot tongue around after it. What a sensation! My whole body melted into his mouth as he kept doing this with strawberry after strawberry. Then, to heighten the passion, he sprayed whipped cream on my pussy, and sucked it off until I thought I would climb the walls. I wanted his cock so bad I could taste it. That was next as he finally turned around so I could see and feel his hard, throbbing muscle.

As I licked his balls, he kept going down on me, licking and sucking off the strawberries and whipped cream until I couldn't stand it. He finally gave my hot, dripping pussy our favorite toy—a multispeed, multiposition, vibrating cock, which at this point took me to another world. As he worked it in and out I dripped strawberry oil down the crack of his ass and onto his balls as they bounced in front of my mouth. I watched his cock get harder until I had to have my mouth on all of it.

He was making me come nonstop with what he was doing with our toy and his mouth. I had to have his cock in me, and he must have sensed this as he turned around and pushed his hard thing into my pulsating cunt. We both came in waves of ecstasy instantly.

After a ten-minute break, it was my turn. I took the strawberries, rubbed one on the head of his cock, and nibbled at it with my teeth. The juice ran down over his balls as I followed it with my tongue up and down over the head. It tasted luscious. Then I took the whipped cream, dotted his nipples, and made a trail down his stomach to his hips and down across his thighs and back up his hard cock. My tongue followed the same path and slowly sucked at the cream until I had it all over both of our bodies. Then I devoured his prick all the way down my throat as his come sprayed into my mouth in a hot shower of pleasure. As we lay there with the cool breeze on our sticky bodies, we decided that Mondays weren't all that bad, and without a doubt, strawberries are our favorite food.

—P. T., Rhode Island

Sundaes on Sunday

Every weekend my boyfriend Hank and I go out for hot-fudge sundaes—it's his favorite dessert. One day I decided to give him a sundae he would never forget. I reserved a hotel room so we could have complete privacy, then headed for the grocery store. I bought whipped cream, cherries, chocolate syrup, and one banana. To get him to the room, I told him I wanted to get away for the weekend and he should meet me at the hotel.

I was already waiting in the room when he walked in. When he saw me his eyes bulged out and his penis started to do the same. There I was, lying spread-eagled, naked on the bed. I had put the whipped cream around my nipples and trailed it down to my juicy cunt, where I had sprayed some between my wet lips and inside my hole. I had also placed one maraschino cherry inside of my pussy, leaving the stem hanging out. I took the banana and started teasing my clit with it.

Hank had already started undressing, and his erection was growing even stronger. Then I put the banana in my mouth and started giving it a blowjob. Hank couldn't handle it anymore. He jumped on the bed and plunged his face deep into my pussy. He licked and sucked up all of the sweets and soon found the cherry stem. He grabbed it with his teeth, pulled it out with slow force, and fed it to me. With incredible force he shoved his tongue deep inside of me and tongue-fucked me until I came with a huge orgasmic release.

Next Hank started to lick the cream off of my nipples—but I took control. I rolled him over and teased *his* nipples with my tongue until they became erect. At the same time, I was letting his balls slide back and forth between my fingers. I could tell he was ready for more—his penis was dying for attention. I took the can of whipped cream, leaned back, and sprayed it into my mouth. Without swallowing, I bent down and took his fully erect tool into my hungry mouth. He groaned with pleasure and begged for more. I was sucking hard and knew he would come any minute, but I wanted him to wait. I took the chocolate syrup and poured it all over him, retracing the lines with the whipped cream. I took a cherry, dipped it onto his chest, and fed it to him. Then I licked up every last drop as I lavishly stroked his penis. I wanted this to be the best orgasm of his life! I took the chocolate syrup and the whipped cream and filled my pulsating cunt. Then I made him put his hands behind his head and told him not to move. I straddled him—carefully so none of what was inside me would fall out—and eased myself onto his rock-hard dick. He let out a loud moan as he felt my warmth and wetness engulf him and my crotch grinding against his.

I wanted us to come together, but the intense pleasure was too much for me, and I couldn't help but explode. By the time he was ready to erupt, though, I started to feel another orgasm coming on. We started moving together slowly, then faster, then all of a sudden he burst inside of me with full force, and I came seconds later. We both fell in exhaustion and I could still feel his sweet juices inside me. Nevertheless, it was the best sundae I ever had, and one that I don't think he'll soon forget.

—L. K., South Carolina

Heaven in a Jar

On the way to a weekend-long rock concert, my lover and I spotted a roadside shop in the country advertising "new honey." Both being lovers of this sweet, sexual fluid, our mouths watered at the prospect of buying some on our way back home. Since we had a third passenger in the car, our obvious excitement had to be contained. We sucked and fucked throughout the weekend, but I knew that I was really saving the best for last. For three days I imagined what I would do with a fresh pot of country honey. I had teased myself into complete horniness, and was especially happy to hear that our passenger had found his own ride home! As we made our way back to the city, we eagerly pulled into the shop to buy the precious liquid.

Once we got back on the highway, I cracked open the sealed lid and swirled my finger into the thick, sticky substance, feeling the juices of my already hot pussy starting to flow. It coated my finger seductively and I slipped it into my lover's mouth, who sucked it eagerly while he drove. Wearing a baggy, kimono-style pantsuit allowed me easy access to my aching cunt. I fingered myself slowly, a fresh stream of honey dripping down my clit to my hole. My lover was straining against the tights he'd borrowed from me for the long drive. I placed my hand on his throbbing cock and rubbed it firmly. It felt incredible beneath the soft, feminine material. We teased each other physically and verbally all the way, trying hard to stay in control of our senses due to the dangerous weekend traffic.

We finally arrived home, and it was almost as if we had forgotten our long, horny trip. In my mind I knew it was only a matter of time before I would have my real honey treat. We put our things away and fed the cat—the usual things people do when they've been away for days. All the while my honeypot was soaked and ready, and the honey jar was waiting on the table.

I found my lover on the bed making a phone call, and the heat was intense. I could not hold off. I pushed him back on the mattress, and our tongues danced in a hot, wet kiss. The teasing and the conversation on our journey home came flooding back. My button was so hard it ached. I got him on his hands and knees and told him to wait. I ran to the kitchen, came back with the jar of sticky liquid, and told him to stick his hard cock deep into the honey. It looked huge under the glass, encased in this thick ooze. I slowly pulled the jar down and watched his cock slowly emerge, dripping his bodily fluid, mixed with honey, back into the container. This was so erotic I repeated it twice, licking his honey-coated, smooth-shaven balls and cock clean each time.

He flipped me onto my back and poured the cool, smooth nectar down my steaming hole—what a contrast it made. He licked and sucked and nibbled my pussy until I exploded, filling his mouth with my own natural sweetness. Then I dipped his cock into the jar one last time and begged him to fuck my hot, tight cunt with all the sticky honey that coated his shaft. I stood up, and he entered me from behind, giving me a sensation that has to be one of a kind. Feeling my slick, slippery juices meeting with a very sticky hard-on brought me to another orgasm.

My lover wasn't finished with me yet. He pulled his cock out of my heat and asked me to suck it, which I eagerly did. We repeated this a few times. I could taste my come and the honey together as my hungry mouth pumped anxiously on his now purple and ready shaft. When he finally erupted into my mouth, I had a heavenly taste sensation of three different flavors.

Every time I have my honey in the morning, I think

of the honey I had that afternoon. I just can't wait to have a friend over for tea with cock-flavored sweetener.

—D. V., Canada

Instructions for a Sunday Morning

Instead of going to church like we always do, my roommate, my boyfriend, and I went to the doughnut shop just up the street from where I attend college. We bought a dozen cream-filled eclairs: six vanilla, five Bavarian cream, and one mammoth chocolate-filled. We had them microwaved.

We sped back to the dorm room with the bounty. We had only just sneaked past the security guard—which was hard to do, considering how many doughnuts were in our possession—when my roommate, Natalie, grabbed the chocolate eclair from the bag and bit off the end of it, licking the excess cream off her lips with the tip of her pink tongue. She handed the remainder to my boyfriend, John.

By this time, we had arrived back at the room. Before the door had even closed, John had unzipped his pants and pulled out his stiffy. He forced himself inside the eclair and moaned in ecstasy as he slid himself in and out of the tasty little pastry.

In the meantime, Natalie had pulled off all my

clothes and pinned me to the bed, an eclair in each hand. I could feel her hot and wet against my leg. She pushed my feet and hands to the sides of the bed. I writhed in anticipation. She paused above me and bit off the end of the sugary snack and squeezed the filling inside my hungry pussy. She filled her own with the other eclair while we watched.

She began stroking, licking, and teasing my nipples as I struggled to do the same to her. Finally, I flipped her over and began to feast on her sweet filling, straddling her head. I felt her tongue begin to probe my own sugar factory.

The eclair had brought John to the explosion point. He cast it aside and leapt atop the writhing female flesh on the bed. He thrust himself urgently into my ass, moaning about how tight it was. "Oh baby, you're better than any eclair," he cried. "I do like chocolate filling best."

I felt the tension in his loins, and suddenly he erupted inside of me in a hot, filling gush. He moaned and fell insensible to the floor. His shot of life flowed through me like an electrical spark, and I felt Natalie's orgasm arriving beneath my pulsing tongue. We came together, exploding like overloaded transformers.

After a few minutes, we all sat up and ate the rest of the eclairs with coffee. We highly recommend this particular Sunday morning activity.

—*A. W., Texas*

Cherry Charge

It's the Fourth of July and we're having a heat wave. Our clothes are clinging to us like second skin. Every fan we own is on and blowing, yet nothing helps to keep us cool. I go for a tall, cold glass of iced tea and a cherry Popsicle. I sit back down and try to relax, but to no avail. My clothes are so sticky that I decide to strip. In an effort to keep cool, I continue to suck on my cherry Popsicle. After a few minutes pass, I get a small surprise. A couple of drops from the Popsicle fall on my breasts. What a great feeling. I start to get an idea.

All the while my husband is in taking a shower, trying to keep himself cool. When he finishes drying off, he comes out to a very cool scene. He sees me and my cherry Popsicle doing some very cool things together.

I rub the Popsicle on my nipples. Oh, what a feeling. I feel the coolness of the Popsicle working on my breasts. One problem: I am getting hot in between my legs. So I run the Popsicle down my body, leaving a cherry trail right down to my very hot box. I rub the tip of the Popsicle over my clit and go crazy. The heat wave must be getting to me by now. I slowly push the head of the ice pop into my pussy in an effort to cool down.

As you can imagine, it isn't working very well. The cherry ice has become my newest obsession. I'm losing all control. At this point I have my eyes closed. I can see nothing but the heat wave. My cherry Popsicle has all my attention. I am pumping it in and out of my pussy at a slow and cooling rate. But after a few minutes of this, I open my eyes to a mind-shattering picture—my husband and his huge, rock-hard dick, standing right in front of me and my pussy. He is mesmerized by my cherry Popsicle, and all of my pussy juices mixing together. I tell him to get down on his knees. I make him suck off all of my juice from the Popsicle. And then I start all over again by reinserting the instrument into my hot, dripping pussy.

I make him fuck my brains out with the ice. Right after a cherry-blowing, mind-shattering orgasm, I make him feed me my come-covered snack as he goes down on me. He eats my pussy like it was the last meal on earth. He runs his tongue all over my clit, licking up every last drop of my cherry come, making me come all over again. After this second mind-shattering orgasm, he eats my pussy clean. Not leaving a single drop of come or Popsicle. Talk about Fourth of July fireworks!

—P. S., Pennsylvania

Strawberries and Cream à la Ray

I can't remember what led to the experience, but the incredible combination of strawberries, whipped cream, and Ray will never be forgotten. He had planned the evening to include dinner out and dessert in. The champagne was chilled, the strawberries were cold and clean, the whipped cream waited by the bed in the hotel room. We sipped champagne as Ray slowly and tenderly massaged my feet and ankles, moving his hand up my legs until it rested just below the juncture with my pelvis. I was completely relaxed, my eyes shut, and I was hot and wet. The sound of whipped cream being sprayed enticed me to imagine the feeling of it against my skin. I could smell a strawberry as Ray's mouth brought it close to my lips. As he put it between my lips and his tongue explored mine, I savored the sweet strawberry taste. I kept my eyes closed, enjoying the sounds, smells, and touches.

The next strawberry must have been designed for its purpose. It fit the contours of my neck perfectly. Ray slid it down from my earlobe to the valley between my breasts, his tongue lightly tracing along the line of strawberry juice and whipped cream. My skin tingled all over. Then a feeling of unexplainable contentment overcame me as, feeding me the strawberry, he drew a warm, wet cloth across what had been its path, leaving no trace of the sweet, sticky juices.

I cried out as I felt a cool, soft texture circle first my right nipple, then the left. I opened my eyes and looked down to see a pink mixture of strawberry juice and whipped cream coating the dark circles around my aroused nipples. Ray's tongue circled slowly, then he drew one nipple into his mouth, sucking gently, then harder, until my breathing become shallow and my hips were rising off the bed. He moved to the other breast, and as he gave it the same treatment, I came. With the warm cloth sustaining my excitement, he removed all evidence of the juices. Using another strawberry as the brush, he painted a trail of whipped cream around my navel. His tongue followed, teasing, caressing, dipping inside.

As the final sweet strawberry was covered with whipped cream, I felt my own juices sliding slowly down my thighs. The sensation of the satiny cream as Ray slowly and softly slipped the strawberry between the lips of my moist pussy and against my clit cast me over the edge again. I couldn't contain my cries of pleasure as he caressed and massaged and urged me on. I screamed louder and came harder as he continued to move the strawberry against my clit. Just when I was certain the intensity could go no higher, I felt myself soaring to heights never before reached, crying out without restraint and coming so hard that Ray thought the strawberry juice had been crushed from the fruit. He calmed me with his quiet voice and soft caresses, then sent me over the edge once more as he held me tight and slid his cock deep within me. If the lovemaking could have been even more heavenly, Ray achieved it by holding me through the night, giving completely and asking nothing in return.

—S. H., Florida